THE CROSSING

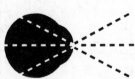

This Large Print Book carries the
Seal of Approval of N.A.V.H.

THE CROSSING

JASON MOTT

THORNDIKE PRESS
A part of Gale, a Cengage Company

Farmington Hills, Mich • San Francisco • New York • Waterville, Maine
Meriden, Conn • Mason, Ohio • Chicago

**LIBRARY OF CONGRESS CIP DATA ON FILE.
CATALOGUING IN PUBLICATION FOR THIS BOOK
IS AVAILABLE FROM THE LIBRARY OF CONGRESS.**

ISBN-13: 978-1-4328-5129-3 (hardcover)

Published in 2018 by arrangement with Harlequin Books S.A.

Printed in the United States of America
1 2 3 4 5 6 7 22 21 20 19 18

THE CROSSING

■ ■ ■ ■

LAUNCH

■ ■ ■ ■

The whole world was dying but still everyone made time for one last war. The Disease had entered its tenth year and the war had entered its fifth and there didn't seem to be any cure in sight for either of them. Some people said that because of the nature of The Disease, the older generation, seeing that their end was finally near, decided to settle all the old scores. One final global bar fight before last call.

The world had already lost twenty percent of its population by the time Tommy and I began our trip. The Disease took the old — killing some, simply putting others into a long, soft slumber — and the war took the young and everyone else tried to lose themselves in whatever they could: drugs, alcohol, sex, science, art, poetry. Everyone had impetus and direction now that everything was falling apart.

When it all first began, Tommy and I were

too young for the war and far too young for The Disease, so we only walked in the shadow of it all, watching and waiting for our turn. Our parents were already dead and we didn't have any other family. We'd never live long enough to catch The Disease, so we viewed it with a detached interest and sympathy.

The Disease started in Russia, but because Russia tends to be tight-lipped about what happens within its borders, it's been difficult for anyone to say just how long it had been happening before the rest of the world found out about it. The UK was the first country beyond Russia to notice the outbreak. It began in a retirement home in London where one morning the staff went to their patients' rooms to find all of them asleep and unable to be awakened. Within hours there were reports coming in from other countries about the extremely elderly falling asleep and never waking.

The Disease garnered a lot of different names in those first frightening weeks: The Lullaby, The Long Goodnight, Sundowners Disease. The last one was meant to make fun of the elderly. After all, those at the end of life were expected to pass away eventually. So for a while, the world was concerned, but not alarmed. It wasn't until The

Disease had been quietly shutting the doors on the oldest of the population that someone at the CDC noticed a decline in the average age of The Disease's victims. Something that began affecting only those in their midnineties and above had progressed to affect those about five years younger. Then the world watched as, over the next couple of years, the average age was reduced even further.

The Disease was coming for everyone. It would begin by emptying out the nursing homes, then progress to the retirement villages, then on and on until, eventually, it would hollow out the office buildings, the nightclubs the youth had once filled with reverie until, one day, there would be no one alive old enough to reproduce. Not long after that, whatever children left would turn out the lights on humanity by drifting off into one long, peaceful slumber.

The world would not end with a bang or a whimper, but in a restful sigh.

Staring down the barrel of that future was what sparked the war. As people panicked they began to blame others. And that blaming donned a coat of nationalism. Russia was the primary target in the beginning since that was where The Disease had begun. Before long, the war spilled over from its borders and into the rest of the world.

Now, five years later, America was the last uninvaded country on the planet. But that wouldn't last. The average age of victims of The Disease had reached sixty — the age of most politicians and military officials. The war was losing its direction and ambling on the shaky legs of enlisted men and women who didn't see any point in fighting when there was a disease coming for them. So the government turned back to the draft.

The Disease was too far away for seventeen-year-olds to really understand or fear. Youth has always been a haven for invincibility, and this was no different. The papers from the draft board went out, scooping up boys and girls in its bloody hands. And one after another they went, they died, and the world grew a little lonelier.

Though it all felt far away from me and Tommy, I knew, of course, that it couldn't last.

Our parents had been dreamers. Our mother was a teacher and believer in things magical, like newspaper horoscopes and the ability of whispered fears to manifest in a person's life. Our father believed in magic of a different kind. He was a writer and, sometimes, amateur astronomer. His magic was a distant moon named Europa.

He fell in love with it at an early age and then passed that love on to my brother and me. He could never know where his obsession with a small ice rock located over three hundred million miles away would lead his children. Like the stars led our father, the memory of our father led my brother and me.

For me, our journey started before I was even born, in letters my father wrote to me and my brother. For Tommy, it all started with a letter from the Draft Board.

For three hard days my brother failed to find the words to explain his impending death to me. With furrowed brow and taut jaw he tried to find a way that, when he laid the news out in front of me, its hardness would be sanded off like a pebble rubbed smooth and glossy over the life of an old river. We were all each other had. Brother and sister. Twins, seventeen years from the womb. How I'd get on without him once he was dead, he didn't know.

In the end, because he had never been any good with words, my brother never did find out the right way to say it. After failing to come up with an alternative he only handed me the brown envelope, with his head hung like a penitent child — even shuffling his feet a little, suddenly making himself smaller than he had been in years — and he said in a low voice, "I won the lottery, Virginia." Then he smiled, as though a smile meant a person was actually happy.

I took the envelope, knowing immediately what it was. Everyone knew what the draft notices looked like. They were a spreading plague, a dark shadow that came for friends and loved ones, took them away and never brought them back. The war was going from bad to worse. As if war had ever done anything else.

I only looked at the letter that would eventually take my brother to his death. I pointed to the awkward font that printed his name in that excited, prize-winner's way, clucked a stiff laugh and said, with no small amount of derision: "Terrible. Just terrible."

■ ■ ■ ■

ESCAPE VELOCITIES

■ ■ ■ ■

ONE

In the middle of a pockmarked crossroads someone had painted the word PEACE in six-foot-tall white letters on the edge of a crater. The night was late and the road black, but the word — what was left of it — caught the starlight and glowed. The lettering was sharp and formal, placed by a steady hand. Someone had cared. About the letters. Maybe even about the word. So I couldn't quite understand how PEACE had met such a bad end out here in the middle of nowhere.

And it truly was nowhere.

If you've never been to Oklahoma, you should go. It's a beautiful place, a place where everything seems to stand alone. Lone trees strike out of the distant horizon, so far away from anything it makes you wonder how a lone seed could ever have gotten there in the first place. In Oklahoma, far houses stand and watch over grassland oceans that shimmer in the dim moonlight. In Oklahoma, the wind has long legs that carry rain clouds on stalks of gray. In Oklahoma, the sun rises far, reigns high, and then comes close in the evening and sits beside you until you doze off on the front porch.

Oklahoma is a place where loners have formed a community. It's a place where people are both alone and together at the same time, like Tommy and I always were. It's a special thing: always having someone with you. It gives you legs to stand on.

I was seventeen when Tommy and I ran away from the war and started on what would come to be our last trip together. Seventeen's an odd age. Too old for dreams, too young for reality.

It was a hard January when this all happened. Any promise of spring was far off as I walked the frozen highway. The ground was still locked from cold and every particle of snow had been swept away so that there was only brown, barren earth. The cold swelled up around me like static on an old television. Now and again the starlight seemed to exhale and the wind raced over the empty winter fields and passed through me hard enough and frigid enough that it frightened me.

To keep my hands from trembling, I turned them to fists buried inside my pockets. To keep my teeth from chattering, my jaw was locked. The muscles ached from holding station. I stomped my feet to keep my toes connected to my body. Now and again they drifted off on their own accord. I was never quite sure if they would return.

But even with all of this, there was beauty. Several hours before, I watched as the failing light went dark and a fistful of bare winter trees jutting up from the sides of the road swung from being thick gray arteries to thin purple veins to black silhouettes that might have been calligraphy of some exotic language, punctuating the black cursive of the small highway scrawling through the countryside. Then the last of the light went away and all the ways the trees had looked became just another memory I would always carry in me.

I was alone that night . . . sort of. I hadn't seen a house since passing through a small, sleepy town before sunset, where the one stoplight on Main Street flashed off and on. Yellow in one direction, red in the other. Even though lights sometimes burned inside the bowels of the homes — a mixture of trailers and two-story farmhouses with clapboard siding and old paint peeling like

19

psoriasis — the town looked left behind, a city desiccated by plague. Everything was weathered and empty, ready to be filled by story and myth. I could imagine dragon eggs hidden in storm shelters, elder gods tucked away in attics. I've always had a tendency to drift off into imagination.

In the window of a darkened diner a sign — lit garish red by the town's single stoplight — declared God Blesses the War. Directly across the street, almost like a bookend, another sign hung in the window of a home and alleged God Left. So The Disease Came. I still don't know exactly who was right.

At one point I almost knocked on the door of one of the houses. A large gray-and-white affair with a tire swing dangling from an evergreen in the backyard and a late-model car parked in the front. I thought I saw someone in one of the upstairs windows. I stared up at them and they stared back down at me. It wasn't until my eyes adjusted that I realized it was only a teddy bear placed in the window, looking out, keeping diligent watch the way only loyal stuffed animals can.

For a moment the feeling of being watched caused me to think it was him. He was coming for me and he wouldn't stop. That's just who he was.

My palms were sweating and my heart was a frightened bird beating against my rib cage. All because of a teddy bear standing watch.

I waved at the guardian, laughed at myself and walked on until the houses stopped appearing and the town sank into the earth behind me. The moment was relegated to history and memory, which, for me, have always been one and the same.

Tommy and I called it "The Memory Gospel."

The Memory Gospel was simple, really: I remember everything. Truly and honestly everything. Every second of every day. Every conversation. Every place I've ever been. Every person I've ever met. Every word I've ever said. Every news report I've ever seen. Every letter of every sentence of every page of every book I've ever read. Every shaggy tree that slanted at an odd angle and was dappled by the dying sunlight in a way that might never again repeat and made a person say to themselves "I hope I never forget this. Never ever."

I don't forget any of it. Not a single moment. I carry all of it inside me.

Every laugh. Every schoolyard bully. Every foster parent who tried. Every social worker who failed. Every time I've stood outside and looked up into the sky and counted the stars until there were tears at the corners of my eyes because I remembered — as if I could ever forget — that my parents were still dead and would never be able to come and stand beside me and take my hand and point up to the night sky and say to me, the way people did in movies, "It makes you feel so small, doesn't it?"

My memory was, is, and always will be, immutable.

The Memory Gospel is the one thing in my life that I can believe in. It's always with me, filling me up and hollowing me out all at the same time, like the way a person can stand before a mountain in the winter and see the light spilling over its craggy shoulders and understand, in that brief instant, that life comes and goes and one day we all will. Like you're part of something and a part of nothing all at once. The Memory Gospel is all-encompassing and inescapable. A forest I can neither get lost in nor find my way out of.

And so I've come to consider myself the chronicler of the last days of the world.

I kept walking with my head down and my shoulders up and the past swirling above my head. I wished for a peaceful, silent cold

— the way it sometimes happened in the nights when the snow fell like dust and you woke in the morning to a world you knew but didn't recognize, like a childhood friend you haven't seen in decades. But the wind stayed hard and unreasonable. It swept down off the mountains in a roar that shoved me forward and almost put me on my face a few times. I always managed to catch myself just before I fell. Eventually I decided to let the wind help. It was heading in the same direction I was, after all. Why not let it push me along? Why not let it carry me off into The Memory Gospel . . .

. . . I'm five years old and hanging upside down in a crashed car. The seat belt holds me tight across the waist and my ears are ringing and there is the sound of water falling outside and Tommy is on the ceiling of the overturned car crying and looking around. "It's going to be okay," my mother says, and suddenly I'm standing in the middle of the road staring down at the word PEACE and I'm terrified and hanging upside down again and I'm in a foster home and I'm attending the funeral of my parents and the social worker is saying, "It's going to be okay," and I'm squeezing Tommy's hand and staring up at a black, starry sky and staring up at the ceiling of the overturned car and Tommy is still crying and

there is blood trickling from his head and our father is dead and our mother is saying, over and over again, "It's going to be okay . . . It's going to be okay . . ." and her voice is softening with each recitation and I'm standing alone in the world and the wind is cold and I am seventeen and still trapped in my five-year-old self watching my parents die and I don't want to see it so I close my eyes . . .

. . . like fists and pushed the memories away.

It's like I told you: I have a tendency to drift.

I stopped walking. When I had finally clawed my way out of what was and into what is, I opened my eyes and looked up at the stars.

Andromeda was brighter than usual that night. One trillion stars burning, raging. Reduced by time and distance to little more than a pinprick of noiseless light. That's how memory was supposed to work. A narrowing down. A softening that made it possible to let go of unwanted or painful memories. Maybe that was why I liked astronomy as much as I did — and still do. It proved that with enough time, even the brightest stars burned out. Everything faded away eventually.

But I understood that, because of distance

and time, when you saw a star you only ever saw the way it used to be. Even the sun was eight minutes in the past by the time you saw it.

"Andromeda," I began, smothering the memory of the car crash with bare, calm facts. "Officially designated as NGC 224. Coordinates: RA 0° 42m 44s | Dec 41° 16.152' 9". 2.537 million light-years away. Two hundred twenty thousand light-years across. 1.5×10^{12} solar masses — estimated. Apparent magnitude of 3.4." On and on I continued. Definitions of mass, luminosity. It was a spiral galaxy and I quoted the composition of each of the spiral's arms. Fact after fact after fact, pulled perfect and undiminished from memory.

I built a levee with each fact, and the recollected dead receded back into their holding places.

"Ten more miles," I said, looking off down the cold, empty, dark road ahead. "Seventeen thousand six hundred yards. Fifty-two thousand eight hundred feet. Six hundred thirty-three thousand six hundred inches . . . and a partridge in a pear tree." I sang the last part. Badly. But the starlight didn't seem to mind.

I took one final look up at the sky. I found Jupiter. I found its moon Europa — nothing more than a whisper of light so difficult to see it made my eyes hurt and I wondered if what I saw was real. But whether I actually saw Europa or only imagined seeing it didn't seem to matter. To some extent, we are all solipsists. I started walking again, heading toward Florida and the last shuttle launch of human history.

I had just passed the crossroads where PEACE was written when the headlights rose out of the far darkness behind me. It had only ever been a matter of time. So I stopped and waited for what was coming.

The headlights approached in cold silence, then the silence shifted into what was almost the sound of applause as tires sizzled over the cold pavement. A chill raced down my spine as the blue lights atop the car flashed into existence.

The police car stopped in front of me. The headlights glared bright enough that I had to shield my eyes. The car shifted into Park and sat idling for a moment. A small plume of steam rose from the exhaust, effervescing into the darkness. The door opened. Booted feet thumped onto the pavement like punctuation at the end of a grim declaration about life. The lights still shone too brightly for me to see who had stepped out of the

26

car, but I didn't need to see in order to know that it was him.

"Got pretty far," he said finally. "I'll give you that much." His voice was as hard as steel, like always. Because of the headlights, he was only a deep shadow and a deeper voice, like thunder come to visit in the late hours of the night. His breath steamed from his lips and expanded into a small anvil head cloud above him.

"I could explain to you why it's important, but you wouldn't understand." There was arrogance in my voice and I knew it, but I didn't try to curb it. At this point, there was no turning back, nothing to be said that would undo what was already done. I knew, better than most, that time's arrow only moves forward. "I'm going to be there to see it," I said. "And I'm never coming back."

He stepped away from the car door and walked out in front of the headlights. I counted each one of my heartbeats, if only to keep myself calm. He was tall and broad as he had always been. His hair cropped close as a harvested field. The backlight of the car's high beams turned him into a monolith, eternal and omnipotent. Something to be worshipped, if only for its cruel disinterest.

He looked around, scanning the open field

of darkness surrounding us. Then he sighed. "You Embers are something else," he said. Then he spat. "You've had your fun. Now, where is he?"

No sooner had the words left his mouth than the blow landed against the back of his head. A tremble went through his body and he slumped to his knees with a pained groan. Then Tommy was there, standing behind him, his fist trembling.

"Run," Tommy said, as our foster father fell unconscious at his feet.

ELSEWHERE

The hardest thing was convincing herself not to be afraid of falling asleep. Each and every evening she watched the news and watched talk of The Disease. Her friend over in Alamance County had come down with it. Fell asleep on the sofa one night and then, when morning came, nobody heard from her until her children found her. And this was back near the beginning. Her friend was eighty-seven years old, but spry for her age. Still, spryness doesn't do anything to repel the unexpected. But wasn't that the way it had always been?

And now nearly ten years had passed and The Disease was creeping ever closer to people her age. So, like many people of a certain age in this world, she figured that the best thing she could do was to get herself away from everybody. She went down to the store and bought herself as much food as her dead husband's pickup truck could carry and she came home and loaded up the house and then went back and filled the truck up again and, this time, she also picked up as many sheets of plastic as she could. And duct tape and disinfectant and even a gas mask — which were slowly becoming all the rage even though nobody knew whether or not they would do any good.

When all was said and done she had everything she needed to live for at least a year. Yeah, it might be a year of eating potted meat and crackers until she was blue in the face, but Lord knows there were worse things in this world.

She lived far enough outside of town that she could live the type of life she wanted. The farm was big and old and her dead husband's pride right up until the day he dropped dead, still sitting atop the same tractor he'd bought when they first got the farm. He'd been dead for nearly twenty years and she was glad that he didn't live to see the world get to where it was: the killing, the dying, the slow fading away of everything that the whole damn species had spent thousands of years building.

No. He was always too softhearted to be able to stand for such a thing. If that heart attack hadn't done him the pitiful kindness of taking him when it did, he would have turned on the news in the world today and died from a plain old broken heart.

She thought about her husband a lot in those first few months of living alone, isolated from the rest of the world. Mostly she thought about him as a way to keep from thinking about everything else that was going on around her. She stopped turning on the news in the mornings because it did nothing but let in the worst parts of the world. Nobody said anything good anymore.

And so she would get up at the crack of dawn — always thankful and amazed and terrified to have woken up at all — and piddle about the house before time came to go out and tend to the garden and she would think about her husband and maybe she would hum some song that he used to love — he'd always been partial to Frank Sinatra — and, as the weeks stretched out into months, maybe she would even talk to her dead husband even though she knew good and hell well that he was dead and she wasn't the type to believe that the dead could hear the breath of the living. But she did it anyway.

Some mornings she talked to him about the past. She told him about the children they'd never had and how she, finally, after all these years, could say that she was glad that they'd never come along. "I just couldn't live with myself if I had to watch those pretty blue eyes worry over this world," she said. The only answer the house gave back to her was the gentle *clunk-clunk-clunk* of the grandfather clock in the living room that never kept the right time but that she wound up anyway because, even if it wasn't doing a good job, it was important for everything in this world to have a purpose.

That old clock made her think about her own purpose. What was it? Her purpose?

What was a woman without purpose?

What was anyone without purpose?

She asked her dead husband that one night when she woke up from a bad dream — a dream that she'd fallen asleep and been unable to wake up from it. Her palms were sweaty and her long hair matted to her brow and her cheeks were slick with tears, and the words trembled out of her lips like a newborn foal. "What's my purpose?" she asked.

And her dead husband did not answer her back, even though she sat and waited to hear his heavy, soft voice for over an hour with the darkness and the clunking of that clock down below counting off its irregular and inconstant seconds.

That was the night that she made a promise never to go to sleep again. She'd stay up for as long as she had to, until The Disease came and went and burned away the rest of humanity and all that was left was her and then, by

God, she'd know what her purpose was. She'd have the answer she'd been waiting for and she wouldn't wake up at night sweating and calling out for her husband because, in the end, she couldn't go on like this: afraid of sleep and afraid of life both at the same time.

She didn't make it a full two days before falling asleep again.

She tried everything to stop it from happening. She drank coffee until it made her head hurt and her chest tight. She went back to watching the news, hoping that the fear the news gave would make her more able to sit up in the late hours and not fall asleep. The news told her about seventeen new cases of The Disease that had been found around the county and that did give her just the right amount of terror that she needed to stay awake for a little while longer.

But she was an old woman and, try as she might, she could feel the sleep walking her down, as steady as that old clock in the living room and, just before she finally fell asleep — a sleep that she would never wake from, something she knew in the pit of her stomach — she thought she heard her husband's voice one more time. He said a single word: "Love."

And her final thought before she fell into the deep, timeless slumber of The Disease was that her question had finally been answered.

Two

For what felt like an eternity, I was unable to breathe. Seeing Jim Gannon at Tommy's feet, I realized I hadn't really expected for it to work. Gannon was six-foot-two and built like a bad dream. All angles and muscle. More animal than man. And that was before you took into account the police uniform that filled him out with cold authority and made you nervous about crimes you hadn't committed.

When I finally did breathe again the air rushed into my lungs, air so thick you could drink it, choke on it if you weren't careful. I felt light-headed and gritted my teeth until the feeling went away.

Standing there in the cold darkness with our foster father lying at Tommy's feet, I thought of all the ways it could have gone wrong:

Tommy could have stumbled on the uneven earth as he climbed up out of the darkness along the edge of the road, stumbled just loud enough for Gannon to hear him and turn and draw his pistol and squeeze the trigger and put an end to everything. It wouldn't have been anything other than a reflex action for Gannon. Law enforcement training taking over. But it still would have ended Tommy's life. Just a sudden flash like a lightbulb bursting, then the long darkness.

Or he could have gotten caught in the headlights of Gannon's car long before he noticed them. It had been my idea that Tommy follow along at a distance, away from the road, buried in the outer dark, orbiting like some phantom planet. "It won't be long before he catches up," I had said. "Do what I tell you and we'll be okay." And so he did.

Only now that Gannon was unconscious on the cold, deserted road did Tommy and I laugh.

The laughter was fleeting, but wonderful, like a meteor slashing across the night sky.

"We've got to get him out of the road," I said.

Tommy flinched. He looked up to see me still standing there in front of the car. "I told you to run," Tommy said, his voice steady and even.

"We've got to get him off the road," I repeated. I was already jogging around and opening the rear door of the police car.

Tommy reached down and took the pistol from Gannon's holster.

"Take the bullets out of it and throw that away," I said.

He placed the gun on the highway. He fumbled through the pockets on Gannon's belt. "Hold these," he said, handing me the man's handcuffs. "Hurry up," he barked.

I took the cuffs. "You don't need these," I said.

Tommy rolled Gannon over and, after a few awkward moments, managed to pull him up off the ground and lift him over his back in a fireman's carry. He'd wrestled off and on growing up. Most of the schools in most of the foster homes he and I had been shuffled through over the years had wrestling programs in some form or other. He'd actually managed to get pretty good at it. The physical side of it — all of the strength and muscles required — were just a matter of deciding to do it. The mental aspect required a lot of thought and Tommy wasn't much of a thinker, but he had gotten pretty good at that too. He could always tell what his opponent was planning. He always knew, milliseconds before it happened, when someone was going to shoot their hips forward or try to spin out or go for an underhook. And his mind reacted to it all on its own. He didn't have to think about it. It was one of the few things in his life, maybe even the only thing, that had come naturally to him. If he'd ever stayed in a single school for more than a season, maybe he would have gotten recruited by some college. Maybe in one of those places where wrestling was a pastime and boys like him could be someone people admired.

But he never did stay anywhere longer than a season and so he never had gotten really good and there were no college recruiters looking for him. The only person looking for him was the unconscious foster father he carried on his back.

Just as Tommy got Gannon to the car, I opened the door and there, sitting in the back seat and as quiet as a corpse, was the Old Man, Jim Gannon's father himself. He'd had a stroke years ago and been confined to his body ever since. The doctors said that he was aware, but paralyzed and unable to speak. The most he ever did was blink, and even that came only on rare occasions.

Gannon had dressed him in khaki work pants and a flannel shirt and a pair of soft-soled nurse's shoes. The Old Man didn't seem to register me as I opened the door and took a moment to stare at him.

"What is it?" Tommy asked.

"It's the Old Man."

"What?" Tommy looked past me. "Is he sick?" Tommy asked. "The Disease?"

"No," I said.

Gannon groaned a little, in the early stages of coming around.

"Give me the handcuffs," Tommy said.

"You don't need to handcuff him," I replied. "Just shut the door. It can only be opened from the outside. He won't be able to get out."

"Give me the handcuffs, Virginia!"

"You. Don't. Need. Them," I said, laying each word out like a brick. Then I turned and tossed the handcuffs out into the darkness. "Don't be so simple."

Tommy was deciding whether or not to run out after them when Gannon, suddenly back to his senses, grabbed his arm. "Tommy . . ." Gannon said, groggy and slow.

Tommy snatched Gannon's hand away and shoved him to the far side of the back seat. Then he bolted back just in time for me to slam the door closed, locking the man inside. "Tommy!" Gannon called. He looked out at the boy through the window, a firm calmness in his eyes. "Tommy . . . open this door."

Without a word Tommy walked around to the front of the car and picked up the pistol that still lay in the middle of the street.

"I told you to throw that away," I said.

He tucked the gun into the pocket of his coat. "If you want it, come over here and take it." His voice was a hard, low warning, something that would let his sister know that for all of my intelligence, despite that flawless, unbreakable memory of mine, he was powerful in his own right. He'd saved me. Not for the first time, and not for the last.

"You're welcome," Tommy said.

"It was my idea," I replied.

"You're still welcome."

Then we stood there in the dark and the cold, looking at the man trapped in the back seat of the car. It would be up to me to figure out what to do next. And it would be up to Tommy to do whatever needed to be done. Just like always. I would get us both to Florida in time to watch the launch and then, after that, I wouldn't need him anymore. And, at the same time, he wouldn't need me anymore. He'd go off to the war. Do his duty the way his draft notice demanded. He would die.

It was the only way things could turn out for us, no matter how much we wanted it to be different. We couldn't know that at the time, but years later, the past would be immutable, and I would have to live with it, perfectly preserved in the halls of memory. And, years later, I would be able to speak for my lost brother, to see this trip the way he had seen it. The last great gift he gave to me.

Tommy hadn't been a smart boy and he would never become a smart man. But that wasn't what really bothered my brother. Neither was it that The Disease or the war would one day find him. The latter, in fact, I'd almost say Tommy always saw as something inevitable. Maybe even welcomed.

Tommy told me once that he could never be like me. Not even if he tried at it every single day for five hundred years, cloistered away like a monk. He'd only ever come up short. He said he'd known that for about as far back as he could remember — which wasn't very far. To be sure, he had memories. As many as most other people did, he figured. He remembered important stuff: the first girl he'd kissed, the first time he got in trouble in grade school, a smattering of song lyrics, a handful of lines from movies. If he was supposed to show up somewhere at a certain time on a certain day he could, for the most part, hold that much in his head. Maybe he'd have to check the calendar again and again in the days before and tell himself, "Now, don't forget!" But that's how it went. That's how it was with everybody.

Everybody except me.

In the last few years before our final trip together, perhaps sensing his growing unease, his body no longer looked like a copy of mine. He had shot up four inches above me and filled out wide and strong. He was all muscle and intention. In spite of the changes to his body, he and I still shared much of the same face. Sometimes when we were together I could look at Tommy and find myself overcome with a feeling of both loneliness and togetherness all at once. Being a twin was cruel in its own way. From the moment you were born you were let in on the dark secret of humanity, the thing that no one wants to know about themselves: that a person is both unique and, at the same time, mass produced. And therefore no better than anyone else.

Hell of a thing for a child to have to grow up knowing.

By the age of twelve Tommy was already being told that he was handsome. Not cute, the way people told it to the other boys his age, but handsome, the way people spoke of grown men. He was athletic. Strong. Everyone knew he would grow up to do something physical. Maybe he'd be a boxer or a wrestler, but never a bully. And then, assuming he lived long enough, the architecture of his physique promised that he could be the type of man that made people feel safe when they had every reason to be afraid. Maybe after he'd been wrestling for a few years he would become a firefighter. Policeman, perhaps. He had a good smile. "A soft smile," people told him, girls especially. Maybe he'd become a doctor with a stern voice but a soft smile, the kind you trusted to save you no matter what harm you had brought upon yourself.

But that was before things started falling apart. Back when young people like us still thought they could grow up to be something other than what they would come to call us: "Embers." It was our job, or so the joke went, to be the last remnants of the flame that had burned so long. And, like all Embers, to eventually burn out.

From the time we were five Tommy and I had been shifted from foster home to foster

home. Nothing to do with The Disease —
that was still years away. But simply because
our parents had already died and left us and
we became "difficult" children. Maybe it
was just the way we were. Or maybe it was
because, after their deaths, the only thing
we had to remember our parents by was a
stack of letters that I'd read once and
burned the next day.

After the letters were gone there were only
Tommy and me, and we were always together. Only twice had anyone tried to
separate us. Tommy had been the one they
wanted.

The first time, no less than a day after
Tommy had gone, I ran away from the
group home in which he had left me behind
and found his new home. It wasn't difficult.
Just a matter of getting the records from the
social worker's paperwork when she wasn't
looking. I snuck into Tommy's room at
night, took his hand and left. We made it a
day and a half on our own before we were
found. The couple who had taken him in
gave him up after that and the two of us
returned to the same foster home we had
been in before. We were together again.

The second time it happened — again, he
had been the one the adoptive family
wanted — we were thirteen. We ran away

again and made it alone together for almost a week. During that week, Tommy thought of a dozen good reasons why we should keep going. He had this idea of picking a direction — any direction — and simply going until that direction ran out. The world was big and we could get lost in it. And even though we would be lost, we would be together the way we had always been.

"We're too young to keep running," I said. "Nobody searches for anyone as hard as they search for lost kids."

"We're not kids," Tommy said, and in just saying so I realized how young he sounded. "They'll break us up again if we go back, Ginny."

"Don't call me Ginny," I answered. "It's what you called me when we were babies. And I'm not a baby anymore."

We were standing beneath an overpass just after sunset, listening to the sound of the cars racing by in light rain, their tires sizzling like bacon. When the big trucks went by overhead there was the *calump-calump-calump* of the expansion gaps in the concrete.

"We'll go back and I'll tell them what they need to hear to make sure they keep us together," I said. I tucked my hands in my pockets and stared off into the distance. The entire conversation was only a formality to be endured before it led to its obvious conclusion.

Tommy's face tightened into a knot. "Dammit, *Virginia!*" he said, leaning hard on my name after planting the flag of "dammit." Curse words were still new to him and still had power. "We can find somewhere to live." We could both feel the momentum of words building inside him, like a shopping cart just beginning to rattle down a steep hill. "We can go off and make a home. We're each other's home when you really stop to think about it!" He belted the words out. He opened his arms, proudly, like a carnival barker making his greatest pitch.

He searched for words that would undo me, but found only the empty breath inside his lungs. If he tried to press me he knew I could always bring up facts and figures, numbers and math enough to break down anything he said. I could recite articles verbatim about the survival rates of runaways if I wanted. True stories of children found dead. Statistics about how badly everything could go for us if the world so decided. I could crunch the math in my head and rattle off the probabilities: such and such a chance of getting kidnapped, such and such a percentage of turning to drugs or prostitution or anything else. On and on, I always knew how to break down any resistance he ever had to anything.

Tommy looked at me, his face soft and afraid and frustrated all at the same time. His mind reached for something to say but his lips knew the fact of futility. Only I could change it. Only I could let him win the argument that he so desperately needed to win.

And he knew — we both knew, and hated — that I wouldn't let him win.

Rather than fight it, rather than try to make the case for the things he thought we should do, he conceded. Tommy's life was always easier when he just did what I wanted.

"So be it," he said.

"Tommy?"

"What?" he answered, sighing the word as his body slumped upon its frame, resigned to defeat.

"They're never going to break us apart," I said.

"Then why do they keep trying?"

I walked over and wrapped my arms around him. He was outgrowing me already and my arms had to work to surround him, but the work was rewarded by the feeling of my brother captured, like some splendid and frail animal, in my arms. I had to protect him. It was my job.

"We won't ever be separated," I said.

"But —"

"I promise, Tommy."

"You can't know that, Ginny. Mom and Dad said they'd always be here too."

Tommy's body shuddered and I knew that he was crying. He wrapped his arms around me, if only to keep me from seeing his tears the way boys and men are known to do.

"Mom and Dad haven't left," I said. "They're in me. In The Memory Gospel. And they're in you too."

"I can't remember like you can," Tommy said, almost as an apology.

"It doesn't matter. They're in you. We're together. A family. And we'll always be that."

"You promise?"

"Just as sure as my name's Ginny."

We stood for a long time, holding one another, and the world passed us by.

. . . *calump-calump-calump* . . .

Like a beating heart fading into nothingness. And when the sound went away, when the world had drifted off into silence, we were still there, together. The way it would always be for my brother and me.

After that we went back to the foster family who had taken him in and, just as before, the family didn't want Tommy unless it was without me. So we found ourselves lost in the system. But at least we were lost together.

Four years later, we were seventeen and running away again, but this time, we wouldn't go back. The launch in Florida wouldn't wait for me the way the war and death would wait for Tommy.

In three days, when this would all be over.

So be it.

To My Children,

We could do nothing to stop the towers from falling. We could do nothing to stop the workplaces from being shot up. And when the shootings spilled out of the office buildings and into the schools, we could do nothing to stop that either. The government began watching everyone because we had given them permission. Climate change. Bankers. On and on and on. All day every day the news outlets came into our homes — slipping in through the waves and cables, screens and surfaces that bound us all together. The television became a hole in the ice through which horror shambled each night, the way it used to in old black-and-white movies. But in those movies dying was all corn syrup. Back then, the world only pretended to be after us and, inevitably, the thing we feared went away, born into darkness on a tide of end credits.

But now the dying we saw on TV was real. The world grew more thorns with each sunrise, tightened in a little closer with each sunset. And all the while we watched. We stared at the news and shook our heads in dismay. We wept. We sat up at night, sleepless and fretting.

Asking ourselves, over and over again: What right did we have to bring children into this world?

Your mother and I went back and forth for years. We felt we had a duty to wait for things to get better. A duty not only to you, but to everyone else. This world, in whatever form it takes, is a product of us all. We forge hope or sow terror. We dole them out in measurements of our own choosing.

But still, it's a big world. I was just a small-town newspaper writer. She a science teacher. How much could we really do about anything?

At some point in your life, you'll want to know where we were when everything changed. It's a hard question to answer, like trying to find the moment when a little hill of rocks became a mountain. It happens suddenly and all at once, like a lightning strike, and after the flash fades, you turn to see that your home has burned to the ground.

While there are a dozen days in which the world changed, and some of them I will tell you about, I'll answer your inevitable question about the moment when things went from the way they were to the way they would become:

We were in North Carolina visiting your mother's parents on the day the towers fell. Your mother, your grandparents and I all spent the morning huddled together in front of the television, watching it happen, just like everyone else. Your grandfather, a stoic man by nature, sat unmoving in his chair for hours, letting what was happening wash over him like floodwaters sweeping over a headstone. When he did finally speak, all he said was, "I'm sorry."

By sunset we were all wrung out. Raw and frayed at the edges. We wanted to sleep, but it was early yet and, even beyond that, we knew that it would be a sleepless night. So your mother and I went for a walk. Her parents lived in a small community on the Intracoastal Waterway where large houses smelled of seawater. Small cars steered gingerly over the earth, guided by retired hands. The ocean thinned out into tendrils of tributaries only a stone's throw from the bedrooms of children.

The streets were empty because the television was still full of tragedy. Your mother and I walked the vacant roads alone. Sometimes the wind carried the sound of sobbing from nearby houses.

We pretended it was the sound of laughter. A lie, but one we felt it was okay to tell ourselves.

Eventually we found a sandy road leading off into the woods. It led to a collection of abandoned buildings. Once upon a time, it had been a summer camp of some sort. Square, concrete buildings held empty wiry bunks, rusting and half-reclaimed by underbrush. A large, high-ceilinged classroom stood at the center of the complex, covered in graffiti and shaggy with kudzu that trembled like grasshoppers when the wind blew.

We moved through the empty, forgotten buildings, stepping slowly, detached from everything, even ourselves, like ghosts. When we had seen enough we followed the edge of the property and found that it led to the ocean. The sun was setting behind a wall of clouds. Just before it disappeared, it flared, shifting colors, from beautiful to ominous, the way a goldfish swimming in a bowl can, with the proper play of lighting, suddenly become an apostrophe of blood.

Then the sun was gone and the moon rose above the water.

As we stood and watched, the light from the moon poured down onto the ocean water. The water swung from black to gray to silver. And then it continued to change. From silver to turquoise to, finally, a glowing, electric blue. I can't remember ever seeing that particular shade of blue. And I have never seen it since. The water looked like lightning, lightning that coiled itself into waves, only to flatten and bubble against the shore, still glowing. Just then, your mother and I could believe we had stumbled upon another planet. Some near-dimension mirror-image earth. A horror-beauty of a world where planes leveled buildings and lightning became water at moonrise.

Wordlessly, your mother stripped off her clothes and, without testing the depths or the dangers, dove in. She disappeared and reemerged, glowing like a glacier. "We don't know what this is," I said.

"It'll be okay," she said.

I wasn't sure I believed her, but I followed anyway. There was never any choice. Not really.

We swam into this new world.

Later that night we told your grandfather what had happened. "Heaven's Tide," he said. "You don't know how lucky you are to see such a thing."

After a bit of research, I learned that it was just a strain of bioluminescent algae. A completely natural occurrence that had happened before and would happen again. The only thing different about this time was that your mother and I had been there to bear witness to it. It was our old, familiar world all the while. It had only chosen to show us something rare and wondrous.

"It's not all horrible," your mother said to me later that night. It was her way of saying, "Let's try a family, even in this world."

It would be years before we succeeded. In the interim the world continued to change. I responded by writing these notes, letters, whatever they are. I write them for you, in case it all falls apart. I write them for myself, to say that it doesn't have to. I write them to prove that the world has always been this hard. I write them to prove that the future was always meant to be a promise, not a threat.

THREE

"There are bad ideas, and then there are bad ideas," Gannon grumbled from the back seat. The sick Old Man beside him said nothing, because that was the way it always was with him.

Behind the wheel Tommy clunked the car into gear and steered it gently off the highway. I sat in the passenger seat, pointing ahead through the window at the path we should take. "Head toward that tree line," I said.

"Those trees won't hide a car," Gannon said. He chuckled a little, then hardened his grin, as though he hadn't meant to find anything funny just now. He looked over at his father, checking to be sure that he was okay, then turned back to Tommy. "Hell of a right hook you've got there." He pressed his hand to the back of his head and checked his palm for blood. "But you always were strong as an ox, weren't you?"

"Can you just stop talking?" Tommy asked.

"It doesn't matter if he talks," I said. "Don't listen. Just get us over behind those trees."

"It's a hell of a world we live in, I suppose," Gannon said with a sigh, as though resigning himself to something. Then he leaned back and closed his eyes and hummed so quietly that the sound was only there for a moment before being swallowed up by the lope of the engine as the car bobbled up and down over the rough-hewn field.

"I'm not the one who sent you that draft notice, Tommy," Gannon said. "You've already let her get you into more trouble than you had to, son."

"He's not your son," I said.

"You're just a strong back to her, Tommy," Gannon said, as though I hadn't spoken. "She'll never make it without you and she knows it. That's the reason she's dragging you along on this. Don't you dare think it's anything different than that. I'm the only person that can make this right with the draft, son. I'm trying to help you. They don't treat dodgers too good."

"Yeah," I replied, "they send them off to war."

Tommy let out a stiff laugh.

Though the ground was frozen and hard now, the winter had come with fits of warmth that had unlocked the earth into a bog only for it to refreeze days later, misshapen and awkward, like a heart riding the highs and lows of love and hate over the course of a long marriage. Here and there the ground dipped, long and deep as a starving belly, and the car was thrown down into a depression and all Tommy could do was hold tight to the steering wheel and keep his foot on the accelerator, uncertain whether or not we would be able to climb out of the hole in which we found ourselves. But Tommy was good behind the wheel and he got the car over to the trees that jutted out, dense and bare, on the far edge of the field.

"Right there," I said, pointing ahead.

"I see it," Tommy said, aiming for where the trees were thickest. There was a scrub of green pines and bare oaks. Not much, but enough to make the car difficult to see from the road when the sun finally came up.

"You kids really should think this over," Gannon said. I thought I heard genuine concern in his voice, but whether it was for us or for himself was hard to say. As the car plunged into one final dip that sent us all bouncing, Gannon grabbed his father to steady the man. "It's okay, Pop," he cooed. "I got you."

Tommy pulled the car to a stop and put it in Park. "Now what?"

"Leave it running," I replied.

"What about poison?" Tommy asked.

"What poison?"

"Carbon dioxide."

"Carbon monoxide," Gannon corrected him, turning and looking at me through the thick Plexiglas divider. "He's afraid we'll suffocate while we're sitting here waiting to be found," he continued. "He's got a right to be scared. It's bad enough that you're locking a sick man like my father in here, but if something happens to me while I'm waiting — anything at all, even if I have a damn heart attack from boredom — that's manslaughter for the both of you. If you're lucky. But they won't let you have luck. Not with a dead cop on their hands. So they'll swing for the fences. Try you both as adults. Murder. First-degree. 'With foresight and malice.' That's what they'll say."

"Is that true?" Tommy asked.

Even I wasn't immune to what Gannon had said. He'd managed to paint a picture in my mind — Tommy and me in a courtroom, on trial; Tommy would get the harder sentence because that had always been his lot in life; they'd send him to the electric chair and put me in prison; but they wouldn't keep me there on account of how smart I was; they'd figure some way out for me on account of how I was special; that had always been my lot in life.

I walked on water. Tommy only choked on it.

"Just do what I told you, Tommy," I replied. "We'll leave the heat on medium and crack the windows. He'll be fine. I promise."

Tommy nodded in assent. He switched off the headlights and set the heater temperature as he had been told.

"Good," I said. "Now get out."

"Why?" Tommy asked.

"Just go, Tommy. I'll be right behind you."

Tommy stared at me. "I'm not going to do anything," I said. I rapped my knuckles against the Plexiglas dividing the front and back of the squad car. "Couldn't even if I wanted to. And you've got the gun, after all."

"That's right," Tommy said, his voice full of sudden authority. ". . . that's right." Finally he opened the driver's door and stepped out into the cold.

I turned in my seat, looking back on Jim Gannon. "Once the sun comes up it won't take them long to find you. It'll be a little embarrassing, so you're welcome to tell them whatever story you want about how you wound up here. If I were you, I would say it was a prank."

Gannon barked a sharp laugh. "A prank?"

"Yep," I replied. "Just the local cops having a little bit of fun with you. You can say that you and them go way back. You just happened to run into them as you were passing through, on your way home from a law enforcement training seminar. That'll explain why you were three states outside of your jurisdiction in your squad car and uniform."

"Jurisdiction doesn't apply with runaway children," Gannon said. "But you already know that, don't you, Virginia? You're the smart one." He slumped in the seat and checked the back of his head once more to be sure it wasn't bleeding.

"Just say that they were some friends of yours and this was their way of being funny. They put you in the back seat of your own car and left you out here. It's believable."

"You got one hell of a mind on you," Gannon replied. "But you already know that."

"And he'll be okay," I said, looking at Gannon's father.

"Are you asking me or telling me?" Gannon replied.

I looked out the car window at Tommy. He was standing just beside the car, watching our conversation.

Gannon's eyes followed mine.

"Just let us go, Jim," I said. My voice was softer than I had planned. There was a levee inside me that was on the verge of breaking all of a sudden. I didn't know when it had begun swelling — I've never been particularly good with emotions. The energy it takes to keep all of the memories at bay tends to push down the feelings connected with those memories. It's the only way that someone like me, who lives as much in the past as they do in the present, can exist without reliving everything again and again. So I learned to keep my feelings at arm's length, but the problem with that is that they always eventually push in, suddenly and without warning. "Just go back home and let Tommy and me have this trip. And once it's over . . ." I hesitated, then pushed on. "Once it's over I'll talk Tommy into coming back. It'll be like nothing ever happened."

"You just don't get it, do you?" Gannon

said. "He showed me his papers. He's already overdue. That means they've already put him on the dodge list. That means jail first and then the war. But if I bring him back, I can help soften that. I come from three generations of lawmen. My name counts for something. I can smooth all of this out for him. Make it so that, when he goes off to fight, he does it with honor. The way he's supposed to. There's a principle at work here." Gannon clucked his tongue. "The thing that amazes me the most is how proud Tommy was when he showed me that letter. Never seen him so proud. Like getting drafted was the best thing that ever happened to him."

"Living was the best thing that ever happened to him," I said. "I'm just trying to keep that going for as long as I can." Then I opened the door before any more could be said and stepped out into the cold, leaving Gannon alone with his father and, perhaps for the first time in his life, powerless, in spite of all the instruments and ornaments of the Law.

Go back far enough and you'll find that Jim Gannon came from a long line of policemen. He called them "lawmen" on the night when he sat me down and recounted to me the names and stories of the three genera-tions that had come before him. He had never called them lawmen before. But once he was finally convinced that I truly did remember everything I ever saw or heard, he brought me into the living room and sat down in front of me with an old scrapbook filled with photos and news clippings and recounted to me all the stories he could remember having to deal with his father, William Gannon Jr.; his grandfather, William Gannon Sr.; and his great-grandfather, Thomas Gannon. "All good lawmen. Each one of them," he said.

It took him a full hour and a half to talk about what was important. There was the story of how his great-grandfather had come over from Europe and immediately gone out West, back before the West was settled, back when the Indians hadn't yet been treatied into submission. And Tom Gannon, seeing the way things needed to be if this country was going to work out, took up the badge as a United States marshal. Years later, when his own son shunned being a marshal but took a fancy to the art of sheriffing, Tom was only slightly upset about it. And when William Sr. passed on his badge to William Jr., it was already decided that, when Jim Gannon was born, he would take up the mantle. But then Gannon's father had a stroke when he was young and never recovered and a new sheriff won the election. Gannon hadn't been old enough to run and now, fifteen years later, he still hadn't managed to get beyond being a deputy.

Something in Gannon's voice told me that maybe he actually hated his job.

"At least I'm still a part of the way things used to be," Gannon said proudly. "There's honor in that." He took a deep breath and stared at me. He sat with his back erect and his chin thrust forward, as though he were posing for a picture. "You make sure you remember that part," he said.

And, of course, I did remember that part. And all the other parts as well. I remembered the way he looked a little afraid when he talked about his not yet being made sheriff. I remembered the way his voice quickened when he talked about the sudden decline of his father — the way a child speeds up their pace as they pass an old abandoned house whose walls and gables have become nothing more than an empty husk. I remembered everything, with unrelenting clarity. To hear Jim tell it, his father had been a smiling, confident man. The type of man that other men wanted to be. The type of man Jim Gannon wanted to be.

And then, one day, that man was gone and all that was left behind was an invalid.

No matter how much he took care of the man, I'm not sure Jim Gannon ever forgave his father for that.

When Gannon had finished speaking, his wife and Tommy were pulling up in the yard. Gannon got up in a hurry and returned his scrapbook to his bedroom and came back out. "No need to talk to them about this," he said to me in the solid, familiar voice I hadn't heard in an hour and a half.

"I hadn't planned to," I replied.

And then, in a whisper, just before the front door opened and his wife and foster son came in, Gannon said, "Thank you."

He had been like every other foster parent in the beginning, back when Jennifer was still with him. Back when The Disease was becoming more aggressive and the war seemed like something that might come to an end just like every other that had come before it. The two of them couldn't have any children on their own — his fault — and so they decided to adopt and with him being well-off in the police force, it wasn't too hard to make happen.

Everyone was trying to have children back then. The population of people over eighty had dwindled and those in their seventies were beginning to go. Back then there were still theories about being able to stop it. And some people say that's what really started the war: the hope that some other country knew something about The Disease and was keeping it to themselves, hoping to outlive the rest of the world. Pregnancy rates tripled in those first years. Everyone hoping to fix the end of people by simply making more people.

And for those who couldn't have their own, adoption became the fix. That's how Tommy and I found Gannon and Jennifer. They came to our group home that day wearing their best Sunday outfits and smiling with the pleased euphoria of people in magazine ads. They'd both been told about how special I was and Jennifer had made it a point to say that "All kids are special." At which point Tommy looked over at her with something akin to pity in his eyes and said, matter-of-factly, "That's bullshit."

Jennifer laughed a nervous laugh, and eventually Jim joined in and it wasn't long before the laughter wasn't nervous anymore. It was as good of an introduction to foster parents as we had ever had. Not that it really mattered. We were fifteen by then. Jennifer and Jim would be the last stop before we were too old for the system.

Over the next two years I watched Jim Gannon harden for reasons no one in the household seemed to be able to understand. He came home after work and talked a little less each day. Mostly he settled in front of the television and heard what it had to say. When the news wasn't talking about The Disease it was talking about the war. And Gannon seemed interested only in the war.

Night after night he watched the reporters wearing bulletproof vests atop polo shirts as they hunkered down inside bombed-out buildings. They yelled about "total destruction" or "total resistance" while gunfire clattered like microwave popcorn somewhere off screen. Now and again they covered their ears and pressed their heads against the ruined floors of faraway war zones and they waited, mumbling to themselves, trying to look both brave and terrified all at once. Then there would be an explosion big enough to make the camera shudder. Maybe followed by a cloud of dust. Then the reporters would lift their head from the sand and look around with bewilderment and say, "Thank God. That was a close one."

Every day Gannon was there watching. Sometimes he gripped the arms of the chair beneath him until his knuckles went white and his face reddened because he didn't know he was holding his breath. Then he would realize and the air would rush into his lungs and he'd have to go outside for a smoke to calm down.

Jennifer would go out to him sometimes. I listened from the upstairs window as Jennifer begged Gannon to tell her what was wrong. Begged him to seek help for whatever it was. Begged him to "come back to me." She even took time to blame herself for their inability to have a child and fix the world like everyone else was trying to do.

None of it worked, though.

He grew harder.

He drank more.

They drifted apart.

Sometimes when he was drunk he would fly into a fit of rage. Thundering voice. High-flying hands that threw dishes and put holes in drywall. And when the rage was over he would retreat to his wife's bedroom door and knock, gently, like a child, and whisper, "I'm sorry, Jen. I'm sorry, okay? Just open the door. Please."

And Jennifer, because she was a soft woman capable of forgiving anything, always opened the door and let him in. Then I would sit in my bedroom, usually with Tommy not far away, and I would listen while Gannon slumped to his knees like a sack of potatoes, sobbing apologies into the late hours of the night. All the while his wife would whisper — the soft sound of her voice drifting through the walls like an incantation — and her whispers would be full of forgiveness and something more. Absolution maybe.

I had once asked Jennifer why she forgave Gannon the way she did. "Because," Jennifer said, "the heart can break and break and break again, but then turn around and love like it's never known how."

Jennifer held out hope for her and Gannon's emotional resurrection. But I knew better.

If this had all happened when I was younger, I might have been inclined to lie awake at night worrying about the fate of my latest set of foster parents. But The Memory Gospel was full of foster parents whose relationships didn't last. Foster parents who had taken in foster children in the hopes that by filling the empty places in their home they would fill the empty places in their hearts. That's all children really were when you got right down to it, I figured: just a person's attempt to create someone who loved them wholly and completely, from birth. Someone who would carry that love forever.

Children, in the end, were gods of our own design. And when you couldn't build your own god, you called social services and had one delivered. But I was tired of being someone else's therapy.

It was during one of Gannon's outbursts a few months ago that I made the decision that Tommy and I should run away.

"To Florida?" Tommy asked. It was late and Gannon was in the living room screaming and Jennifer was in her bedroom refusing to let him come in. The house trembled and shook, but continued standing.

"To the launch," I replied.

"This is that whole Jupiter thing again, right?" Tommy asked.

I sighed a long, slow, damning sigh. I would have to explain it all yet again to my brother. "Not Jupiter," I began. "Europa. One of Jupiter's moons."

"Still don't care," Tommy said.

"They're sending a probe up there that might find life."

"They won't," Tommy replied. He was lying on the floor, staring up at the ceiling as we talked. Whether he genuinely didn't believe in what I was telling him or whether he just wanted to frustrate me, I couldn't decide, but the latter was the one that was working the most. "And no," Tommy said, "I don't need you to explain the math to me about how they actually might find something there. That whole Frank's equation of whatever."

"The Drake equation," I corrected him.

"The Bobby equation. The Joe equation. The Captain America equation. I don't care what it is," Tommy said. "It's not going to happen."

"I don't know why I bother," I said.

"Because I make frustration fun," Tommy said. Then he smiled a self-satisfied smile.

"Do you remember Dad's letter?"

"Nope," Tommy replied, almost before the question could be asked.

"He said, 'Even back then I knew that Europa was important.' Do you know when people first had the idea that there might be life on Europa?"

"Nope, but I'm sure you're going to tell me."

"As far back as 1989," I said. "That's when the Galileo mission was launched and sent back all that data in 1995 that showed there might be an ocean under the surface. Dad was just a kid back then, younger than us, but I bet he heard about it and fell in love with Europa immediately. He knew it was special. He knew we'd have to send a probe there one day to find out. He always knew."

"Good for him," Tommy said. He rolled over onto his side, tucked his forearm beneath his head and closed his eyes. In the living room the sound of Gannon's yelling was starting to subside. He'd be asleep soon, and then Tommy would fall asleep, but never before.

"Let's do it for Dad," I said.

"Dad's dead," Tommy replied. "He'll never know whether we do it or not."

"We'll know," I replied.

"I'm not going," Tommy said. There was finality in his voice, like a door being closed. "And if I don't go you won't go."

He was right, of course. And I knew it.

So that night, while Gannon descended from shouting to slurred mumbling to that final, incomprehensible bit of soft gibbering that always swept over him in the moments before sleep, while Tommy was on his side, falling asleep, I began being buried in The Gospel:

. . . Tommy is twelve years old and wants to be a magician and I know that he won't be any good at it but I sit patiently as Tommy stands in front of me with a cape made out of a foster father's jacket and a top hat that is nothing more than a baseball cap and Tommy

clumsily holds a deck of cards and shuffles them back and forth in his hand and he has forgotten to say the magic words and he has forgotten everything else so that when he holds up the seven of hearts and asks, "Is this your card?" I say to him, "Yes!" even though it isn't my card and Tommy, because of his knowledge of his own weakness with memory and planning, doesn't trust that he has chosen the correct card and so he turns it around and looks at it and then looks back at me and his eyes ask me to confirm whether or not he has chosen the right card — because he knows that I will remember what he doesn't and he has come to trust The Memory Gospel and trust what I tell him to be true — and he stands waiting, never looking more like a child than right now, and he asks a second time, "Are you sure this was your card?" and without hesitation I say to him, "Yes, that's it," and Tommy smiles stiffly and doubts himself and his lack of memory even more and I know that, because of this one moment, he always will and so I decide, right then and there, to always be the keeper of not only the past, but also the future . . .

ELSEWHERE

He was checking on his father every single day and, when he was honest with himself, he didn't know how much longer he could keep doing it. They had never gotten along. He'd always been a burden to the Old Man — as least, that's how it felt to him — but now with things going the way they were in the world, the good thing for him to do was to make amends before the end came in that soft, quiet way it was coming these days.

It had been his girlfriend's idea. "Make up with your father," she said. And she said it in that gentle, movie-of-the-week way of saying it. The way a person says it when they have no idea what they're asking of someone.

It wasn't that he hated his father. Not anymore, at least. He'd gone through that period of hating for years. He'd spent every single day of his life gnashing his teeth on the memories of everything the Old Man had done to him. The beatings, the name-calling. The

Old Man had even gone so far as to lock him in a closet for a full day because he hadn't come home on time the day before. And there were worse things. Things that he didn't want to remember. Things that he probably should have gone to see a therapist about — at least, that's what his girlfriend told him — but he never did. He had been raised by the Old Man to believe that a man takes care of his own sadness.

But visiting the Old Man now was something that he felt he could do. More than that, he felt that he had to do it. Between The Disease and the war, everyone was trying to make amends, to settle the old debts and put things to rest on their own terms. People called it "Settling Up." And, whether the Old Man knew it or not, his son was coming to him over and over again in the hopes of Settling Up, even though he didn't really know what that meant. He just knew it was something that needed to be done.

So for over a month he went to the small retirement home and he walked through the antiseptic-smelling hallways with a knot in his stomach and all of his muscles tense and as soon as he saw the Old Man the knot hardened and the muscles got even tenser, yet he smiled and said the familiar words, "Hi, Pop," just the same way he always had.

The Old Man had been wasting away for years, but he was still strong. He sat up straight — a military man through and through — and every time his son came into the room and said, "Hi, Pop" the Old Man replied to him by saying, "You're late."

But the man had gotten used to the way his father was and, nowadays, he actually did show up late since he didn't particularly want to be there, but showing up was the right thing to do and people were all about doing the right thing these days.

So the cycle went for months.

And then one day the man showed up and said, "Hi, Pop."

"You're late."

"How are you feeling?"

"Good enough." The Old Man jutted his lower jaw forward like an anvil. "You heard about these damn kids? These Embers?" He spat the word like snake venom.

"Yeah, Pop. I heard about them."

"Goddamn cowards," the Old Man said, almost at a growl. "Too afraid to go off and fight the way they're supposed to. Goddamn bleeding-heart cowards." He tightened his fist and slammed it on his chair and tried to stand but his legs hadn't worked in years on account of a car accident that had broken his back and he sometimes seemed to forget that. Or maybe he was just too stubborn to accept it.

"I can't say I really blame them," the man said.

The Old Man ignored his son's opinion and continued on: "The fact of the matter is everybody's got a job to do and these kids ain't doing it. They think they're the first ones to be afraid of a war? Well they ain't. Problem is they think they're special. They feel like they're too good to go off and fight and maybe die and, mark my words, that'll be the exact thing that brings an ending to everybody and everything on this planet."

"What about The Disease?" the man asked his father.

"What about it?" the Old Man replied. "People been getting sick ever since people came into existence. And we're still here. The world is still spinning and we're still crawling all over it. No, there ain't no getting rid of people. There ain't no getting rid of humanity."

"Well, maybe this time is different." The man swallowed, looking for courage.

"Nothing's ever different," the Old Man butted in. And then he cleared his throat and looked over at his son, and suddenly the Old Man's ever-present anger seemed to lessen, like a muscle that had become fatigued. "They found two people this morning. Right down the hall. Couldn't wake them up. Wasn't neither one of them any older than me."

And there it was. The Old Man was scared. Maybe for the very first time in his life.

Seeing that, the man was afraid. Because if the Old Man could be afraid that this was the twilight of the world, maybe this was, truly, as everyone had been saying, the "end of the party" for all of humankind. Which meant that he would die and his girlfriend would die and, even more terrifying, the Old Man — a man so mean and full of spite that Death had been too afraid to take him for years — would finally die as well.

All of a sudden, the man loved his father and all of the energy he had spent being angry with him was gone.

So he looked away and said finally, in a low voice, "I forgive you."

The Old Man didn't reply, which didn't surprise the man. But it still made him angry. "God dammit, say something!"

When he looked back at his father, he found the Old Man sleeping — his head lolled forward at the end of his neck, a small drop of spittle already forming in the corner of his lip.

The man would try to rouse his father but it wouldn't work. He would call the nurses and they would come and, only because it was what they were paid to do, they would inject the Old Man with stimulants and race around

78

shouting about blood pressure and heart rate, knowing that the Old Man wouldn't wake just like no one else had wakened from The Disease.

The man eventually walked out of the retirement home thinking to himself that, finally, he had said the words to his father. Wondering if he had been heard.

FOUR

Years later Tommy would tell me about this
moment, about this whole trip. He would
give it all to me so that I could remember it
and write it all down. He said to me that
when he stopped to think about it, he had
been expecting the draft notice all along.
Since the day he turned seventeen. Since
the day the letters started going out. Since
the day the politicians decided to reinstate
the draft. On and on, all the way back to
before the start of the war. It was like he'd
been expecting that letter from the president
for his entire life. And so, when it finally
came, he found himself confused and disbe-
lieving, the way we all are when the world
finally does the terrible thing we knew it
would.

The letter from the Draft Board came in a
plain brown envelope with the presidential
seal — which some people had mocked by
calling it "The Free Chicken" — in the up-

per left corner. He'd just gotten home from school and opened the mailbox and there it was, like a foundling, waiting for him. It stated Mr. Thomas Matthews in a typeface so bold and straight that he could almost hear the president himself sounding out his name.

He put his thumb over The Free Chicken for a moment and rubbed it back and forth. When he looked, the chicken was still there. So be it. He'd been preparing himself for this moment. Watching Gannon's ever-growing collection of war movies when he wasn't at home, just to get a sense of what Hollywood had to say how war was. He figured it was a pretty good way to get a handle on things. Sure, there were books out there that he could read, but he'd managed to get through only one of them: Tim O'Brien's *The Things They Carried.* It wasn't a difficult read but it was a difficult book. Everybody kept dying and Tommy couldn't predict when it would happen or who it would happen to next. In the movies, you knew that the more familiar the actor, the longer it would take for Death to find them. But with O'Brien's book there weren't any actors to recognize and so Death took who it wanted whenever it wanted. That notion left Tommy shaken and unsettled for a few days after he'd finished the book.

But then, as it always happened with Tommy, O'Brien's book and the memory of everything it had made him feel began to recede and, before long, it was almost as if he hadn't read the book at all. If someone asked him he could say, "Yeah, I read that." But that it was a book about soldiers was all he could ever say about it. And because he was so gifted in his ability to let go of things — including fear of Death itself — his confidence could always come back to him.

As he stood there that day staring down at the president's chicken pressed beneath his thumb, the fear came rising back up inside him. He remembered that he had read some book about soldiers and war and dying and he remembered that it had made him afraid, but he couldn't remember why. So he simply folded the letter from the president and stuffed it into his pocket.

In the three days before he showed the letter to me, Tommy spent a lot of time watching the news. There was bombing in Baltimore. Where the war was happening, fifty-three soldiers had died in an ambush. In France there was a handful of killings. London caught a bomber before any damage could be done. Police and soldiers — one barely distinguishable from the other anymore — stood before the cameras with pride bursting from their chests in the way only the English can.

The war, terrorism, however you wanted to slice it up, was transforming everyone. But Tommy was too young to be able to see and understand it. Tommy only saw the way the world was and he couldn't imagine it ever being any other way. So when people talked about how much better things used to be — the way his father did in his letters — Tommy listened and pondered what was being said but, ultimately, saw it all as little more than fiction. Memory was always fiction, Tommy figured. And maybe that was why he chose not to buy into it. Maybe that was why he chose not to remember anything. To Tommy's mind, the whole reason the war was still going on was that everyone was too busy wishing the world was the way it used to be. It would be better, he figured, if people just accepted their world.

He got in two fistfights the day after the draft notice came. Won them both, of course. Because he was strong and hard and because he had started them both before the other boys involved even knew what was happening. There was one boy — big as a wildebeest and almost as ugly — who Tommy had walked up on while he was tying his shoe and stepped squarely on his foot. The boy rose up and towered over Tommy and Tommy knew good and well that he should have been afraid, but he wasn't.

After he'd beaten up the boy and walked away, Tommy told himself that he should feel bad for what he had done. And maybe he actually did feel bad. It was always hard to say. What he really felt was the adrenaline racing through his veins like lava. He felt the bruises forming on his knuckles. He felt the throb in his left ear where the boy had brought around a haymaker and found a home for it. He felt a small quiver in his legs that was the sign that the adrenaline would soon be leaving him and he'd come crashing back down to earth.

Dinner had come and gone and Gannon was asleep when Tommy got home later that night. I was sitting in my bedroom reading on account of how I rarely ever slept.

"Did you win?" I asked.

"What?" Tommy replied. I made a motion to the side of my face. After a moment, Tommy realized what I was saying. "Oh," he said, touching the back of his hand to the welt on the side of his ear. "It's nothing."

"Who gave you that nothing?"

"No one," Tommy replied. Then: "Everyone."

"That's pretty existential."

"It's pretty what?"

"Nothing."

Tommy sat on the floor and looked down at his hands. His knuckles were bruised and the fingers of his left hand trembled. He made a fist so that he didn't have to see them shake.

"So, are you going to tell me what it is?" I asked.

"Nothing," Tommy said. "I guess I'm just experimental or whatever."

"Existential."

"That's what I said." His brow was furrowed. His clenched fist wound itself even tighter. He heard a soft, muffled pop and looked up to see that the sound was that of me closing my book and focusing my attention on him, which I didn't do often enough. I realize that now.

"Whatever it is," I said, "I'm going to figure it out eventually."

"I know," Tommy said.

"Not because I'm smarter than you."

"No?"

"No," I replied. "I'm going to figure it out because you're my brother. And because I love you."

"Thanks, Ginny," Tommy said. "You're a good sister sometimes."

"Don't go ruining my image," I said, grinning in spite of myself. "You want me to read you one of Dad's letters?" I asked.

"No," Tommy replied. He looked down at his hand. Finally it had stopped shaking. "Why do you read them?" Tommy asked.

"What do you mean?"

"What's the point?"

"Because keeping them matters," I said.

"Why does it matter?" Tommy replied. I could see the thoughts taking shape in his mind. "I guess I just don't understand how holding on to the past does anything good for the future," he said slowly.

He exhaled. He'd passed the candle that was burning inside through the crevices of his mind and body and he'd said what he felt. He'd achieved that miracle. "I'll see you in the morning," he said immediately, before I could ask more questions.

He went to his room and pulled out the draft notice from his pocket. It was wrinkled. He looked again at the strong, indomitable font that they used to tell seventeen-year-old boys that it was their turn to pick up a rifle and go off and get killed, and then a voice was in his head, sounding like the president himself, saying, "No way in hell you can do this."

Tommy stood in his room and it seemed smaller all of a sudden. Or maybe he seemed larger. Maybe he was swelling up, overflowing the inside of himself.

It was just after midnight when Tommy started out for the river. It was over two hours of hiking before he began to hear the roar of the water and feel the chilly spray rising up and misting through the January air. He had brought his backpack along — complete with camping supplies — on the off chance that he might run into someone and need an excuse.

He was almost upset when he met no one on his way to the river. One of the few times in his life that he'd actually thought ahead and there would be nobody to see it.

Then he found himself standing atop a large rock on the edge of the river, staring down into the water as the moon shone overhead and turned the water to light. The rock moved a little under his weight, like it knew why he had come there and wanted to help. When the rock shifted and settled again Tommy just stood there and waited for the bottom to fall out from beneath him. He straightened his back and stuck his chest out and looked like the statue of a hero who had conquered everything in this life and had gone on to conquer everything in the next.

Tommy knew that he was supposed to be afraid. But he wasn't. Just tired. Like he'd carried too much for too long.

He inched closer to the edge of the rock. It shifted again beneath him, but still didn't give up. Tommy waited for Death with the patience of a crocodile. He wasn't sure when it had happened, but somewhere along the way he had decided to put his life into the hands of Fate. So he waited for The Inevitable Lady to make her decision.

Time passed and the rock never gave way. The wind never came along and pushed him off. The river itself never reached up and plucked him out of the air. The only thing that happened was that time passed and he was still alive and, finally, the more he realized he was still alive, the more afraid he became.

Afraid of the war. Not afraid of dying in it, but of going to it and not being smart enough. Afraid of failing the man next to him. Afraid of messing things up the way he could sometimes and getting somebody killed. Afraid he'd go there and get it all wrong and be sent home and I would be waiting for him and I'd look at him with eyes that looked just like our mother's and I'd say, "It's okay, Tommy. You did your best."

And he would be forced to live with the fact that his best hadn't been good enough. It never was.

The fear never broke. Not even when he stepped back from the edge and started home. He didn't cry, even though he thought that was probably what he should have done. That's what a person was supposed to do at these types of moments. But there were no tears. Not until he got back to me.

He came inside the house just before sunrise and found everyone asleep just as they had been. He took off his backpack and placed it in the closet. He walked into my room and sat on the floor next to my bed and, finally, he began to cry.

He sobbed like a child until the new day broke.

When I woke — from a dream of rain and sadness — I looked down at him and saw him crying and I climbed out of bed and sat beside him and put my arm around him and said, as though ending a long conversation the two of us had been having, "Thank you."

He clucked a sob-filled laugh.

"I never know how to do anything right," Tommy said.

To My Children,

Your mother always smiled more than I did and I never understood why. She planned trips we knew we weren't going to take. She bought old photos at yard sales of people we didn't know and she told me the fictitious narrative of their lives in her best storyteller's voice. In the mornings she assigned me the most interesting horoscope she could find, regardless of what sign it fell under. We lived in a small apartment that she turned into a home. She filled it with items rooted in the both of us. The scarf she wore on our first date. A fistful of sand from a night shared on a beach. She always found a way to present these small things like holy relics so that we were never far away from the things we love.

By the end of the first month of knowing we were bringing a child into the world I couldn't sleep. At night I sat up reading while your mother snored in that catlike way of hers. I reread old books, certain I had missed something important but never exactly sure what. When the morning came, I had slept for maybe two hours. My eyes stung and my body felt as though it belonged to someone else. Then your mother would roll over and kiss me — she was always touching, always trying to prove to me that we were connected — and my body would become my own once again.

At work, I wrote a personal interest column. "Keeping hope alive" is how Clarence, the old man who owned the paper, referred to it. It was my job, he felt, to stem the dismal tide that seemed to be rising. I was supposed to undo everything that was being done in the world.

Clarence — a stout man with wide shoulders, round glasses and an even rounder bald head — told me one day, "It'll never matter more than it does right now."

"What's that?"

"It's all knocking on the front door. And we've got to answer it, for better or worse. But that doesn't mean we have to give up."

"You lost me."

"Like hell I did."

Whenever possible, "Like hell I did" was how he ended conversations. There was nothing those four words couldn't do. They made him enigmatic and wise when, only a moment ago, he had been just a fat old bald man with arthritic knuckles and a newspaper that was draining his life's savings.

That night in bed, I told your mother about Clarence and what he'd said.

"I think he's right," she mumbled. It was early still but she was already half-asleep.

"Right about what?" I asked. "What he said didn't make any sense."

"Wise words coming your way," she said, just as she fell asleep.

It was that morning's horoscope.

It felt like everyone was talking about something but had forgotten to clue me in on the conversation.

Meanwhile, the world and the things that happened in it made my job a little harder every day. But still, I did my work, and each and every Sunday, Clarence's newspaper came out with my byline and some story that made it seem as if everything in life made sense. And all the while insomnia was my friend and I felt like a fraud because there you were, growing, next to me in the bed inside your mother, and I was just perpetuating a lie. I was saying that everything was okay and that everything would continue to be okay. Parenting 101: The

Art of Hopefulness.

Then one day, Clarence came in and canceled my column. "It's all just getting too big," he said.

"That's no reason to cancel me," I said. "I've got a kid on the way."

"I know," he said. "I didn't say I was firing you. I'll still find something for you to do. Sports maybe. Or crime. There's enough of that to spread around."

I didn't want sports and I didn't want crime. I wanted people. I wanted to write about the fair that had just arrived. I wanted to describe the way the lights lit up the sky until they reached the clouds. I wanted to talk about the laughter that could never drown out the familiar and strange music that seemed to rise up from everywhere at a fairground, sounding unlike anything else over the course of your life. I wanted to tell people about the Whirl-and-Twirl, the Teacup ride, the Rocking Ship and the Rocket Ship, the Bumper Cars, the cotton candy that promised heaven and diabetes at the same time. All of it mattered just then. It wasn't hope anymore, it was doctrine. People needed to know it still existed just like they needed to know that there was someone who heard their prayers in the late hours of the night.

And that someone, in a certain type of way, was me. By writing it all down I was saving everything. Preserving the moments that can be easily forgotten. Saving them not for me. Not even for you. But for everyone.

Clarence published me only once a month after that. He added crime. He added sports. He added terrorism. He added politics. He poured it all on. Milk onto cereal. But once a month people got better news. They got to hear about that fair. And after it had come and gone, I wrote another piece on it, so that they would know that just because they couldn't see it anymore didn't mean it wasn't still out there. Still alive. Still pouring light up into darkness.

We changed the title of my column to The Art of Hopefulness not long after that. It was your mother's suggestion. "Hope," she said, "is just imagination put into practice." I couldn't tell if it was my horoscope for the day or her own idea.

FIVE

"Keep walking," Tommy said. He nudged me in the back and got me going again. I didn't know that I had stopped walking. I only knew that I was cold and tired and that, in spite of myself, I couldn't stop thinking about Gannon and his father.

"Do you think they're okay?"

"Of course they are," Tommy replied. "You wouldn't have let us leave them if they weren't going to be okay." He looked off into the distance. "We need to find a ride before they find them."

"I know," I said.

"I know you know," Tommy said. "But do you know your hands are shaking?"

I looked down and found my hands trembling. "When did that start?" I asked.

Tommy took my hands in his and held them like small birds. He took a deep breath and exhaled over them, then rubbed my fingers and blew on them again. "Come on, you Ember. Let's get you warmed up." My warming fingers felt of pins and needles.

"Don't call me that," I said.

"Why not? I think it's a cool name."

"Jesus, Tommy."

"Did I ever tell you the one about the Ember who walked into the blacked-out bar? . . . He asked for a light beer." Then he smiled but, as usual, didn't laugh.

"That doesn't even make any sense."

"Whatever," Tommy said. "How about this, then: What's hypothermia?"

"What?"

"Just tell me something about it," Tommy said. "The weirder the better. There's always something weird in that brain of yours." He smiled, still rubbing my hands together like kindling.

"Hypothermia," I began, my words shivering just a little, "is when the body core reaches a temperature below thirty-five degrees Celsius or ninety-five degrees Fahrenheit."

"Ain't it always like ninety-six or something?" Tommy interrupted.

Whether he was doing it to annoy me or didn't honestly know, I couldn't tell. "No," I said. "Normal body temperature is ninety-eight-point-six."

"Well, ninety-five isn't too far off," Tommy

said. "Hardly anything when you really think about it."

"Can I finish?" I asked, more than a little annoyed at the interruption.

"I mean, think about it," Tommy said. "Three degrees? Just three degrees? Come on!" He laughed a goofy, ignorant laugh that arched his back and seemed to show all thirty-two of his teeth at once. It was the first time I'd seen him laugh like that in over a year.

When we first got into the foster care system Tommy had become obsessed with telling terrible jokes. Jokes like, "Two flies are on the porch together. Which one is the actor? The one on the screen."

When they didn't get a laugh, they got a grimace. Either reaction gave Tommy the same amount of delight. He would throw his head back and laugh and show all of his teeth just like he was doing now and those were some of the few occasions when Tommy seemed to forget himself and be happy.

But then I stopped laughing at his jokes and so he stopped telling them and I got to see him smile less and less often because, no matter how much I wanted to, I couldn't smile. Somewhere along the way I had forgotten how and, in doing so, I had stolen my brother's laughter.

But he had somehow found it again in the days since receiving his draft notice. Maybe waiting to die is something we should all be able to laugh about.

"I'm ignoring you," I said.

"Not very well," Tommy replied. "Now keep talking."

"Hypothermia symptoms depend on how far the body temperature has fallen," I said. "It usually starts with shivering in the extremities on account of how they lose temperature the fastest and exhibit vasoconstriction."

"What's vasoconstruction?" Tommy asked. "Is that like building something out of Vaseline?"

"Vasoconstriction," I corrected him.

"That's what I said," Tommy fired back.

"It's when the blood vessels constrict in order to reduce blood flow," I said. "Basically the body begins trying to hoard all of the blood . . ." My voice trailed off. I took a deep breath. The cold was suddenly swelling up around me like a fog.

"Don't stop now," Tommy said, managing a smile. "That vasoconstruction thing's got me on the edge of my seat."

"Vasoconstriction."

"Again: that's what I said."

Tommy's smile was wide and proud.

"Don't do that," I said.

"Don't do what?"

"Handle me. Don't handle me like this. I'm fine."

"You're not fine, Ginny," Tommy said. "You're freezing and I'm just trying to remind you that you're smart enough to know it. The first symptom you mentioned was shivering, right?" He let go of my hands. We both watched. For a moment they were okay, but then the trembling returned.

"I'll be fine," I said. I shoved my hands into my pockets and started walking again. Though the sky was still dark the thin light I saw in the distance began to grow, back-lighting the trees. They became ghosts, beautiful and eternal.

After a few steps, Tommy was at my side again. "Okay," he said. "You'll be fine. But in the meantime, where's my weird fact? You still owe me one."

"You're still trying to distract me," I said.

"Yep," Tommy replied. "Now come on."

After a few more steps, I began, "Okay. Two things: terminal-burrowing and paradoxical undressing."

"Is that like getting naked at a party?" Tommy asked.

"Neither has been studied very much," I said, ignoring the interruption, "but basically in the late stages of hypothermia there's a thing called terminal-burrowing. Basically, people will try to dig a hole and curl up, even if that might not be the best thing to do."

"Well, that doesn't sound so bad," Tommy said. "It's like digging one of those things in the snow for yourself."

"An igloo?"

"That's what I said."

"No," I replied. "It's totally irrational. People will crawl under beds, behind desks, under couches. And to make it worse, a lot of the time they're naked when they do it."

"How'd they get naked?" Tommy asked with a smirk. "Because that seems like the best part of the story and you skipped right over it."

"Paradoxical undressing," I replied. "Somewhere around thirty-five percent of people that die of hypothermia are found naked. It's believed that what happens is the vasoconstriction —"

"Vasoconstruction."

"That's what I . . . Screw you, Tommy." I cleared my throat to drown out the sound of Tommy's laughter. "The blood vessels eventually get exhausted, like a muscle that's been tensed too long, and so they suddenly stop constricting and let all of the blood flow. The body warms up all of a sudden and, even though you're literally freezing to death, you feel hot. Sometimes people even start sweating."

"So people start taking their clothes off?"

"Yeah," I said. "And then sometimes, after they've taken off all of their clothes, they get that burrowing instinct. They're found naked and frozen in some hole someplace."

"Next time I ask you for a weird fact," Tommy said, "just stop me. Or better yet, just tell me something to do with numbers. Numbers can't be as bad as people getting naked and dying in a hole someplace."

"You're going to be okay," I said.

"I know," Tommy replied, no small amount of pride in his voice.

"I mean you're not going to die in some hole," I said. I felt my voice soften.

We walked several steps before Tommy answered. His eyes had narrowed and his chin stuck forward like the bow of a tugboat. It was obvious he knew that I was trying to tell him something subtle. Trying to make a point without hammering him over the head with it. I could almost hear the gears working in his mind, grinding in their slow, methodical, limited way.

"I hear you," Tommy repeated. A patina of doubt clung to his voice.

"I can't get along without you," I said.

"I hear you," Tommy repeated.

"Hey, here's another weird fact for you."

"Oh no," Tommy said, palming his face.

"No, this one's fun. So in ancient Greece they used to believe that, in the very beginning, men and women were one creature. Two heads, four arms, four legs, all of that."

"First naked people digging holes and now this," Tommy said from behind his hand. I could hear him holding back a laugh.

I reached over and pulled his hand away and, sure enough, there was Tommy's wide, toothy smile. The one he didn't show nearly as much as he used to. "Don't interrupt me," I said, and I was smiling too, even though I hadn't intended to. "So men and women were one and then the gods threw down lightning bolts and split them into two. But the thing was that it split the soul in half. So men and women are always trying to find the other half of their soul."

"That sounds like some weird kind of horror movie."

"No," I said and laughed. "The thing is, the story is about dating and marriage. It's about how people fall in love. But what if it wasn't? What if it was about brothers and sisters? What if you're the other half of my soul and I'm the other half of yours?"

Tommy's toothy smile faded, replaced by a warm, contemplative grin that bordered on embarrassment. "Leave it to you to think of a thing like that at a time like this," he said.

"If I could be half of anybody, Tommy, I'd want it to be you."

The words came from somewhere I hadn't intended. But I meant them all just then. Looking back now, I wonder how I ever drifted away from believing them. I wonder how I betrayed my brother, who really was the other half of my soul, like I did.

The miles came and went. I counted off each footstep as a way of keeping my mind from drifting back to the cold that was always gnawing at the edges of me. I followed in Tommy's shadow as the wind came down from somewhere in the world far, far away and poured over us both. No matter how hard the wind, Tommy never wavered. It was easy to follow him if I let myself.

Without speaking Tommy reached back and took my hand and pulled me off the road and down into the large ditch bordering it. When I started to ask what was going on he put a finger to my lips and slid closer to the grass and turned and looked up at the sky and seemed only to wait. After a few seconds I heard the sound of the car coming.

I held my breath and waited as the sound hissed closer. The wind pushed and pulled the sound so that the car seemed to be coming from all directions at once, like standing inside a bell after it's been struck, but the glare of the headlights showed that the car was coming from the direction from which we had just come. There was no reason to believe that it wasn't Gannon.

The seconds stretched out long.

The car came and the car passed, giving no indication that it had ever seen us.

After it had passed Tommy lifted his head and watched the car recede into the dark. "We should get off the road," he said. "At least for a while."

I only nodded and followed my brother's lead.

He led us down the embankment toward a wall of dark trees that grew up along the road in dark, scruffy shadow. The bark shone in the dim starlight and bounced a reedy light off the cold, hard earth. The air inside the forest was denser, warmer. The sound of our footfalls and rustling of our clothes bounced around from tree to tree and came back to us sounding like the movement of a dozen other people. As if, at any moment, we might turn a corner and find our own faces peeking out at us from behind some tree.

"Stop," Tommy said.

After a few seconds of standing in the cold, dense forest, I heard the sound. It was a gentle rustling at first, like canvas rubbing flesh. And then came the low, rhythmic thud of footfalls followed by young lungs pushing and pulling at the cold, thick air.

A light flared in our eyes, blinding us both.

"Who are you?" a hard, female voice hissed. "What are you doing out here?"

She held up a hand to beat back the light just as Tommy did the same. Then he took a step forward, putting himself between me and whoever was behind the flashlight.

Tommy lowered his hand and looked directly into the glare. Then, having nothing productive come of it, he shielded his eyes and over his shoulder whispered to me, "Who do you think they are, Ginny?"

I already knew who they were, even before the light was lowered and our eyes were able to adjust so we could finally see them.

There were almost ten of them standing in the forest before us, beneath the dim starlight. Embers, each and every one. And all of them old enough to be drafted. All of them trying to get away from the war.

Save for one, they stood with their heads down, coats pulled up to their ears, legs trembling from cold and fatigue, as though everything in their lives was being carried on their shoulders and was pushing them into the earth, grinding them down with each moment.

"Hey!" Tommy said before I could stop him.

In unison, they all trained their eyes on him. "We're not police or draft," Tommy said. "We're just on our way to Florida," he continued. "Heading down to watch the launch. How about you guys?"

After a long moment and a watchful stare, the person holding the flashlight spoke. She was dark-skinned with her hair cut close like a soldier's. She had hard eyes. And when she spoke, her voice was confident as steel. "You both about the right age," she said, looking us up and down. "You been drafted yet? You don't have to go. None of us has to. If you're smart you'll come with us." Her voice was still firm, but there was sympathy in it. Almost pity. In spite of whatever compassion might have been there, she never let her eyes leave me as I

107

moved closer to Tommy and placed my hand inside his pocket. Gannon's gun was still there.

"Like my brother told you, we're heading down to watch the launch," I said.

The girl with the hard eyes barked a sharp laugh. "Is your map broken? Because you're a long way from Florida."

Tommy managed a smile. Then he squinted, looking over the group, and I could see that his brain had finally figured out what it was seeing. Now if only I could stop him before — "You're dodgers, aren't you?" Tommy asked, almost happily.

A tremble went through the group. The girl with the hard eyes seemed to harden even more. "And if we are?" she asked, the question bordering on a threat.

All over the country there had been groups of Embers running from the war. In some parts of the country it was becoming a rite of passage. The biggest case had been dubbed "The Dublin Disappearance." Twenty-seven high school seniors simply didn't show up for school one day. By the time the school and the parents found out about it, the kids had a three-day head start. They'd orchestrated it so that their parents had given them permission to go off on a weekend camping trip. But by Sunday night the kids weren't back and then on Monday morning when time came for school, the kids still weren't there.

It was late Monday afternoon when a package arrived at the school containing all of the students' cell phones and all twenty-seven draft letters with the words NO THANK YOU scrawled across them. It had become the slogan of the movement, a polite refusal to be a part of things, a deference so polite that it seemed as though they were only turning down an offer of dessert at the end of a meal. All across the country NO THANK YOU began showing up in the empty beds of seventeen- and eighteen-year-olds who had been drafted.

It was just over two months ago — seventy-seven days, to be exact, which my memory always was — since The Dublin Disappearance.

In the beginning the story filled the news outlets. The people came on television and blamed the government, blamed the war, blamed the parents, blamed the students. There was no shortage of places to point. But when the days turned to weeks and the students still weren't found, the concern shifted. They were called cowards and deemed "lacking in moral fortitude" by one of the pundits. "A generation of polite cowards" is what some people called them.

Slowly, compassion for frightened kids hardened into anger at cowardly brats.

More weeks came and went and a couple of the students were found. They were caught not far from the Canadian border by a pair of local hunters who had been chasing both deer and dodgers — their words. The pair was sent to jail and there they sat right up until one of them couldn't take it anymore and decided that the war would be better. So his lawyer spoke to the judge and, sure enough, he went off to the war and died a miserable death but got called a hero for it.

Still, NO THANK YOU showed up spray-painted on walls, plastered on websites, written on abandoned draft notices and left in the middle of schools increasingly diminished by the war's insatiable appetite. The three words, I understood, weren't a refusal, but a plea.

"Where are you guys from?" Tommy asked, sounding as clueless and trusting as he always sounded.

"Nowhere," the girl with the hard eyes said. "Just passing through."

"Good," I replied.

"You really headed to the launch?" someone behind the girl with the hard eyes asked.

"Yep," Tommy replied brightly.

But I couldn't take my eyes off the girl in the lead and she wouldn't take her eyes off me. My hand was still in Tommy's pocket, clamped around the handle of Gannon's gun. I stared at the girl's close-cropped hair, the eyes that didn't seem to blink, only watch and wait, as if she had seen beyond the darkness surrounding them and was able to observe everything, maybe even the whole world, in one swift movement.

"You've already been to the war, haven't you?" I asked.

The girl's eyes narrowed, then relaxed. "Yeah," she said.

"Tell me," Tommy said, almost breathless. "Tell me how it was."

"It's a war," the girl replied. "How could it ever be anything other than terrible?" Her eyes lowered and she was no longer looking at us. She was looking inward, remembering, perhaps. Tommy and I both wanted to know what she saw. There is always a foolish curiosity about war. So many writers and filmmakers have tried to tell us about it, so many veterans, poems, songs. The oldest stories are stories of war. But still, all of us who have never been there wonder how much of the stories is true.

"Really?" Tommy asked, a bit of awe in

his voice. "And you made it back okay. You really came back okay." He turned to me and pointed at the girl with the hard eyes. "You see? I told you. I told you!" Then he laughed and took my hand out of his pocket, making me let go of the weapon. "It's all going to be okay," Tommy said, but whether he was speaking of now or of the future was difficult to say.

"Did I mention that I got drafted?" Tommy blurted out.

"You don't have to go," one of the other teenagers said. Then, "Just say, 'No Thank You.' " Their eyes cut from Tommy to me and back to Tommy, pleading.

Tommy dismissed them with his hand. "I'm going to go and come back and be okay."

"Good for you," the girl with the hard eyes said.

"You'll see," Tommy replied, and he turned to me as he said the words. Then he turned and looked back over his shoulder, as if he was able to see Gannon in the distance, still locked in that car on the side of the road. "But for now," Tommy said, "my sister and I need to get going."

The girl with the hard eyes waved her hand, and with military precision, the others behind her started forward. Tommy and

I stood motionless as the crowd of young faces passed us by. I tried to see them all, tried to capture their visages into The Memory Gospel so that no matter how they fared in the war, they would not be lost. I would always remember them, perfect and undiminished.

I could save them that way. Save them all.

But then, no matter how much I tried to resist it, the moment came when the group has passed. Tommy and I lingered, turning to watch the teens disappear into the darkness, opening the distance between us. "Maybe they've got the right idea," I said.

"What do you mean?" Tommy asked.

"Maybe you should go with them. Maybe we should."

Tommy clucked a hard laugh.

"Gannon would never find us if we went that way," I said. "As far as he knows, we're heading to Florida. So he'll be looking for us along that path. But if we went with them . . . we'd be okay."

Tommy scratched the top of his head for a moment, thinking. "Nope," he said finally. "We started this. We've got to finish it."

He started off into the night, continuing into the forest, which had become deep and swollen since the passing of the others, who were headed north, maybe to Canada in the hope of getting away from the war, away from everything. But that would only delay the inevitable. Of course, none of us knew that then.

I closed my eyes and remembered their faces, one by one. But it was the face of the girl with the hard eyes that I remembered most clearly. I saw myself in the girl's face, in spite of the dark skin and the close-cropped hair. It was the face of someone who had been changed.

I watched the girl with the hard eyes until she had disappeared into the darkness and the cold and, perhaps for the first time in my life, I wanted to be someone else. I wanted to be her.

ELSEWHERE

The money would last for another month and then, after that, well, they didn't really know what would happen. Rather, they didn't *want* to know what would happen.

Diane knew the truth of it. She knew that as soon as the money ran out their parents would pass away like so many other people in this world. And she had come to terms with that. But it was worry over her sister, Helen, that kept her up at night more than anything else. Helen had always been the type who cared too much, the type to keep crying over what was lost. In fact, on the right day, she could still be found getting tight in the throat and watery around her eyes over the family dog, Sprite, that died when they were both children. And when Diane asked her sister about it, Helen would only reply by wiping the corner of her eyes and saying, "I can feel how I want to feel."

Day after day, Diane watched as Helen went

on feeling how she wanted to feel about their parents, both of whom lay sleeping in their bed together, connected to feeding tubes and heart monitors and everything else that did nothing but stave off the inevitable one more hour at a time, and at the end of every day Diane sat down and reviewed the expenses and saw that the math of it all wasn't ever going to come out fine. In the end, this would break them both and, in all honesty, maybe it already had.

And so, finally, tired of watching everything fall apart, there was nothing left to do but try to save something.

"Helen?" Diane called, her voice soft yet firm in the way it had always been.

Helen was sitting at their parents' bedside as usual. Helen was as delicate physically as she was emotionally, Diane thought. She was thin and long, angled like a heron sculpted from brass. Her face had been knotted in frustration or worry as far back as Diane could remember. Even when her sister smiled, it was clouded by anticipation of the frown that would soon follow behind it.

Diane spent years wondering how she and her sister had been born of the same blood.

"Helen?" she called again.

"Yes," Helen answered, snapping out of her thoughts. She looked around, confused for a

116

moment, then found her bearings. "What's the matter?"

"We need to talk about the finances," Diane said.

Helen shook her head. "Not this again."

"It's not going away," Diane replied. "Have you even looked at the bills? In another month there'll be nothing left."

"Then we'll sell whatever we have."

"That's what I'm trying to tell you. There won't be anything left to sell."

"Then we'll take out a loan. We'll borrow it from somebody. Anybody." Helen straightened her back and folded her arms across her chest and looked at their parents who lay side by side, sleeping, just as they had been for the last six months. "I told you I don't want to talk about this type of stuff in front of them."

"They can't hear us," Diane said, but she wasn't sure whether or not she believed that, so she said it more softly than she normally would have.

"It's been proven that coma patients can hear voices and find comfort in the sound of their loved ones."

"These aren't coma patients, Helen. It's The Disease. They're not coming out of it."

"You don't know that."

"I do. And so do you."

They went back and forth this way for half

an hour and by the end of it nothing had changed. When it was all said and done, Diane knew that her sister wouldn't be dissuaded. All there was left to do was to cut ties. So she did. She emptied out her part of the savings and then, without much effort, decided not to go back to her parents or her sister.

It kept her awake for the first few days. She sat up in the late hours of the night imagining the sight of her parents sleeping and Helen sitting at their bedside with no one to help her. But the difference between Diane and her sister had been that, just like with the family dog, Helen never knew when to let things go. Diane, on the other hand, had always known when to sever ties and get back to life.

And with the war happening and The Disease burning through people, there wasn't much life left to get back to. A person had to take advantage of everything they could get their hands on. So that's what Diane did.

Having finally mustered the courage, Diane took to heart what so many others in the world were saying, that this was the end so a person might as well enjoy what they could.

She'd always wanted to go to Las Vegas so, finally, after years of not doing it, she went. Most of the flights were canceled due to growing hysteria over the war, so she loaded up her car and made the long, dusty drive into the desert and found Las Vegas waiting for her.

It was everything Diane had dreamed it would be. Lights and music and people. Neither the war nor The Disease seemed to be able to find purchase here. Diane was able to forget about her sister and her parents and everything else. She drank and she gambled and she made love to a man with a nice face who reminded her of one of the boys she'd fallen in love with back in high school and she stayed awake for days and the lack of sleep only seemed to spur on more excitement and so she had fun and lived and was able to truly forget about everything that was going wrong in the world.

A week later, when she finally decided to call home and check on her sister and her parents, she found them both just as she had left them. The money was all but gone, but Helen was still at their bedside, determined to burn every remaining penny to hold on to them for as long as she could. And when Diane said to her sister, "You need to let them go," Helen simply replied, "Neither of us is wrong."

Six

We climbed up out of the forest almost an hour later and found the world burning.

In a long, glowing line along an inky black highway, great plumes of flame burst out of the earth and licked at the dark sky. The fires were big enough to burn buses. At intervals like telephone poles, the pyres roared and shook the air, driving the cold back into the darkness. The air was suddenly hot and thick in our lungs. Beads of sweat sprang up on Tommy's brow and all he could do was stand there with his eyes wide and his mouth agape as he tried to count the pyramids of flame that stretched along the highway as far as his eyes could see. The most he was able to manage was a whispered, awestruck ". . . Wow."

"It's so warm," I said, as the fire's breath swept over me.

Once our eyes adjusted to the alien light, Tommy and I could make out large, insect-like creatures picking at the fires. Steel backhoes and bulldozers housing men with glassy, drowsy eyes chewed at the earth and loaded severed trees onto the fires. The flames leaped. The machines worked. The earth died a little. And on and on it went.

"What do you think they're doing?" Tommy asked. He looked down the road, squinting, trying to see where the pyres ended and sanity began again.

"Pipeline," I said.

Tommy thought for a moment. "What's the point?"

"We should get going," I said, looking up at the sky. Finally the sun was breaking the horizon. The sky swelled before us, defying gravity in its usual way, filling out the corners of the world like paint rolling out over a ceiling. I stared up for a moment, then turned on my heel and started east along the road.

Tommy followed. He looked back over his shoulder now and again, probably half expecting to see Gannon's car crawling up the road behind us. It was only a matter of time, Tommy and I knew, like everything else in life. Everything that could happen would happen if you gave it long enough. Tommy had heard someone say that once and he'd come to believe it. It made sense to him, for the most part. And that was all he could ask out of most philosophies. So, given enough time, he knew that Gannon would find us. And yet he also knew that I would make it to Florida somehow. And he knew that he would make it off to the war. It would all come to pass, just so long as we were given enough time.

Life was all about time.

We walked along the highway, watching the earth bloom into the new day. Trees grew from shadow to substance, like water hardening into ice. A flock of blackbirds bolted from the underbrush along the roadside not far from one of the bonfires, their wings pummeling the air. The men in the bulldozers and backhoes worked mechanically until the sun had climbed the backs of the trees. The men looked thin and hollow in the dawn, like puppets made of paper.

Tommy and I outwalked the pyres. Miles came and went. The air became cold and clammy again. A chill fog rolled in around us, so dense that we could almost wrap it in our arms and squeeze it into rain.

The tremble of cold returned to my hands. My stomach gnawed at itself. All the fatigue came pouring over me but there was nothing left to do but continue on.

I walked with my head down, counting footsteps.

Tommy saw the house before I did.

"Ginny," Tommy said. "Ginny!"

"What?"

"We should go to that house," Tommy pointed. Off in the distance, beyond a field and at the end of a dirt road branching off the highway, stood a small farmhouse. A porch light burned like the eye of a cyclops in the foggy day.

"Come this way," he said, tugging me off the pavement and onto the soft crunch of the dirt road that led to the farmhouse.

I didn't want to follow, but I didn't have the strength to protest.

The farmhouse climbed up out of the earth one angle at a time. A sharply pitched roof. A porch that wrapped the house in old wooden arms. Milky white windows that looked like eyes casting aspersions. The smell of burning firewood that peppered the air.

"I'll do the talking," Tommy said.

"Don't be stupid," I replied. My voice was still far away, barely present, but it was stern and confident. "They'll be more likely to be nice to us if they see me first."

"Why?"

"Because I'm a girl. I'm less threatening."

Tommy thought for a moment, trying to find a flaw in my logic. As usual, he came up short. "What if we just both stand side by side? That way they see us both at the same time. They'll know we're not hiding anything, you know?"

I took a deep breath and clenched my jaw. "I'll do the talking."

"Okay," Tommy said finally.

When the old woman opened the door, she was backlit by sun that had finally begun piercing the fog and had come to rest just above her shoulders, rushing in through a back window. It was difficult to make out what was giving her such a strange, bug-like appearance until, finally, I realized that like so many people since the arrival of The Disease, she was wearing a gas mask. The light on her shoulders turned her grand and ethereal, like some creature of myth discovered after uncounted ages. But the double-barreled shotgun held in her hands and leveled at us reminded me that there were no more oracles left in this world. Just frightened people.

"Good morning," I said brightly, as if the woman had only been offering a handshake rather than twin barrels of a twelve-gauge.

The woman squinted, peering at me

through the lenses of her gas mask, and then past me, at Tommy. He waved and smiled.

"First of all," I declared, "we're not going to hurt you."

All over the globe there were reports of Embers like Tommy and me attacking — and even killing — anyone old enough to possibly be infected by The Disease. The idea was that you could stop its spread by snuffing out its potential victims. A dark thought of starving The Disease, but there was no sign of it working. It was, at the end of the day, simply an act of murder in a world that was slowly losing its mind. No one understood how The Disease started or was spread.

The old woman had every right to hold us at gunpoint.

"My name's Virginia," I declared. "That's my brother, Tommy. We're twins, can you tell?" I smiled a wide, toothy smile that made it seem as though I might have been a traveling Bible salesman in another life.

"What do you want?" the woman's muffled voice said. I couldn't see much of her face, but from her hands I guessed her to be somewhere near sixty. Maybe older. Which was a rare thing since The Disease.

She had silver hair that was cut short like a boy's. She was short and wide, like an old refrigerator. Her gun darted back and forth between us as her breath came and went in ominous gasps through the gas mask.

"We just want a little respite," I said in my brightest "Please Don't Shoot Us" voice. "We've been walking all night and we're just hoping to get a break from the cold. Everything's starting to feel disconnected and far away." I held up my hands so that the woman could see the way they trembled.

"Let's hear him tell it," the woman said in her muffled voice, eyeing Tommy. He was still standing some distance behind me, just far enough away that, if he were up to something, it would maybe give him some way to take advantage of the old woman.

"It's like she said, ma'am," Tommy said. "We're just cold. Really cold." His voice trembled from genuine fatigue. Plumes of steam rose from the house as the warmth exhaled into the cold world. Tommy and I both longed for that warmth, like a flower thirsting for sunshine.

The woman watched us for another moment. Somewhere off in the distance there was a deep booming sound, like thunder or an explosion. All three of us turned and looked in the direction of the sound. We waited, but nothing ever followed that would explain what we had heard.

"Who you running from?" the woman asked.

Before Tommy could speak, I said, "Our father."

The woman considered this for a moment.

"You infected?" she asked.

"Actually," I said, "they don't know how The Disease is spread. So —"

"No, ma'am," Tommy interrupted. "We're not infected. Just cold. That's all."

Then, as if she had seen this all before, she lowered the shotgun and simply said, "Come on in."

Her name was Maggie and she seemed the serious sort. The type of woman who always knew more than she cared to say. The type of woman who asked direct questions and demanded direct answers.

"Sit down and I'll feed you," Maggie said, ushering us into the old house. It smelled of mildew and the sweetness of old wood, of dust and children come and gone decades ago. Maybe it was the scent of crayon wax cured into the wood over a lifetime of child rearing. It was difficult to say. Whatever it was, I liked the house and Tommy did too. He later told me that it felt more like home than anywhere else he had ever been before.

I expected to find her house filled with

bottled water and canned food. There were doomsday preppers all over the globe who were finally seeing all of their years of planning suddenly become a valuable commodity. Even though things weren't yet in that pure lawless state that most of them expected, it was hard to make a case for the world not soon descending into just that.

But Maggie wasn't a doomsday prepper or a hoarder. She was just an old woman who was afraid that a pair of strange children might infect her with something that would make her fall asleep one night and never wake up again.

"Thank you," Tommy said. It was the fourth time he had thanked her. And for the fourth time she said, matter-of-factly, "You're welcome."

Maggie was already fixing our plates — without ever removing her gas mask — as we stood next to a large, old fireplace in the living room. The fire crackled and roared and embers popped now and again, flaring briefly like an idea and then disappearing.

"It'll take me a few to get more eggs going," Maggie said. "I'm used to cooking for one."

"Thank you," Tommy said again.

I left the fireplace and took a seat on the couch. I was still too cold. Still not able to connect to my body, only able to connect to my memories again. The living room faded away, less real than the time when . . .

. . . *I'm five years old and Tommy and I are sitting together in the back of an ambulance and a paramedic named Alice is wiping the blood, staring at us as if we carry some form of contagion, and she smiles now and again but it's a weak, sad smile and she says, after a moment of not being able to come up with anything else, "I'm going to step out for a moment, but I'll be right back." And then Tommy and I watch her leave and it's like a hollow place opening up in the sky because now Tommy and I are alone and all we can do is hold one another and listen to the sound of the people outside the ambulance and all they're saying is how sad they are for us and how terrible it is and how much they pity us and Tommy can't stop crying. I put my arm around him and it's like holding onto an earthquake and this is what losing someone feels like. This is what it would always feel like . . .*

"Have you ever tried talking to them?" Tommy asked. He was sitting beside me, holding me.

"What?"

"You were remembering Mom and Dad, weren't you? You're always remembering

129

them. Have you ever tried talking to them?"

"You can't talk to memories," I replied.

"But they're not just memories for you, though. They're real. So maybe you can talk to them. Maybe you can find a way to stop remembering them."

"Who says I want to?"

"You'd be surprised how good forgetting is," Tommy said. He took his arms from around me. He ran his fingers through his hair. "I hardly remember them. I'm not even sure I do remember them. It's like hearing some song in your head and you think maybe what you hear is how the song sounds but you're not really sure. That's what Mom and Dad are for me: a song I half remember." He shook his head, looking guilty. "I guess I'm supposed to want more than that. I guess I should want to remember everything about them — and sometimes I do. But other times, I'm glad I can't remember them. Because forgetting them means forgetting what I lost." He looked at me long and hard. "Maybe you can't forget anything because you don't want to."

Hate is a hard thing to let go of. It's the kind of thing that burrows into your skin until it changes the very way your skin feels, and eventually, you can't remember feeling any other way.

I hated Tommy in that moment. And in a way, I still hate him. But that's my sin to bear, one that would sting all the sharper later when Tommy was gone and all that I had left was my memory of hating him.

"Come on up," Maggie said, leaning in from the kitchen.

"Yes, ma'am," Tommy said. Then to me, "Food."

We went in and sat at the table. Maggie had plated eggs and bacon and two large biscuits apiece. For someone who was used to cooking alone, she seemed well-practiced in tending others. "There'll be more up in a bit," she said. She coughed behind her mask. "Then the two of you can be on your way."

"You sure we can't rest just a little?" Tommy asked. "We're really tired."

Maggie mulled this over for a moment, then shook her head.

"Oh," Tommy said, and he tapped the back of my hand.

It was a signal dating back to our earliest days in foster homes. It was our way of letting each other know that we needed to convince someone of something for the sake of us both. I knew my part and Tommy knew his.

"You'll have to excuse my brother," I said,

firming up my voice to sound like the know-it-all most people took me for. "He's not the most communicative of the bunch. He's what you call an iceberg: just that little bit ever gets to peek up through the surface. But he's a good kid underneath."

"That a fact?" Maggie asked. She stood with her back to the stove, watching us closely.

"A fact it is," I said. "He tries hard, but he's just not much of a wordsmith. Or rather, he just doesn't really like to talk."

"Good to know you don't have that problem," Maggie said.

"You bet I don't." I scanned the house. In the corner there was an old, dusty chess board. "Do you play?" I asked.

"Not particularly," Maggie said. "Know how to, but never quite could get the hang of it."

"It's a complicated game. Invented in Eastern India sometime between 220 and 550, in the Gupta Empire."

"The what empire?" Maggie asked, moving her jaw back and forth.

"The Gupta Empire," I answered. "Founded by Maharaja Sri Gupta. He lived from the year 240 to 280."

"You some kind of expert on him?"

"Nope. I just remember everything."

Maggie clucked a laugh. "I bet."

"No, ma'am," Tommy added. "She's telling you the truth. She remembers everything."

"Nobody remembers everything," Maggie said.

"I do."

"She does," Tommy said, almost at the same time.

Maggie watched us both anew, and again her lower jaw grated back and forth behind her mask, like a cow chewing cud. After a moment, she laughed and waved her hand dismissively. "Bull," she said. "But you almost had me."

Tommy looked over at me. "Go ahead."

I closed my eyes. "Your kitchen counters are almost nine feet in length," I began, "and sitting across the top of it, in order from left to right, are a white toaster with three scratch marks along the side. The middle scratch mark is beginning to rust. Next to the toaster is a ceramic container holding three spatulas — two of which are the exact same — one wooden spoon with a nick in the handle shaped like a crescent moon, one metal fork for turning meat, one large green plastic spoon for soup or broths, and a pair of chopsticks with black marks on their tips."

"Do the living room," Tommy said.

"The chess table has seven pieces on the board: one white queen, two white pawns, a black knight and rook, and both kings. The white king is on G7. The black king is on C2. The knight is . . ."

"Hold on," Maggie said.

Finally I opened my eyes and smiled as politely as I knew how. "And I'll never forget," I said. "Not any of it. I remember everything."

Maggie's eyes were as thin as reeds. "That . . . that can't be true," she said. Her voice was hardly a whisper behind her mask. I could barely hear her, like an echo at the bottom of a well. Tommy cut his eyes from Maggie to me. Tommy's job now was to mend the bridge.

It's human nature not to trust intelligence. And memory is a key element of intelligence. So being able to remember everything makes people nervous. It inspires a sense of inadequacy which, in turn, makes them defensive and suspicious. After all, a person who remembers everything may just as well know everything. And a person that knows everything could know parts of you that you aren't proud of.

Tommy told me that once. Then by the next day he had forgotten.

"She won two chess championships," Tommy said. He smiled to show that he was being sincere. "But I was never any good at it. I'm more like you, Miss Maggie. I tried for years to get good, but I can barely keep the rules straight in my head." He laughed, an offering for Maggie to not feel as small as he knew she felt. "That one there," he said, pointing to me, "she's a bit of a freak."

Finally Maggie smiled too. I was the only one who didn't.

"Seems that way," Maggie said. Then, after a moment, she cleared her throat and said, "I guess you could rest here for a little while."

"Thank you! We won't be here long," Tommy said. "We'll move on just as soon as we're rested up a little."

"Fine by me," Maggie said. She sipped from a cup of coffee. "So, you say you're running from your daddy?"

"Yes, ma'am."

"No," I corrected him. "Not our daddy. Our foster father."

Tommy reached over and squeezed my hand. "Just let me talk," he said in a hard whisper. It was clear that Maggie heard, but she offered no response. "It's a long story, but basically we're going to Florida. Down to Cape Canaveral to watch a shuttle launch."

Maggie considered this for a moment. "Seems like a long way for something you can watch on TV, especially with things the way they are. Did you hear what the Russians are doing now? Word is they're going to use the nukes. With all that going on, I don't know how some damn rocket launch is still happening."

"Because it has to happen!" I exclaimed.

"Why?" Maggie replied. "It's a waste to me. By the time it gets wherever it's going — if the Russians don't shoot it down first — won't be nobody left down here anyhow. Makes me believe what people say about it being some kind of secret weapon or maybe something for the president and the rest to escape."

Everything she said was stupid and foolish. She was just like all the rest who didn't know anything about anything. People who didn't understand that the Europa mission was all we had left. All that mattered. It was one last gasp of wonder in a world drowning in blood.

I wanted to tell her all of that, but I held my tongue and let Tommy do the talking.

"I guess," Tommy said. "But the freak here is a big fan of the space program."

"Don't call me that," I said.

Tommy ignored me and kept his focus on Maggie. "One day she's probably going to work for NASA. And this is an important launch, so we're going to watch it. And our foster father didn't want us to go."

"So you're runaways," Maggie said.

"We try not to think of it that way," Tommy said. "We like to think of it more like an adventure."

Maggie returned her attention to me. "You really don't forget anything?"

"Nothing at all," I replied.

"That's some kind of a blessing," Maggie said.

"Some kind of freak," Tommy said.

Before breakfast was over there came the long, loud whine of the emergency alert system from the television. We stopped and turned as the sound went away and a news broadcaster appeared. Solemnly, he said simply, "We interrupted your programming for this message from the President of the United States."

And then the president was there standing behind a large wooden lectern bearing the presidential seal. He stood tall and solid, like always, but there was also a look of exhaustion on his face. "My fellow Americans . . ." the president began.

137

"They've got nukes now," Maggie's almost robotic gas-mask voice said.

New York had been attacked again. They were still estimating the death toll, but the current count was in the hundreds. Someone in Times Square had exploded.

Every explosion, every gunshot, every flash of light and sound and steel that ended someone's life chipped away at the remnants of what the world used to be. There is always someone dying, always someone in pain. The world doesn't spare anyone. No person nor country nor creed.

Tommy and I learned that early. America was learning it late.

Then came the latest news of The Disease. A man in his midthirties had been found in his apartment, unable to awake. It was a case of The Disease affecting someone far beyond the bell curve of its spread. Up until then the youngest person affected had been a fifty-year-old woman from Tennessee, and even she was considered an outlier. But now The Disease was escalating, as if it was competing with the war to see which of them could extinguish humanity first.

Maggie talked off and on through the president's speech. Neither Tommy nor I interrupted her, even though her talking made it difficult to keep up with what was going on. The president mentioned "escalation." The president mentioned "armaments." The president mentioned "necessary force."

"I can't believe it," Maggie said. "It's terrible . . . I always knew it was going to happen . . ."

On and on the conversation continued as he piled on the horrors of the world and the war. The president told Maggie that there would be a need for even more soldiers. Maggie told the president to go to hell. The president told Maggie that there would be an executive order coming soon to reduce the age of the draft by another year. Maggie told the president to go to hell. The president told Maggie that extreme measures had become necessary in the face of further escalation. Maggie turned the president off, making him disappear into a pool of blackness.

After she sighed, her hand, maybe of its own volition, reached out and turned the TV on again.

The troops were mobilizing. The ships were engaged. The planes were flying. The drones had never left the air. Tommy watched and listened and believed, in spite of himself, that it would all be okay. It was something in the way the president stood there in that perfect suit with his perfect hair and his perfect skin and his perfect elocution that could do nothing to disguise the fatigue in his voice and the rings of sleeplessness carved around his eyes. All of it told Tommy that, even if things were getting worse, someone was in charge. The ship was being steered. It would not go running over the edge of the waterfall.

It meant that, when it was finally Tommy's turn, when the Europa shuttle had launched and Gannon had caught up to us and turned Tommy in and sent him off to the war, there was a chance that he would be fine. The president would get him through. It would be the way it was in stories. He would leave home and return a hero. Changed, certainly, but unharmed overall. Finally, for the first time in his life, he would be lucky. He was overdue for his share of luck. And what better place to use all of your good luck than in a war?

"It'll all be okay," Tommy whispered.

"Everyone's going to die," Maggie said.

After the president was done, Maggie switched the television off again. The house felt small and tight all of a sudden.

"Does she really remember everything?" she asked, turning to Tommy. "I ask you because I feel like she could put one over on me if she wanted to. But you seem like . . . well, like you wouldn't lie, even if you could."

"It's true," Tommy said.

Maggie nodded, confirming something to herself. "Okay."

After a moment, she got up and walked over to an old record player standing in the corner of the room. Sorting through a small stack of vinyl, she plucked out a selection and eased it delicately from its sleeve. She stared at it, as though remembering something.

She placed the record into the player but didn't switch it on. She turned to us, then cleared her throat and slowly removed her gas mask. The face beneath it was beautiful: aged but firm, filled with years that had given her thick, deep laugh lines around her face so that she looked as though she was perpetually smiling. She looked like the type of woman I wished our mother had gotten the chance to become.

"I ain't done this in years," Maggie said. Her face flushed and her mouth trembled. "But since everything's going to sod and . . . and since you'll never forget it, maybe it'll mean something." She looked, all of a sudden, like some small and delicate bird, trying to remember its way home. "Okay," she said finally. Then she switched on the record player.

An orchestra billowed out of the record player speakers. The sound was low and grainy, like wood given form. After a handful of measures Maggie took a deep breath, held it for a moment, then began to sing.

Tommy had never heard opera before. Not really. He knew what it was. He knew the general idea of it. The rise and fall of the voice, the sustained notes, that loud, thunderous presence. But he knew as much about it as he probably knew about computer programming: just theories and the occasional piece of pop culture reference that one inevitably comes across. He'd never met an opera singer before.

Now that he had, he didn't know how he could live for the rest of his life if he never met another one. Maggie's voice was louder than he could have imagined. It swelled out of her mouth like a tidal wave, shoving him back down inside himself. He was overcome by that familiar feeling of smallness — like he felt when he tried to compare himself to me. But there was something else too. A sense of calm that came over him. He closed his eyes and the sound of her voice became a thing he could fall into. Every note, every tremble, all of it consumed him. The world washed away and, before he knew what was happening, the song was over.

The silence lingered for a moment, before it was swallowed up by reality.

Tommy kept his eyes closed, still feeling the heft and sweep of Maggie's voice shake his bones. The echo of her song reverberated around the inside of his skull and, for once in his life, he felt that he truly and fully understood something about the world. Exactly what that something was he couldn't say. But it was a big, grand thing, like understanding that everything in life was cruel and beautiful and that neither was any better than the other. Tommy understood, for one lightning-strike moment, what he was supposed to do with his life.

And then the flash was gone and he was just Tommy again.

The sound of Maggie's voice inside his head — now only a memory, like closing your eyes and still seeing the sun burning — was something that would disappear soon. He knew that and he didn't want it to happen. Because that was the way it always happened and he hated himself for it. He would forget this feeling just like he had forgotten a thousand — a hundred thousand — other things in his life.

Tommy closed his hand into a fist and

rubbed his thumb against his forefinger, concentrating, concentrating so hard it hurt. But still Maggie's voice slipped away and no matter how tightly he clutched at it with his mind, the light that she had lit inside of him grew dimmer and dimmer, second by second.

And then the light went out, never to burn in his mind again.

To My Children,

The first miscarriage took our legs out from under us. She was asleep and then there was blood in the bed and then we'd lost our first child. The horoscope she read that day had offered no warning. I think that was what hurt her the most. She felt like she had let tragedy blindside us. For a while after it happened she gave up reading only the good fortunes to me. She still read them over breakfast, but if the stars called for me to be cautious, she let me know.

We went to the movies a lot after that. We watched the heroes save the world. Heroes always have their powers. Even when they're taken away, they're never really gone. They still serve as symbols. So we fed on that. We made it our gospel. And when the movies let out we shuffled wordlessly into the night and came home and she would read a book until she drifted off to sleep — which was fitful now, though it had never been before — and then I would take her book and read the same pages she read, as if doing so could tell me what she was thinking, how she felt.

It was a full year before we decided to try again. She was back to reading me

145

good fortunes in the mornings and her sleep wasn't fitful anymore. Then we lost the second child too.

We fought a lot after that. We'd never been the type to fight. We had to learn how to do it. She said I didn't tell her often enough that I loved her. She said I didn't "see" her anymore.

I said she'd forgotten what love was. I said she'd cursed us with astrology.

We went back and forth this way, neither of us willing to tell the truth: we hated each other because we knew that the loss of this second child hadn't hurt us as deeply as the loss of the first.

When we found out we were pregnant with the second, we tied our emotions down and kept them there. We wore masks — laughter and grins and pleasant surprise — but underneath the surface there was only stone. And, sure enough, when the second child failed to come into the world, the stones that we had built around our hearts held. We cried. We trembled with grief. We hurt. But not like we had before. And we refused to forgive ourselves for that.

It only took us six months to get pregnant again — something else we wouldn't forgive ourselves for. In those six months of wandering through the haze of self-hatred, I survived by getting lost in Europa.

I fell in love with it back when I was a kid. Galileo sent back all those beautiful, grainy images that started people studying, thinking, learning. This was how we learned about the possible ocean beneath Europa's surface.

It was a good time for science. All the ways we developed to spy on ourselves and kill each other had given us new and exciting ways to look outward, to see the rest of the universe. Yeah, we still spent most of our time taking cosmological selfies, but every now and then it was possible to see beyond ourselves.

Tidal flux had been discovered on Europa. The ice covering the surface showed signs of distress, signs of change. It wasn't a static, flat rock. There was heat beneath it. From the looks of things, that heat melted enough ice to create an ocean beneath the surface. There were fissures and bulges on the face of the moon as Jupiter and Io pushed and pulled at it, making Europa's core hotter, making the ocean — and therefore life — more likely.

Late at night, after your mother had

fallen asleep, I would find articles on Europa and read them aloud. Whether I was reading them to her or to the child it was hard to say. I just knew that I wanted to pass on the possibility that there might be something wonderful happening out there. Something that I would probably never live long enough to see for myself, but perhaps my children could.

Every night I read of Europa to you. Stats, figures, math, theories. And on and on. Where there were gaps of information, I filled them in with my imagination. I put a playground in the Argadnel Regio. In Falga, I placed a dog that grew larger every year but still was ever a puppy. I created a forest in which the trees always bloomed in red and gold and their leaves tasted like cold pineapple. The sky was always a thousand different colors. I placed these made-up things on Europa and I poured them all into your mother's sleeping ear, letting them drain down into that world inside her.

I wanted to convince you that there was something out here — in the meat grinder of existence — that was worth your time. Something that you could be excited about. Something that you could tie yourself to and love, the way I wanted to tie myself to you and love you.

I wanted to say to you, "Good fortune awaits you." I wanted to say, "Don't fear the adventure." I wanted to say, "Don't leave us again." I wanted to say, "I promise I'll break the stone around my heart and love you this time." I wanted to say, "Please."

Imagine the joy when the two of you answered our prayers in unison.

Seven

It is the middle of spring and my father is behind the wheel and my mother is in the passenger seat reading and, now and again, singing along with the radio. She has a high voice and is rarely on key, but she sings with energy and vibrancy that makes it not only acceptable, but pleasurable.

The sun is high and my parents have the windows down, letting in sweet, wet air. It is not long after sunrise and the air is still as thick as a down pillow. My father brims with pride for reasons only fathers know and plays a game of calling out the names of cars on the highway and then calling out the names of cities that begin with the same letter. Sometimes my mother plays along but, mostly, it is a game the man enjoys on his own.

Around noon we stop off at a small diner in a small town because Tommy is hungry and his hunger has made him fussy. Hunger gnaws at my stomach too but I'm not the fussy type.

The diner has a long, chrome-lined counter in a 1950s style with chrome-plate stools growing up out of black-and-white tiles covering the floor, and along the wall of the restaurant burgundy booths made of faux leather huddle around sticky wooden tables, waiting.

"This is just perfect," my father says as he lifts me out of my car seat. His arms are massive and protective to my five-year-old self and I rest my head on his shoulder, and for a moment, The Memory Gospel quiets inside me . . . and I am finally able to separate myself from the memory.

My mother took Tommy by the hand and helped him out of the car. He rubbed his eyes and tried to pull away. "I'm hungry," he said.

"I know," our mother replied. Then she lifted him into her arms.

The diner served breakfast all day and Tommy and I had always been partial to pancakes. The pancakes were flavored with a hint of cinnamon. It was the first time I had ever had cinnamon.

Our parents sat on the outside of the booth. Our father had brought along an actual paper map, saying that his father "never needed GPS." He unfolded the map in front of him, taking up half of the table, and stared down at it. He placed his finger on the highway lines and traced down the long path ahead.

"We're making good time," he said. "Perfect time, actually."

"Watch the syrup," Mom said, removing the corner of the map from Tommy's plate.

"Virginia?" he called. "Virginia, how many moons does Jupiter have?"

"Sixty-two," I answered. "But they keep finding more, so who knows how many there will be a few years from now."

"And which one is the largest?"

"Ganymede."

"What about Titan?"

"One of Saturn's moons. And not as large."

"And where does the word *titan* come from?"

"Greek gods," I answered while reaching over and stealing pancakes from Tommy's plate as he stared out the window at a man fixing the chain on his bicycle.

"Are you sure about that?" my father asked.

I swallowed Tommy's pancakes. "They were the parents of the Greek gods."

"Excellent!" my father barked. He slapped his hands together and laughed. "You're an amazing kid," he said to me. "Do you know that?"

"Don't do that," my mother said.

"Don't do what?"

"That," she replied. "Don't treat her like she's different."

"But she is different," he replied.

"Exactly," she replied. "And she's going to be known for that for her whole life. She should at least be treated like a normal person by her family."

My father chuckled. "You make it sound like she's got some kind of defect or something. She's a genius. That's a good kind of special."

My mother sighed. "And what about Tommy?"

"What about Tommy?" my father asked. Then he reached over and tousled Tommy's hair. Tommy, for his part, was still staring out of the window, watching the man wrestle with the chain on his bicycle. If he heard or understood what our parents were saying, he gave no indication. "Tommy's perfectly happy," my father said.

"I want my children to know that they're equal in our eyes," my mother said.

My father gave another laugh. But this one was nervous, stiff. The laugh was a lie. "Of course they are," he said. Then he returned his attention to his map. "Where are we headed, Virginia?"

"Cape Canaveral," I replied.

"And what did I tell you about Cape Canaveral?"

Before I answered I reached over to Tommy's plate and stole another portion of his pancakes and, without hesitation, threw it across the table and hit him square in the forehead.

"Daaaaaaad!" Tommy yowled.

Mom laughed. It was an embarrassed, unintentional laugh, as though she'd not meant for her children to see it. "Virginia, don't hit your brother with pancakes." Then she reached down to her plate and picked up a piece of bacon and flung it across and hit me in the forehead.

An hour later we were in the car and the car slid off the road and tumbled down the side of a mountain and both of our parents were dead and only Tommy and I were left and every second of that final hour — full of wind and laughter and bad singing and the hum of the engine and the squeal of the tires and the crunch of the metal and the slow way my mother stopped asking, "Are you okay?" — has never left me.

Tommy was able to forget and I hated him for it.

■ ■ ■ ■

I had always known that Tommy wanted to be a soldier. It wasn't even his fault when you got right down to it. Tommy, like so many Embers being charmed off to the war, was a victim of marketing.

The military had long ago seen the way the war was going. They knew that there was little chance of this ending well and, maybe because war has always been this way, they did everything they could to ensure that the next generation was willing and eager to join.

The propaganda started with the television shows and movies, like so much of everything else. On television the heroes were always soldiers, either coming home from the war or going off to it. A good military background was the secret method by which heroes became heroic.

So every day after school Tommy would come home to whatever foster parent we happened to be living with and he would drop his backpack in his room and sit down in front of the television and watch the old reruns of cartoons about soldiers or robots or, sometimes, robot soldiers, and they all shouted orders and obeyed orders and there was always a well-defined chain of command. Tommy or any other child never saw the soldiers question authority.

The military had no qualms about inserting themselves into commercial breaks either. They made joining up seem like some great Homeric pastime. There was one commercial that featured a man in a white T-shirt, climbing a mountain on which the faces of stern-looking soldiers were superimposed. And when he had climbed the faces of enough soldiers from every era of military service, he reached the top of the mountain. But living atop the mountain was a great hell beast armed with a large whip, waiting for the sweaty, grime-covered man.

The whip-cracking hell beast roared fire and ash and smoke, but the T-shirt–clad man seemed unfazed. He reached into the rock of the mountain and retrieved a large sword — exactly who had placed it there? I again deferred to the marketing department who were, it seemed to me, just throwing metaphors into a mixer and shaking them around at this point. And with a single swing of the sword, the hell beast was vanquished in an explosion of fire and light.

And when the light receded, who should be standing there except our hero? But gone now was the ratty T-shirt. He now wore the uniform of a marine. And suddenly, there appeared behind him a long line of other marines. All of them staring straight ahead, past the camera, into that glorious space where legends live.

The commercial having reached its climax, the superimposed words You Are Not Embers, You Are The Burning Light. . . . Join Now appeared on the screen in front of the soldier like writing on a bathroom mirror.

So every day after school I watched as Tommy ingested this message about men in T-shirts fighting hell beasts with magical swords found in mountains. And I knew that it was just a matter of time before Tommy got the idea in his head that he could slay hell beasts.

I tried a few times to help him see the artifice of it all. "None of that is real," I told him.

"I know," he always replied. But he never looked up from the television as he said the words. He only stared ahead, let it wash over him like the tide, and he sometimes looked down at his hands and watched them, as though waiting for some sword to appear.

By the time he was thirteen there was enough of a foundation built up inside him that he began talking to recruiters at school.

When he could, he picked up military magazines — which was a big thing for Tommy since he didn't particularly care for reading. But the photograph-heavy magazines showed enough guns and tanks and drones and rockets and flame throwers and sniper rifles and exotic pistols and bulletproof vests and land mines and armored personnel carriers to keep a boy his age busy for hours.

Tommy began carrying the magazines around with him — rolled up like a baton in his hand — and whenever he wasn't busy he unfurled them and stared at it all. "One day," I heard Tommy say to himself.

But I knew that the military was simply doing what it had always done to boys like Tommy: made them feel special. I saw the way Tommy seemed to live in my shadow. He had always been there to help me and I had always let him. Maybe I even shared a certain degree of guilt. Maybe I accepted Tommy's role as the sidekick rather than star a little too often.

That was the kind of thing that I could barely get a handle on myself, and I was living with it. So I knew that it wouldn't do much good to include other people in the discussion. Only Tommy had ever really known about it. And while I knew that he couldn't possibly understand — I hardly understood it myself and I was living with it — at least Tommy had been there for me.

When I really got down to it, I hadn't been apart from Tommy for very long. The longest we'd been separated was during that small period of time when Tommy had gotten adopted and I hadn't. And both times I hadn't known what to do with myself when Tommy wasn't there.

The first time it happened I had barely understood what The Memory Gospel was. Back then, I almost believed that everybody remembered everything the same way I did. After all, it's only through the slow grind of life that we come to know that others around us are, ultimately, unknowable. So how was I to imagine that it wasn't the same for everyone?

It wasn't until Tommy was taken away from me that I began to understand I was different. It wasn't until that first night when I curled up in bed and Tommy wasn't there to take my hand and hold it and squeeze it the way he always did that I finally missed him. I realized then — in one long, sweeping progression of memory — that Tommy had been there for me every single day since the death of our parents. I saw him, that night when I closed my eyes. I saw every version of my brother, day upon day upon day, for years. His clothes shifted and changed and, at the same time, remained constant and unchanged in my memory. I could see his face every day for years, stretched out behind him and in front of him and everywhere all at once. There were thousands of Tommys in my mind. But none of them could take my hand. None of them could squeeze it and say to me, "It's going to be okay, Ginny." None of them could remind me of the fact that I wasn't alone in this world.

Memory is just another word for loneliness when you get right down to it.

I didn't sleep at all while I was away from Tommy. I only lay in bed at night, weighed down by all the memories of him. I watched his entire life like a movie that played on a constant loop behind my eyelids until I was barely able to tell memory from reality.

Once, during that first night, I sat up in bed and thought I saw Tommy asleep on the floor beside me the way he often did — like some large, hairless dog, guarding me. I immediately knew that he wasn't really there, that it was just a combination of memories and fatigue. Every time he had ever been asleep on the floor beside me came together in one constant image that lay motionless and perfect, showing Tommy through all of the years at once. Almost enough to make him seem real.

But he wasn't and I knew it. Still, I reached out my hand, tried to touch him, failed, and began to cry.

Tommy had watched me every single day and every single night, I realized then. He had seen the way The Memory Gospel began inside of me, the way it shaped me and how I saw the world. He might as well have been given the gift himself. Tommy, in the end, had succeeded in the hardest thing to do in life: making another person feel a little less alone.

And when I scoured all of the memories, I saw that I hadn't always done the same for him. Yes, I looked out for him. I tried to keep him from making bad decisions. I solved his math problems for him or I told him the summation of whatever book he was supposed to read but never did. I had done those small things to make his life a little easier, but I hadn't done anything to make him feel special. I had always treated Tommy like an accessory in my own life rather than the star of his. And that, I knew, was the reason the military was able to get its hooks into him.

The recruiters began coming by the house not long after Tommy broke into his teenage years. The war and The Disease were ramping up, nibbling away at the gene pool from both ends and Tommy looked like one of the perfect ways to fix it. Genetics and time conspired to broaden his shoulders and thicken his hands and even though there was a bit of awkward gangliness about him, it was clearly only a temporary phase. Tommy would one day become a man people feared or loved because of his physical abilities. He would be a hammer in this world if someone used him properly.

At least, that was how the recruiting officers seemed to see the situation.

"You'd be right at home in the corps," the recruiter told Tommy. It was a Friday afternoon not long after school had gotten out. The recruiter's name was Mitch — in my head, I called him Mitch the Bitch just because it was an easy way to make fun of him — and he was a tall, dark-skinned man with almost no hair on any part of his body. He seemed streamlined in the way mannequins or racing dogs are. Like he could fall into a placid lake and never make a splash.

"I tell you, Tommy," Mitch the Bitch

continued, "you've got a future in the corps like you won't believe. We'll push you in ways you never knew you could be pushed. You'll see parts of yourself that you never knew were there."

"Yeah," I interrupted, "your intestinal tract. Or maybe your spleen when you step on a landmine somewhere."

Mitch, Tommy and Gannon all turned to look at me. Gannon scowled. Mitch just seemed annoyed. Only Tommy seemed to be willing to take it as a joke. "Well, it's true," I said.

"Anyhow," Mitch the Bitch continued, "you're the perfect material for the corps, Tommy. You're just the raw clay we're always looking to mold into a man. Tell me: Have you ever wanted to travel?"

"Sure."

"Since when?" I interrupted.

"Since a long time," Tommy said.

I laughed. "You've never said anything about wanting to go anywhere, Tommy. You don't have to tell this guy what he wants to hear. In fact, it's the other way around. He's trying to make the sell to you. It's in his interest to lie."

"I haven't lied about anything," Mitch the Bitch said, his voice hard and cold. It was clear that he was used to barking orders and getting his way. Used to being able to snap his fingers and see soldiers or cadets jump ten feet high. A born and bred military man.

"No," I said, "you haven't technically lied. But you've definitely omitted key pieces of information and you've painted things in a particular light." I smiled. "But that's okay. That's what we all do when we're trying to convince someone of something. That's the heart of rhetoric."

Mitch the Bitch looked over at Gannon.

"Virginia," Gannon warned.

"What?" I replied. "I'm telling the truth."

"Just let the man talk," Gannon said. "It's not like Tommy's going to enlist tomorrow. He's still years away from going anywhere. You don't have to get so defensive."

"Don't I?" I replied, looking at Mitch the Bitch. "He's not old enough to enlist yet but he's old enough to sign one of those Letters of Intent, isn't he, Mitch?" I looked at the small briefcase Mitch the Bitch always carried with him. It was full to the brim with Letters of Intent. All of them waiting to be signed by boys and girls like Tommy. People who didn't know any better. People who had watched the commercials and believed that it was all mountain climbing and hell beast slaying.

"Even if he were to sign the Letter of

Intent," Mitch the Bitch began, "which isn't why I'm here, mind you. But even if he were to sign it, he still has the right to change his mind. There's nothing permanently binding about the letter. It's symbolic more than anything else. A symbol of Tommy's willingness to make a commitment. That's what military service is all about. Commitment. Service. One person's willingness to put the betterment of their country and their community ahead of themselves." Mitch the Bitch's eyes were focused on Tommy. He was in full salesmanship mode now, like a politician or a preacher. "I'm telling you, Tommy," Mitch continued. "My time in the corps has made me the man I am today. You wouldn't know it to look at me now, but I used to be a little bit of a hell-raiser back when I was your age. Drinking. Drugs. Fighting. You name it, I lived it." Mitch the Bitch turned introspective and slid into his own memories, like an uncle at a family reunion. "It wasn't my parents' fault. Not at all. I had a lot of anger about things that, to this day, I still don't quite understand. I acted out."

"You see what he did there, Tommy?" I asked. "That whole thing about being angry about things he couldn't understand. By being nonspecific like that, he's letting you fill in the gaps in your own mind so that you can relate to the story. If he were to say something specific, like how he was angry at his dad for spanking him or that his mom didn't spend enough time with him, then that would give you something to either confirm or deny. And since he knows our parents are dead he can just leave the cause of his anger blank. That way you can say to yourself, 'Yeah, I get angry about stuff too.' Then you'll relate to him and you'll sign that paper and he can make his quota for the month."

Mitch the Bitch seemed flat-out angry now. Whatever pretenses of being civil and of accidentally saying all the right things that Tommy wanted to hear were gone now. He closed his eyes and took a deep breath. Then he turned to Tommy. "Is there any way the two of us could talk without your sister being here?"

Before Tommy could answer, Gannon stood and said, "Come with me, Virginia."

"No," I said. "He doesn't get to kick me out just because I'm making a point. Tell me, Mitch, when you talk to my brother about all of the adventures he's going to have, all that time when he gets to mold himself into something strong and amazing, have you talked to him about the percentage of recruits who find themselves in the basic infantry? And, of those infantry, just how many are sent to the front lines? And, of those sent to the front lines, just how many are killed?"

"Virginia!" Gannon shouted.

But I didn't bother to stop. "And then, even of those who aren't killed, just how many of them are injured? Maimed? So let's say they make it back home. What about the percentage with PTSD? What about the number of soldiers who come home and commit suicide within the first two years of being discharged? Have you told my brother all of those numbers, Mitch? Because I know the number even if you don't!"

There. I had done it. I had given him both barrels. Right here in front of Gannon. And, more importantly, right there in front of Tommy. I waited for Tommy to turn and look at Mitch. Waited for Mitch the Bitch to give Tommy all of those answers, to talk about the soldiers, the PTSD, the suicides, everything that the brochures for the military service didn't tell you. I waited for Tommy to say to Mitch the Bitch, "Answer my sister's questions!"

I waited and I waited.

But all that happened was that Mitch the Bitch, Gannon and Tommy all looked at me with a mixture of surprise, anger and pity. Tommy was the one with the look of pity on his face. But whether it was for me or for himself, he couldn't say.

"Ginny," Tommy said.

"What!" I barked.

"Ginny . . . just let him talk." Tommy's voice was the softest plea I had ever heard.

I swallowed. "Okay," I said. Then I stood. "It's your life, Tommy." I left the room.

Tommy and Mitch the Bitch talked for well over an hour after I left. Even though I was in my bedroom with the door shut I could hear pieces of their conversation. I could hear Mitch the Bitch bring up honor and courage and duty. He was a living, breathing commercial. And every single time I wanted to race into the living room and grab Tommy by the ear and tell him everything that was wrong with what Mitch the Bitch was saying. All of the omissions of fact. All of the numbers that he either wasn't aware of or simply chose to leave out.

But I didn't.

When Mitch the Bitch had gone and the sun had set and the house was finally quiet, Tommy came into my room. I was lying on the bed with my back to the door, but I knew from the soft sound of his footfalls that it was him. I had been lost in The Memory Gospel just then.

"Ginny?" Tommy called. "Ginny? Are you awake?"

"You know I am," I replied.

Tommy came over and sat on the floor beside my bed. "He . . . he wasn't a bad guy. Not really. He's just doing his job, you know? He's supposed to say those things."

"Did you sign the Letter of Intent?" I asked.

"Will you just listen to me?" Tommy replied. "It's not like I'm going in tomorrow or anything. And it's not like I don't know that the war is dangerous. I'm not as dumb as you think I am."

"I never said you were dumb, Tommy."

"You never had to say it," Tommy replied. "I know what I am. I'm regular. That's all. Or maybe I'm even a little bit below regular." He let out an embarrassed laugh. "But I don't think that's a bad thing. I'm not ashamed of it." I knew that was a lie.

"Did you sign the letter?"

"No," Tommy said.

Finally I sat up in the bed. "Thank you," I said.

"Yeah," Tommy replied. Then he eased down onto the floor and curled up into a ball and, before long, he was asleep. Leaving me to think about what it all meant.

I awoke to the sound of Maggie coming into the house in a huff. "Virginia?" Maggie called. "Virginia, wake up. Tommy's gone."

ELSEWHERE

It wasn't that Kevin and Marvin were running from the war like so many other Embers. It was simply that the brothers felt the need to give something back at a time when everything was being taken away. They had money and were just old enough to have been missed by the draft and yet were just young enough to still be afraid that things might change and it could come for them the way it had come for the rest of their friends. They wanted to do something but didn't really know what until the day Kevin had the idea that if the world was going to end it might as well end with a party.

And that was how the "Drifting Party" started.

It was a simple idea: a new party in a new town every night. The very first town they pulled into, they rented out a bar and unloaded the speakers from their van and started the music. By the end of that first night the building was filled to capacity and spilling out into the street and the police finally had to come send people away. And when the morning came and Kevin and Marvin loaded up their bus and started off, they found a line of people waiting to follow behind them. It was like a band that was always on tour, and it wasn't long before their fame spread and the party moved with them.

It began with Embers. Those staring down the barrel of the war got into the idea of one last party with a mass of people who were also awaiting the end of their world. For a single night Embers could come and they could fall into a well of music and light and writhing bodies — which is the way it has always been with pleasure and music — and they could pretend that the dawn would never come, that the darkness was a home in which they could live.

So they did.

And when the dawn came and the party faded into memory and mystique, Kevin and Marvin boarded a large bus — which they had paid for themselves — and started off for the next town. The plan was simple: there was no plan. Just drive and party at sundown and hope that people came and lost themselves for a little while before they went off to the war and lost themselves forever.

Now, six months later, the Drifting Party was

a living, breathing entity that consumed entire towns in the Midwest for a single night. The whole country had taken notice. The Party was being mapped and tracked like a storm, something fearsome and splendorous all at once. It swept over the skin of America in a long, winding line of cars and motorcycles and trucks and buses and everything else that was mobile. There were even people following along on foot, and Kevin and Marvin took sight of this and decided that they wouldn't travel any farther than a day's walk for as long as the Drifting Party continued.

So their small experiment — sponsored by a couple of rich kids who had gotten lucky all of their lives — continued to grow and expand and take on one form after another.

But the problem — which the brothers didn't know about — was that those who didn't want to go off to the war at all were using the Drifting Party as a way to connect with other dodgers for means and methods of escaping the war. The brothers found out the night the police met them in a small Midwestern town that barely had a name. They surrounded the mass of Embers and asked for identification from everyone and it didn't take long before they were finding the draft dodgers mingled in among the revelers and began arresting them.

No one knew how the first gunshot was

fired. But everyone would come to know the aftermath of that gunshot.

When it was over the party was silent and Kevin was dead and Marvin was arrested and there were seventeen dead teenagers found among the ruin and wreckage of the Last Party.

Marvin wept for his brother and raged and wept some more, but there was nothing that he could do to bring back the dead. The next day he voluntarily enlisted. Three months later he was killed.

His story made the news and captured national attention for a few days. And then the fervor passed away like so many other things. The world returned to news about The Disease and the war and the dark days ahead. But for so many Embers who wound up going off to the war, there were glorious remembrances of a time before the end of things when there was music and light and revelry, and being alive was a blessing and not a burden. When all seems to be falling apart, those are the types of memories that can save a generation.

EIGHT

Even though he knew he could never grow up to be like me, Tommy was proud of himself for all the things that he had seen and all the ways he felt he was able to get a handle on the world. It was easy for someone with a mind like mine, Tommy figured. All I had to do was the required reading about the subject and pull it into my mind, able to see everything stretched out in front of me — then if I could sit and think long enough, I could sort out anything.

But for someone like Tommy, somebody who didn't have that ability — someone who had to break the world up into bite-sized pieces and, from those small morsels of understanding, come up with a plan on how to make it through the day, how to treat people who were good, how to stay out of the clutches of people who were bad, how to tell the difference between the two — life was a hard proposition.

Tommy felt he did okay most of the time. He had an inner compass of sorts that tended to tell him what to do, as long as he didn't spend too much time overthinking. Which wasn't to say that he thought thinking was bad. We were supposed to sit down and stick our elbow on our knee and our fist to our chin — like Rodin's *The Thinker,* though Tommy didn't know the name of the sculpture — and then, after we'd done all of that brow-furrowing type of thinking, we would suddenly see the clear path ahead. What we didn't know about something wouldn't matter because that internal compass would intuitively know the differences between right and wrong, good and evil. That was the thing that could put a not-so-smart person on even footing with someone capable of remembering everything they ever saw or read or said or did.

And putting people on even footing was the only thing that made the world fair. The only thing that made life fair. And it was damn important to be sure that things in life were, above all else, fair.

And while he didn't remember everything the way I did, he remembered the important stuff in his life. He remembered all the things that he was supposed to remember in order to become a good person. And it was important to Tommy to be a good person. If he couldn't be a smart one, then being a good one was something that he could be proud of.

Even though he was only seventeen, he'd seen a great many things in his life that had helped his moral compass. Tommy had seen a house burn to the ground and the family make it out in the nick of time. He had seen people stand before the smoldering remains of their life and smile and laugh and cry as though they had been granted the greatest gift in the entire universe rather than having just had it all taken away. He had seen a dog climb a tree — that one was odd, but he felt a lesson was there. He had seen bullies beating up on the weak and he had seen the weak beating up on the strong. He had seen rockets light up the sky like stars. He had seen planes fly so close overhead once — years ago, when one of their foster parents had taken them to a military air show — that when they passed people were bowled over and terrified that it would all come crashing down around their ears. He had seen winters so cold that tree limbs broke in the breeze. He had seen summer days so hot that birds kept out of the sky. He had seen teachers having sex in the bathroom, thinking they were hidden. It had happened not long after there was news of another bombing and people were desperate to remind themselves that there was something other than death in this world. And he had seen his fair share of death, as well, obviously. Death, which seemed hellbent on balancing the scales and reminding those who loved life that, eventually and without exception, it all comes to an end.

Even beyond the death of our parents — which he had seen but could not remember because that was the way his mind worked — he had seen the dead on television. Beds full of Disease victims flanked by weeping loved ones. Soldiers sent back from the war missing limbs. Civilians with blood-drenched bandages on their faces lying on cots in dusty desert hovels. On the internet, once, he had spent the night watching war videos. In the videos people were beheaded by the enemies. The videos were never around long. They lasted for only minutes before the censors found them and took them down, but they were there briefly and Tommy spent the night chasing one video around the web as it was taken down from one site and reposted on another.

Over and over again he watched the man with his hands bound behind his back lose his head. The man was calm to it all, accepting, as though he knew something that Tommy and no one else in the world seemed to be aware of. Whatever the secret was, Tommy wanted to know it. And that, even though he didn't realize it, had been the reason he had spent the night chasing the video, watching the man be killed over and over again. He wanted to know how it was possible for anyone to stare into the void of their own death with calm resilience and acceptance.

Whether he saw his own future in that video or not it was hard for him to say. Soldiers were often captured in the war and killed on video. That was the way of things nowadays. Privacy was more of a theory than anything. Births had been filmed and shown around for years. So, Tommy figured, it made perfect sense that death would get the same treatment.

So maybe one day — he sometimes mused to himself — he would be the man on his knees waiting for the blade to fall and for the lights to go out. He wasn't sure if he believed in an afterlife. Ever since I had made the decision that we were both atheists years ago, he'd struggled with it. He'd tried, now and again over the years, to convince me that there was possibly another option. But trying to outwit me in a conversation was something that he could never really do, so he kept his thoughts to himself.

Life, everything that a person did and saw and felt, couldn't all be for nothing. There had to be more. And it was his job to make me understand it. Life had shown him that. He had seen the country fall further and further into disagreement and arguing. When I read one of our father's letters Tommy would always listen and not really be sure he believed whether or not things were ever better. People were always talking about how much better things used to be. The sun used to shine brighter. Days were longer. The water tasted better. The world was greener. And on and on. Sometimes Tommy could be convinced that he had been born at the wrong time. Everything that had been good was decaying and everything that had been better would never come around again. The whole world, it seemed, was sliding into some place that it could never come back from.

And Tommy had, without a doubt, seen enough bad things to become numb to them. Sometimes it unsettled him just how easy it was to forget that there were, truly and without debate, bad things that happened in this world. It was all too easy to take in so much of what was happening that it overflowed the inside of you and you just felt like, well, like maybe nothing really mattered anymore.

Maybe that was really what was going on inside me. Maybe that was why I always seemed to be able to accept what was happening. Because of The Memory Gospel I carried everything, always saw the big picture, always saw the bad things, and I was never able to get away from them. I never had the luxury of lying to myself and saying that good things mattered more than the bad. Maybe that was why I made such a big fuss about deciding that the two of us become atheists. It was easier to believe in nothing than to believe in something broken and flawed.

But Tommy — even though a good percentage of what he remembered were bad things — was also able to remember the good.

Once he had seen a boy jump into a lake and save the life of a drowning man. He'd seen people give money and food to the homeless. He'd seen a dog fight off a stranger to protect a child. He'd seen stars that shone in the daytime even though such things weren't supposed to happen. He'd seen the sun turn blue once — something to do with the alignment of chemicals in the air. He'd seen the ocean turn a similar electric blue — he hadn't really seen that one; it had been something his father had written about in one of his letters and Tommy had gotten the image in his head and not been able to get rid of it.

He still believed in the world.

But I had seen it all too and I had lost my belief in the world. Tommy knew that it wasn't likely I'd ever get that back. I was broken.

What I needed, Tommy thought, was to find something to believe in. Something like he had. When he stopped to think about it — which wasn't all too often, but it did happen — Tommy knew that he believed in a great many things. He believed in America. In the way the country was always trying to be the best version of itself. Yeah, maybe it didn't always do what it was trying to do, but at least it tried. He believed in people. Really and truly believed in them, in spite of the foster parents that had come and gone over the years.

If he could ever make me believe in something — America, people, God, something — then maybe I'd be happy.

He didn't know when I had become unhappy. It happened the way a sunny day suddenly becomes overcast. The clouds just seemed to appear out of nothing, as if they had always been there.

Tommy was pretty sure that it had begun with the death of our parents. That made sense to him. The course of our lives had changed, pushed us into the cycle of foster homes and group homes and foster parents and adoptive parents and social workers and new schools and new homes and new friends and new bullies and new reasons to be afraid to fall asleep at night — Tommy was haunted by a recurring memory that he might one day fall asleep and wake up in some unknown place surrounded by strangers with no way back to me. So Tommy figured that I was filled with similar fears, a whole host of things that I could never forget — after all, Tommy was blessed with the ability to forget anything and I was cursed with the opposite.

What else could he do but feel bad for me?

So every single day, from pretty far back as Tommy could remember, he made a promise to do what he could to make sure that I was happy and taken care of. He learned not to be upset when I got mad at him or took my anger out on him by showing off just how good I was at remembering things. He learned to forgive, over and over again. And because he had learned the art of forgetting — for truly and honestly letting go of the things he didn't want to keep in his mind — he could truly forgive me.

But since I couldn't forget, I never seemed able to forgive myself.

To this day, I apologized for the time when we were children and I had called him "a retarded oaf." Tommy didn't even remember the incident. Sometimes he wondered if it was all part of my imagination.

I would apologize and he would say, "It's okay, Ginny." And then he would smile to prove to me that it was, truly and sincerely, okay. But sometimes that would only make things worse.

"Do you even remember?" I asked.

"No," Tommy replied.

"Then how are you saying it's okay?"

"Well," Tommy replied, "I think the fact that I don't remember proves that it's okay. It's like it never happened. So, in a sense, maybe it never did."

"But that's not the truth," I said. "It did happen. I remember it." With each word I grew more and more frustrated. My eyes narrowed. The muscles of my jaw firmed up like concrete.

"But if I'm the one it happened to," Tommy replied, "and I don't remember it.

Doesn't that mean it's okay?"

"No!" I shouted, even angrier than before.

It went this way over and over again throughout our lives thus far. Him going one way in the world and me going another. Each argument, each time we felt a little differently about something, Tommy could feel that there was a dam being built between us, pebble by pebble.

Some nights Tommy would lie awake, wondering about that dam. He was smart enough to know people sometimes grew apart in this world. That was just the way of things. A person couldn't be expected to remain who they were from one end of their life to the other. Especially not with the way life had of falling down around your ears without much warning or reason. How can two people, even brother and sister, expect to get through it unchanged?

He saw changes in us. Every day I was drifting a bit further away. Every time he brought up something from the past that he couldn't remember, I would recite the story with a little less energy and interest than I had the time before. He felt bad about making me the keeper of the things he couldn't hold on to, and so he tried to limit it. If he felt himself getting to a nostalgic place — which was rare, because he hardly understood the notion of nostalgia, not really — he would stop himself. He would slow down and think to himself and ask, "Does it really matter?" And most of the time, he would come to the decision that it didn't.

But other times a memory would come into his head and only I could tell him the way things had once been. He would ask me and I would tell him and the gap between us would get just a bit wider.

He didn't understand how I couldn't believe in anything. There was a word for the way I felt about things, the way I believed in nothing. Absolutely nothing at all. I had told him one time that life was just a train ride to nowhere. I'd read it in a book and he knew I believed it — but he felt that it wasn't a good attitude to have about life. A person had a responsibility to find happiness in things. Maybe responsibility wasn't the exact word he wanted to use, but he wasn't good enough with words to be able to say for sure. All he knew was that there were things in this life to be happy about. But it was an elusive thing, like the smell of cedar and jasmine. Happiness was always just beyond the range of what you could see and hear and feel. You had to be on the lookout for it. You had to meet it halfway. You had to get down on your knees, penitent and patient — words Tommy couldn't think of but that fit his thoughts, nonetheless — and you had to say to yourself: "I'm going to be happy."

And if you did that, life could be a bearable thing.

But because of The Memory Gospel, I dragged around all the bad things in addition to all the good things and, maybe just because the bad had always outnumbered the good, I had become the atheist and the pessimist that I was. It was his job to fix that. To fix me. To make me understand that a person could believe in things and be happy and that it would all be okay.

Which was why Tommy didn't mind the fact that I had gotten him out here running from our foster father and from the Draft Board and the end of the world. If a person believed what the old people had to say about such things, we were on course to find the world hammered into a flat nothing by nuclear bombs and war and taxes and politics and religions and racism and sexism and discrimination and gun violence and murders and accidental deaths and rising sea levels and oil spilling into the oceans and oil spilling into the wetlands and oil spilling into the Arctic and whales beaching themselves because of naval sonar and masked madmen and rapists and solar flares and asteroids and tetanus and high blood pressure and car crashes and alcoholism and opioids and water with too much lead and wind and rain and the way the sky shone on certain days. Even before The Disease, it was never going to last.

It was everywhere and it was out to get everyone.

But that didn't mean that life was all bad. A person could find the good things too. Just like he had. Even though he would go off to war and he would probably die, he could still have a few good times before then.

Tommy jolted awake from some dream he couldn't remember, heart racing. When he wiped his hand across his forehead, he found it covered in sweat. "Shit," he swore to himself. He was afraid, but of exactly what he didn't know. He sat up and checked to see that I was still there. I was. I had curled into a ball on one side of the bed. The other side of the bed was unmussed. I always left room for him.

When he saw that I was safe, his heartbeat slowed and he exhaled, long and deep. He had slept awkwardly and his neck was sore. He sat up and rubbed the muscles.

"Ginny?" he called.

When I didn't wake up, he stood and walked into the living room. Maggie was nowhere to be seen. In the kitchen he found a small note on the table that said, "Take what you need." He grabbed some juice from the refrigerator and looked out the window. Maggie's home was in the middle of a beautiful nowhere. Hills rolled out around it like a green ocean and, in the far distance, there were mountains that blended into the sky.

There was a large barn out in the middle of a nearby field. He thought he saw someone moving around.

The sunlight came down in buckets. Birds sang in the distant trees and the wind rolled in and felt like pillow. Tommy closed his eyes for a few steps and listened and felt and let it all take over his body because it was a good feeling and he knew that it might never come again.

When he reached the barn he found Maggie inside, lying on her back beneath a large old tractor. "Hi," Tommy said as he entered.

Maggie stuck her head out from beneath the tractor. She wasn't wearing her gas mask and the sun was in her eyes and she had to squint. For a moment, she didn't seem to recognize him, but then she said, "Tommy." It sounded like both a declaration and a question.

"Yep," Tommy replied. "That's me. Where's your mask?" he asked, caught off guard by how piercing her eyes were in the bright winter's day.

"Just decided not to," Maggie said. "Already gave what I had to give." Then, "Sleep well?" she asked, turning her attention back to the tractor.

"Sure did," Tommy said brightly. "Anything I can help you with?"

After a moment, Maggie's head came back out from beneath the tractor. "You know anything about tractors?"

"Not really," Tommy replied. "But I've got hands. And I'm pretty strong. That's got to be good for something."

"Always is," Maggie said. "Hand me that wrench."

She made a motion to one of the wrenches lying on the ground. Tommy handed it to her and stretched out on the ground beside her. The old tractor was a mixture of rust and oil. Maggie had removed one of the panels. The innards of the machine showed barely like the innards of some alien animal.

"Where'd you learn to sing like that?" Tommy asked.

"Can't hardly remember," Maggie said. Then, "No, that's not really true. It was just a long time ago. You wouldn't know it to look at me, but I've been around. Grew up here. Then traveled around for a few years, singing. Sang in some fancy places. Then came back home and took over the farm." She shrugged her shoulders. "Been here ever since."

"Well, you're awesome." Tommy grinned. "That was the most beautiful thing I've ever heard." He guessed the woman was over sixty, but the more he thought about how beautifully she had sung, when the rise and fall and tremble of her voice came back to him, it was as if he could see the years falling away from her. She seemed to grow younger by the second.

"Would you sing again?"

"What's that?"

"Would you mind singing again?" Tommy repeated. "I'd really like to hear it."

Maggie clucked a laugh. "Thanks for the compliment, but I've had enough of it for one lifetime."

"But you're so good at it," Tommy said. "You're special."

"Not really," Maggie replied. "Lots of people out there better than me."

"More people out there are worse than

you, though."

Maggie made one final turn on the wrench and, groaning just a little, got out from underneath the tractor. "Help me up," she said.

Tommy offered his hand and helped her stand.

"My knees aren't what they used to be," she said. She walked around and tried the ignition. The tractor shuddered and sputtered, but failed to start. "Damn," Maggie muttered.

The two of them worked at it for another hour with similar results. Then they walked out into the day and Maggie wiped her brow.

"Your sister always been like that?" Maggie asked.

"Yep," Tommy replied. "Never forgotten anything. Couldn't if she wanted to."

"That's a hell of a gift."

"Sure is," Tommy answered.

"What about you? You special like that too?"

"Not me," Tommy said. "I've got the worst memory on the planet. Stuff comes and goes with me. She's the smart one."

"Just because she can remember stuff doesn't mean she's smarter than you."

"Of course it does," Tommy replied. "It's

okay, though. I'm fine."

"That's something interesting to live with."

"She's supposed to get treated a little special. Because she is." Then pride filled his voice. "But when this trip is over, I'm going off on my own. I'm joining the army."

"You got drafted?"

"Yep," Tommy said. Then, "But I was going to go anyway."

Maggie thought for a moment. "You know it's not going to be like it is on the commercials, don't you?"

"I know." His voice was sharp. "I've thought about it. For a long time."

"And you still want to go?"

He nodded. "It'll be good for me," he said. "I won't stay forever. Only a couple of years. And then I'll come back and Virginia and I will get back to normal and everything will be okay."

"You mean running away across country isn't normal for you two?" She smirked at him and Tommy couldn't help but return it.

"It'll just be different after I get back from the army," Tommy said, his smirk fading. "It'll be better. I think I'll be someone different when I get back. I'll be smarter. Maybe I won't need Virginia as much as I do now."

Maggie watched him. He could feel her eyes taking him in. He took a deep breath, uncertain of exactly what she was looking for. "Well," she said, "just be sure to take care of yourself. You seem like a good kid."

"I'm not perfect," Tommy said.

"Never said you were."

"I'm not very smart."

"You don't have to be in this world. Just be a good person. The rest will take care of itself."

Tommy's face tightened. "You think that's true?" he asked.

"I know it is," Maggie replied.

They never did manage to get the tractor started. The both of them tinkering, twisting and turning parts, then switching on the ignition like children awaiting a surprise party. The hard edges and cold that had started the day wore off as the hour crept closer to noon. Tommy could almost believe that everything was going to be okay.

Then he heard the crunch of car tires on gravel and Tommy's stomach sank because he knew, without even looking, what was happening.

He stepped out of the barn and into the bright light of day to see a police car pulling up in front of him. When he saw it, maybe he was happy in some strange way. This would make everything simple. It was hard to say exactly what Tommy felt. He had never been much good with his feelings.

■ ■ ■ ■

SEPARATION

■ ■ ■ ■

NINE

"You're just going to go?" Maggie asked.

"That's the only way I'll get there," I replied. I had already filled the backpack with all the food I could carry. I cinched the buckle around my waist and adjusted the shoulder straps. I did it just as I had done it every other time before, as if my brother hadn't been taken away by the police.

"Do you want me to drive you to the station? Into town or something? I know the man that took your brother. His name's Hodges. He's an okay guy when you get right down to it. And you're a smart girl. Probably smarter than Hodges. You could talk to him. Maybe talk him into letting your brother finish this trip with you."

"It's best if I just keep moving on," I said. There was a knot in my stomach that seemed to be swelling with every word, filling me up moment by moment. It would consume me if I thought about it long enough, I knew that. So I closed my eyes and swallowed and, when I opened them again, I could convince myself that the feeling was gone.

When I opened my eyes I found Maggie's face as tight as a prune. "So you're just going to leave him?"

"He'll be okay," I said. "We knew we might get separated. We agreed to meet somewhere if that happened. He'll be there."

"He didn't get separated," Maggie said, her hands forming fists. "He was arrested! Hodges said there was an APB out on the both of you. Said an out-of-state cop had called it in. Probably that father of yours."

"Foster father," I corrected her.

Maggie pulled in a deep breath. When she exhaled, her fists softened again into hands, like ice effervescing into steam. "What the hell is wrong with you, girl?" she said, almost at a whisper. Then, "You should have seen him, that brother of yours. As soon as he saw it was a police car that was coming he turned to me and said, 'Please don't tell them about Ginny. Please.' He was almost crying. He asked me to do it for him like he was asking God Almighty for salvation. And then, when Hodges asked him about where you might be, he said you was already gone down to Florida. That you'd hopped a late bus and was already well on your way. Only reason Hodges believed him was because I said Tommy was the only one that had come."

"Why did you do that?" I asked. "Why did you lie for me?"

Maggie shook her head. "Can't say I really lied for you so much as I lied for your brother. Never met anybody that carried so much on his shoulders."

I barked a sharp, awkward laugh that made the knot in my stomach swell even more. The laugh lasted no longer than a flash of lightning behind a distant mountain. "Tommy's not carrying anything on his shoulders," I said. "That's what makes him so lucky." I straightened my back and prepared to head off. But before I started, I turned and looked back at Maggie one last time.

"Tommy's going to be fine," I said. "I know it doesn't seem like it, but he will. He'll be upset with me when he does, upset because of something I did that he doesn't know about. But . . . well . . . it's too late to fix any of that, I suppose. Maybe he'll forgive me. It's hard to say."

"Forgive you for what?" Maggie asked.

I didn't wait to answer. I lowered my head and started forward.

"Wait!" Maggie shouted. The old woman came chugging up beside me. Her face was red and stricken with fear. Her breaths came quick and shallow, as if she were standing on the thin bridge that had been thrown over an abyss. She reached into her pocket and, reluctantly, pulled out Gannon's pistol.

"Here," Maggie said. "Tommy also gave me this. Said you would need it since he wasn't with you anymore. He also said to tell you he was sorry."

I picked up the pistol and stuffed it into my pocket. "Bye, Maggie," I said, then I started forward again, and this time I promised myself that I wouldn't stop for anything else.

"You're some piece of work," Maggie said, almost throwing the words at my back as the distance between us opened. "If you ask me, your brother got the raw end of the deal when he landed you as a sister. Give you long enough and you're going to be worse to him than the war ever could be."

I walked out into the day with Maggie's words ringing in my ears. I made my way down to the highway, nervous that Gannon might be there waiting for me. According to

Maggie, Tommy had only just been taken. And maybe Hodges, the man Maggie said took Tommy away, hadn't yet had time to call Gannon — which would mean that Gannon could come driving up at any time, even by accident. But, alternatively, maybe Hodges had called Gannon already. Maybe he had been there, waiting and watching from a distance as Tommy was taken. And maybe now he was sitting around somewhere watching here too.

"You're being paranoid," I told myself.

I felt my heart thumping in my chest like a hammer on the head of an anvil. My palms were sweaty and I felt lightheaded. If I'd been thinking about it, I would have called it a panic attack. But why should I have a panic attack just because Tommy wasn't with me anymore? I still had a job to do. A place to be.

"It's going to be okay," I said to myself. But I wasn't sure whether or not I believed it.

When I reached the main road I looked around, reaffirming my sense of the cardinal directions. For a while I waited at the edge, looking back down the road just in case there was a car coming. Then I turned and started east. I walked for nearly two hours

203

before the truck came along. I stood with my thumb in the air, watching the old truck rumble its way up the road. It was dark blue, almost black, and rusted here and there and, because of how the sun was positioned in the sky, there was a glare that reflected on the windshield and bounced into my eyes and made it so that, as the truck passed, I couldn't see the face of the driver.

When it had passed me the brake lights lit up and the truck pulled off to the side of the road and idled, with the exhaust pipe rattling like thunder. The dented license plate was from Arizona and didn't quite seem to belong. Either logic or raw instinct made a chill run through my body.

I stood motionless and watched the idling truck. I could see a man sitting at the wheel. His brake lights were aglow as he looked back at me in the rearview mirror, waiting.

"Instinct is the calling card of animals," I whispered to myself. "It's just a truck and you've got a lot of miles to make."

I made no move toward the truck.

Still the truck waited.

In my pocket, my right hand curled around Gannon's gun and I realized, for the first time, that I didn't know whether or not it was loaded. I had simply taken it and stuffed it into my pocket. But since then, I had been rushing, like I was running away from both Maggie and Gannon. So the gun had become simply a weight in my pocket that made me feel safe and dangerous at the same time.

But if the man in the truck were to step out and walk toward me, threatening to do all the things that were done to seventeen-year-old girls hitchhiking alone, I didn't know what would happen if I pulled the gun from my pocket and squeezed the trigger.

"That's okay," I said finally. A moment later I realized that I had only whispered it, so I yelled, "That's okay! I don't need a ride!"

But still the truck waited. The man looked back at me in the mirror, then looked down at something in the truck, then looked back at me again. I watched him and tried to decide what to do. There was a part of me that wanted to get into the truck. He was the first person who had stopped and, from what I could see of him, he wasn't much of an imposing figure. He was thin-shouldered and didn't look very much like the type of man that would overpower someone.

But weren't those exactly the people who did such things?

The small pickup truck continued to wait.

"I'm okay," I yelled. And I made a shooing motion with my arms and hands, like trying to convince a garden snake that had slithered through the front door to go back the way it came.

Somehow, it worked.

The man in the truck took one final look at me. Then the brake lights went out and, after looking for traffic, the man started again down the road. I thought I saw him shrug his shoulders just before he got back onto the highway, leaving me behind. And that one gesture made me uncertain I had done the right thing.

I was alone again. I walked for another hour and still there was no one. Only open fields and mountains in the distance and trees and memories of the truck and the man who sat inside it waiting for me and thoughts of what might have happened.

"Okay," I said to myself suddenly, stepping away from the road and marching through a field toward a large dead tree.

When I was about thirty yards away I stopped and turned and, without hesitation, aimed the gun at the tree and fired. It almost leaped from my hand. My heart beat in my ears, but I tightened my grip and pulled the trigger two more times. Each time the gun roared and jumped like an angry god of old. The gun was, after all, something built solely for the purpose of taking away someone's life. When there were only three bullets left I dropped the gun and fell to my knees and started crying and I didn't know why.

Rain had begun to fall when a small Honda rumbled down the road toward me. I stuck out my thumb. The car skidded to a stop just past me and the passenger door flew open.

A man with one arm sat behind the wheel shouting, "If-you-want-out-of-the-damn-monsoon-we're-heading-to-the-hospital-Get-your-ass-in-if-you're-going-to-Well-don't-just-stand-there-looking-like-a-damn-statue-Having-one-fucking-arm-ain't-contagious-Jesus-fucking-Christ!"

A woman in the back seat — with sweat sprinkled across her brow and a large, round stomach — placed her hand on his shoulder and she whispered something softly in his ear and the bluster went out of the man behind the wheel like a dragon that lost its pilot light.

"I'm sorry," he said to me, his words muddled in the chatter of the rain pounding on the car, persistent as a tax collector. Then, slowly, "We're headed to the hospital.

Wife's having a baby. You're welcome to ride into town with us if that's the way you're headed." He couldn't even look at me when he said it. He only finished his sentence and sat with his head hung like a child standing before the church congregation with a fist-ful of stolen communion wafers.

I didn't let him linger in his shame. I jumped in the car as if he'd never yelled at me or apologized to me and I said some-thing about being born lucky.

"Nolan and Connie," the pregnant woman in the back seat said between the hee-hee-hoo-hoo of her breathing. She shook my hand while Nolan put his foot on the ac-celerator and the rear tires spun in the gravel before the car finally lurched back onto the highway. Nolan cursed at himself — something about bad tires — while Con-nie and I talked all the way to the hospital with Nolan sawing at the steering wheel with his one hand. Connie seemed happy to have someone to talk to.

They were a pair of "New Birthers." Another of the many couples trying to repopulate the dying world. New Birthers cycled in and out of the hospitals, pushing out children and hope in one fell swoop, all the while certain that something in their creations of life would balance out all of the death and dying that were seeping into everything else around them.

Just like with Embers, the New Birthers weren't working under any unified plan or direction. They were just people doing what they could to quell the fear inside of them. And I always hoped that their efforts would bear fruit. Because it was easier to imagine that than to imagine their efforts being in vain and that those children they worked so diligently to bring into creation would be destined to live the shortest, harshest lives of any of us.

Since the beginning of time children were meant to ensure the future. Now the future couldn't ensure the children.

I asked Connie questions about the baby and about Nolan and I said things like, "It's going to be okay" while squeezing Connie's hand and, sometimes, I did Lamaze breathing along with her. We even laughed now and then, like old friends sitting in the front parlor of an old house, remembering life as it was before everything changed.

Nolan squinted over the steering wheel as if tightening his eyes could make his vision part the sheets of rain like Moses. It went like this the whole way to the hospital. When we pulled up in front of the emergency room I bolted from the car like a scalded dog and came back with a wheelchair and a nurse as if delivering the babies of strangers was a hobby of mine. Nolan was still in the driver's seat, his hand locked on the wheel like a dead man's, like it hadn't received the message from his brain yet that they'd gotten where they were trying to go. Then Connie's hand was on his shoulder and his hand relaxed and released the wheel and his arm flopped down onto his leg, lifeless, like an animal shot through the heart. "Jesus," he said.

"You okay?" I asked.

Connie sat forward in the back seat and wrapped her arm around her husband's neck. "We're gonna get through this," she said.

Nolan sniffled and rubbed his eyes and suddenly looked like a child. "We're gonna be okay," he said. "Everything's gonna be fine."

"Of course you are," I said brightly. It was part performance, part sincerity. Whichever of the two was the majority I couldn't say. All I knew was that, just then, the couple was nervous and maybe I could help them and, for the first time since starting out, I wasn't thinking about Gannon and what would happen when he caught up to me.

"Jesus," Nolan said when the car was

parked and the nurse had taken Connie into the back of the hospital. He and I were standing at the registration desk together.

"You okay?" I asked.

"What's your name again?"

"Virginia," I said. "I'm a student of human nature. And I'm willing to bet hard-earned American dollars — as my third foster father used to say — that this is your first baby and that you'd give anything you could for it all to go ahead and get over with. But don't you worry. Things generally sort themselves out."

"That a fact?" Nolan replied. He pawed at the empty pocket of his shirt like a smoker who had only recently given up the habit.

"It is," I said. "Do you like numbers? I'm pretty good with numbers and, speaking for the numbers, a CDC report from 2014 said that the rate of infant deaths was only 6.1 deaths per one thousand. Not the greatest for developed countries, but —"

"How do you know that?" he asked. Then he turned to the nurse before I had time to answer. "How long's this gonna be?"

"Excuse me?"

"How long?"

"Can't really say," the nurse replied, punching at her keyboard, only half paying attention to him. "Sometimes they pop right out. Other times they do everything they can to stay in there." She snorted a half laugh. "We'll know more in a little bit, once the nurses examine her."

"Is everything okay? With her? With the baby?" Nolan made a fist with his existing hand. Then the fist relaxed into an open hand again and he sighed.

"We'll know more once she's examined," the nurse said. She was watching her computer screen and didn't see the fist he had made and unmade.

"Well, how long is that gonna take?" he asked.

"Not long."

"Well, how long is not long!" He said it sharp enough that the nurse finally looked up from her computer. She looked him in the eyes, and then at the empty, folded sleeve where his left arm should have been. Her face softened.

"Jesus," he said.

I put my hand on his shoulder the way Connie had. "Let's go outside, shall we?" I said. "I think I left something in the car. Plus, there's fresh air out there. Fresh air and rabbits and unicorns, all types of awesome things. That's what a person needs at a time like now: clean air and sunshine.

Speaking of air, sort of, did you know that there's a global helium shortage?"

"A what?" Nolan asked. He fell into step beside me, his face tightened into a question.

"Yep. Not enough helium in the world and less and less each day," I said. "Strange facts are fun facts. Anyhow, while everyone is filling up kids' balloons at birthday parties, helium is also used in MRI machines and other advanced science. But there's only a finite amount here on earth. It won't be here forever."

"So what . . . I mean, what are they gonna do?" Nolan asked.

"Hell if I know," I said. "But it feels good to think about something else for a change, doesn't it?"

Nolan barked a small laugh.

When we got back outside the rain had stopped, as if it had existed only to torment us on the drive. The sun hadn't come out from behind the clouds just yet, but it would soon, I could tell. It was that feeling like false dawn — a small, barely noticeable change, like a dial being turned up somewhere, everything brightening by degrees, a spark becoming an ember becoming a flame.

"You're soaked to the bone," Nolan said,

starting off toward the car. "Don't suppose you've got a change of clothes, do you?"

"Point of fact, I don't," I said brightly, even as my shoes squished with each step and my clothes flapped, soggy and heavy around me.

"Well, I can't let you go off like that," Nolan said, marching across the parking lot like a plow animal. He ran his hand through his hair.

Nolan opened the trunk of the car after fiddling with his keys. There was a large blanket and a gym bag full of Connie's clothes. He unzipped it and flopped the lid open. After riffling through it, he found a flannel shirt of his and pulled it out, careful not to disturb the rest of her clothes. He placed the shirt next to the bag and took off his wet one and put on the dry one. His hand shook so he made a fist and released it and the shaking stopped.

"You going to make it?" I asked.

"I'll be fine," Nolan said. Then: "What are you doing?"

I had already started walking away.

"Where are you going? You can't leave like this. You'll catch pneumonia. Just look at yourself!" He reached into the trunk and grabbed Connie's bag. "There's clothes in here that'll fit you. Get into something dry and hang around for a bit. You just . . . you just can't go off like that. Just . . . stick around for a bit."

"Thanks for the offer," I said. "But I've got miles to make up. A long, long way to go."

"Please," Nolan said. He looked smaller than he had before, like a sculpture made from paper.

Nolan was a good man about to become a father in a harsh, uncertain world. The war, The Disease, and still he had found belief enough to think that another soul in this world could make a difference, could find happiness, could build something out of the rubble and ruin that everyone seemed to know was inevitable. Becoming a parent was an act of courage, just as it had always been.

It started from the moment I got into the car: a vision of my parents. I couldn't help but imagine them heading to the hospital on the day Tommy and I were born. The fact was, and this was something I knew, just as sure as I knew my own name, that all of this whole trip ahead of me, was just my way of chasing my parents' ghosts. I imagined, all those years ago, my parents being as frightened and excited as Connie and Nolan. In the car, I had seen my mother's face in Connie's — smiling, breathing in and out like the bellows of a furnace. And Nolan became my father, desperate and maybe even more afraid than my mother, sawing at the steering wheel as if death itself were driving behind them, headlights flashing and horn blowing. And I couldn't help but become afraid for them both. I knew, even if they didn't, that everything they were afraid of could come true at any moment, without warning.

When Nolan had pressed his luck and drove faster on the way to the hospital, he did it out of a certainty that they would be okay. Maybe there would be a few hairy moments but he and his wife would make it. That was never in doubt for Nolan. God had already taken his arm. There was no way He would take his child as well. And I knew that Connie shared the same confidence. It was their first child — Connie had made a point of telling me that more than once — and the woman was certain that there were only good things ahead for her and her family. That's what they were building, after all: a family. "And families don't get snuffed out in their early stages," I had told them at one point, fully aware and living proof that it was a lie.

But such truths weren't conceived of in

Nolan and Connie's philosophy. Nor the philosophies of any other parents. Who was I to take that away from them?

My own parents were already dead and I would never have the chance to be afraid for them. The longer I lingered in the hospital, the more afraid I became for Nolan and Connie.

"Son of a bitch," Nolan said, flopping down into the seat beside me. "Every single one of them. Just a bunch of sons of bitches." He scratched the back of his neck and then wiped his chin in frustration.

"What's the matter?" I asked, trying to push the thoughts of my parents from my mind.

"Nothing," Nolan said. "Just the damn headache of it all. All we're trying to do is have a baby. People have been doing that since before there were people. And these bastards just want to get their paperwork done."

He fixed his mouth to say more, but one of the nurses came over and smiled and said, "They've got her in a room now. Room 513. You can go on up if you're ready."

"Thank you," Nolan said immediately, and all of the anger was gone from his voice. He sighed and his body relaxed. "Thank you," he said again softly.

I patted him on the shoulder. "It's going to be fine. Like you said, people have been having babies since before there were people."

He flashed a smile and stood and the two of us started off for the elevator. When we reached Connie's room, a nurse came out and motioned for us to go on in. Nolan reached up as if to tip an imaginary hat to her but the movement came off as awkward. The nurse seemed not to notice.

"There she is," Nolan said warmly. He sat on the edge of the bed — so that his missing arm was facing away from Connie — and hugged her and kissed her on the top of the head. "You okay?"

"Feeling fine," she said.

Nolan sat up. He looked her up and down, taking in her sudden calmness. "What's happening? Everything okay?"

"Everything's fine," Connie said. "The baby just decided to slow down."

"Is that normal?"

"Totally normal."

"You sure? What did the doctors say?"

"Settle down, husband," Connie replied. She squeezed his arm. "Everything is okay."

"You're damn right it is," I added. "You've got nothing to be afraid of."

The nurse came back before too long to

218

let Nolan know that there was still paper-work to be done. After Nolan left, I stayed with Connie, who was growing sleepy from the medicine they had given her. She stared up at the ceiling, counting the ceiling tiles aloud, while the medication began to flow through her veins — heavy, thick veins that, when I saw them, reminded me of Europa's Falga Regio — wide, branching lines slicing into the ice like cracks in the floor of an empty riverbed in which the water has long ago gone. Everything reminded me of Europa in some form or another. So, for me, Nolan was Jupiter — the big, colorful gas giant that could have been a star, a life giver in its own right, if things had gone differently, but fate had other plans. Now it was only potential churning in upon itself — still glorious and beautiful, but never what it could have been.

Maybe planets do mourn the lives they could have led as stars. Who's to say?

Connie was Europa. The small, cool orbiter with an ocean of life buried inside her.

Connie let out a long, relaxed sigh. "How you feeling?" I asked.

"It's all free drinks and dancing girls," Connie said with a dopey, faraway look in her eyes. "Where's Nolan?"

"Taking care of the paperwork, I think. There's no shortage of things that need to be filled out."

"How is he?"

"*Pensive* would be the word I'd use."

"He's always been afraid of everything," Connie replied with a smile.

"You want me to go and get him?"

"No," Connie said. "Just hang out with me for a bit if you don't mind. Nolan will come in when he's ready." She adjusted her position on the bed and looked at me. "I don't think I ever asked you where you were headed."

"South," I replied. "Southeast to be more precise. Cape Canaveral. Almost to the bottom of the American map."

"Canaveral?" Connie said. "Going to watch a launch?"

"Yes, indeed," I said. "Nothing more majestic, in my opinion. The summit of mankind's achievements, if you ask me. Hardly anything comp—"

"I did that once," Connie replied. "It's something. What's the launch?"

"Unmanned probe on its way to Europa, one of the Jov—"

"One of Jupiter's moons, if I'm not too buzzed to think straight."

"Dead on!" I exclaimed. "You must be a

fellow fan of the celestial science. Not nearly enough talk about the heavens and far too much talk about Heaven if you ask me. I'm fond enough of the metaphysical and related theories but there's so much here, in this universe, that we have yet to figure out that I feel like people spend too much time thinking on the unknowable and not enough time trying to sort out the rest." I exhaled.

"People you've met so far, you mean?"

"Exactly," I said. "Not complacency, just pattern making. The world is vexing enough, I suppose, without the talk of space exploration and the greater knowledge of mankind. Too much to think about for general people, what with bills and mortgages and divorces and children and everything else that comes and plants roots in a person's life."

"Kids think about it."

"They do, indeed. Children are the future until they become adults, then they simply become furniture — stagnant and unchanging."

Connie laughed. "But not you, huh?" she said. "So why is it so important to you? Why uproot your life to head across the country with the way everything is? Why not just curl up and hide or, better yet, run away like other Embers?" She tried to sit up, then changed her mind. "I can't blame them for running away. Can't blame them at all. And then, look at you: it's obvious that you're not just on a trip. You've got no bags. And you should be taking a bus or a plane. No, you make it seem like this is your final trip in life, like you're taking a one-way trip. You make it seem like there's not going to be anything after Florida, after the launch. Maybe you should hang here in Arkansas for a while. Skip out on that launch. Why are you doing this?" She watched me closely as she asked the question.

"Can I answer a question with a question?" I asked.

"You sorta just did," Connie replied.

"Why do people like you do it?"

"People like me?"

"New Birthers. It's all winding down," I said. "Why pretend otherwise?"

"Because that's what hope is," Connie replied without a moment of hesitation, as if she had been waiting for the question since the day she was born. "You know the great thing about strangers? They don't know anything about you. You can tell them anything and then disappear and never see them again. They make perfect confidants. And since they don't know you or, in a sense, care about you, they don't have anything to gain by skewing their answers.

They can be honest with you and you can be honest with them." The pain was coming back to her and she reached up and took a hold of the self-medication button. "Can't promise I'll be in a state to offer decent advice for very long."

"An interesting thesis," I said. "I —"

"Can you just cut the smoke and mirrors for a moment?" Connie asked. "Please?"

"I'm going because this Europa mission is the last good thing that's going to happen in this world." I spoke slowly. "And I want to be there to see it. I want to remember it, to keep it forever, because that's what you're supposed to do with good things. I'm going because my brother and I don't understand each other anymore. This was supposed to be our last chance to get things back to the way they were. But I guess things can never get back to the way we remember them, no matter how perfectly we remember them." I looked down at my hands and caught them trembling. They looked afraid. "I wish Mom and Dad were here."

"I was wondering about that but didn't want to ask," Connie said. "Where are your parents?"

"Dead."

"How long ago?"

"When I was five."

223

"Sorry."

"It's not your fault."

"I can still be sorry," Connie said. The pain was washing over her again. "So, do you think they'll find life on Europa?"

My smile indicated it was a question I had wanted to be asked for many, many years. "I don't know," I said, sitting forward. "It's the best chance. All of the preliminary data says conditions are right. There's an ocean beneath the surface. And, as a general rule, where there's water, there's life."

"Bacteria?"

"Probably certainly," I answered, excitement filling me up all of a sudden. "But for it to really be meaningful to most people, we'll need more than bacteria. There'll need to be something bigger than that, something that, when you stick a camera into the water, swims up to the lens and dances in front of it."

Connie laughed. Then the medicine hit her like a tidal wave of relaxation, like a cloud moving through her veins.

"What's so funny?" I asked.

"You're a dreamer," Connie replied. "And that's not an insult." Then, "Jesus, this is some good medicine." She laughed.

"I'm carrying a gun," I said softly.

"That's nice," Connie replied, blinking slowly.

"And I hate my brother because he's the only one of us who gets to forget how much he misses our parents."

"That's very wonderful," Connie said, the words slow and drowsy. She was already asleep before the sentence finished, leaving me alone with my confession.

I wasn't there when Connie woke up. Nor was I there when Nolan came back from taking care of the paperwork. I hope that their child came out healthy. I hope they were all happy together. I hope she and Nolan stopped being afraid. I hope the war and The Disease, which were unkind to so many, were kind to all of them.

ELSEWHERE

Justin watched and waited for as long as he could. He'd never been the type to worry and fret and overreact to things, and that's what had made him such a good father and husband and manager of the small retail store where he worked. He was dependable. That's what anyone who knew him was bound to say about him if asked to boil him down to a single word. Dependable.

And being dependable meant that a person didn't run off in a panic every time something seemed to be going wrong. No. Justin prided himself on an attitude that could hunker down and sit out the worst storm until it had passed over and the sunlight finally broke through the clouds and a person could stick their head out into the cool, wet air and know, in the pit of their stomach, that everything was going to be okay in the end.

But this time things were different.

For the first few years after The Disease appeared he didn't think much of it. It was just another mysterious disease — just like all diseases were when they first started off. And just like every other disease that had come before it, eventually people would solve what caused it and how it spread and all those other things that always come to light with enough time and then everything would be okay. Maybe they wouldn't cure it completely, but at the very least things would come under control.

And when the war followed hot on the heels of The Disease a few years later, that too was something that he felt he could wait out and endure. Dependability was a simple way to be brave. Live your life, stick to your routine, and let the vicissitudes of life swim and swirl around you until calm came back.

But then years passed and the war wasn't over and The Disease was still spreading and the economy was slowing and people were being drafted and going off and not coming back and people were cashing in their life's savings and buying guns and bullets and food and water and stockpiling things and traveling around the country behind parties just because they needed something to believe in and none of it was looking any better. Not even a little bit.

It was when his daughter fell sick and he

took her in to the doctor and found out that they didn't have any antibiotics on hand . . . that's when everything changed. She made it through her illness, thankfully. But that was the end of it. If he was going to be dependable, then he would worry less about being there for everyone else — including humanity as a whole — and more for the wife and two daughters he was trying to raise.

So the next week he cashed in his life's savings — which was a good thing because the banks were running low and it wasn't long before there would be no money left and the bloodshed would begin — and when he had the money it only took him another week to find a boat big enough for him and his family to live on.

He'd grown up in the Outer Banks of North Carolina. Learned to swim before he could walk. The idea of hiding out on the water while the world fell down on its knees seemed like a good alternative to anything else that he could think of. It seemed like a good way to keep his family together.

So they packed things up and drove down back to the Outer Banks that they knew so well and he put his family on the boat at the dock and tied it off and told them to give him a few more hours before he came onboard and they all set off. He had one more stop to make.

He hadn't seen his parents in nearly three years and even though he talked to them on the phone nearly once a week, he had never actually said the words to them until he stood at the end of his childhood driveway and they stood on the porch watching him with fear and sadness in their eyes:

"I'm sorry," he said, his voice raised enough to carry his words, but not so loud as to make them think he was yelling at them. He'd never, not even when he was a hardheaded teenager, yelled at his parents. "It's just the way things are," he said.

"I know, son," his father said. His voice was as warm and even as always. The man had been an electrician all of his life. An electrician and a fisherman when the budget called for it. Both careers had given him a hard, grizzled look and an overall sense of capability that, even now that he was in his mid-seventies, had not waned. "You need to do what's right for your family."

A lump formed in Justin's throat. "That's all I'm trying to do," he said. It was hard to breathe all of a sudden. Or, rather, it was hard to breathe without crying.

"Don't you worry about us," his mother said. She was just as small and frail as always, but the sound of her voice calmed him now just as much as it did when he was a child. Once a child always a child, Justin thought.

"I don't want to do it," Justin said. "But . . . it's the girls. I've got the girls and I've got to make sure they're okay."

"We know," his father said.

"It's okay," his mother said.

He wanted to hug them, and all of its own accord, his foot took a step forward.

"No, baby," his mother said. Her eyes were puffy all of a sudden. And then she was crying. "Don't come any closer."

"Listen to your mother," Justin's father said. "We wouldn't forgive ourselves if we somehow gave whatever this disease is to you and then you took it back to those grandchildren of ours."

"But you don't know that you're infected," Justin said.

"But you don't know that we're not."

And that was the truth of it. A truth that Justin swallowed along with the lump in his throat. After a moment he nodded and said, "I'll call. I promise I'll call."

"Please do," his mother said.

"We'll be here," his father said.

He stood there for a while longer, staring and waiting for the world to change, waiting for something to be different than the way it was. But that change never did come and the silence was only broken by the sound of his father saying: "Okay, son . . . go on now."

And what else could Justin do but listen to his father and leave?

When he made it back to his family and the boat, his wife asked him where he had been — even though she knew perfectly well — and he didn't answer. He only took his children in his arms and wept and kissed them and held them tight and did not speak as he pulled anchor and the boat pulled away from the dock, leaving behind home once and forever.

Ten

Tommy watched through the cell bars as Gannon walked in through the front door of the small police station.

It had been only a few moments since Hodges had offered his speech on duty and responsibility as it applied to today's youth. It had been a challenging speech for the man — full of words so big Hodges had to stop and lick his lips and sometimes nibble the word down to its smallest syllables in order for it to be spoken. He used the term "duty." He used the word "privilege." He tossed "God" in now and again, something Tommy tried not to notice. He believed in things enough for that. If Hodges had been a more handsome man or simply a man born with more money, he could have become an elected official. Maybe even president.

But Hodges was here and he had caught Tommy at Maggie's place and called Gannon and brought Tommy to the station and put him in a cell and looked over his paperwork and looked him up in the computer and given his speech on responsibility and now that Gannon had arrived, Hodges looked at Tommy with something akin to pity in his eyes.

The two men greeted each other with mumbled hellos. Gannon hardly glanced in Tommy's direction. He only followed Hodges into the office, with Hodges smiling and with his thumbs tucked into the loops of his belt like a caricature.

They sat in the office with the door open for a while. Hodges sat back in his chair talking, looking over his desk like a king holding court. Gannon sat with his back straight and his eyes on Hodges. After a while Hodges reached onto his desk and picked up Tommy's draft notice. He pointed at the letter and spoke and, once or twice, looked over at Tommy. Then his eyes went back to Gannon.

The conversation ended and Hodges led Gannon out of his office to Tommy's cell.

"Here he is."

Gannon looked in through the bars at Tommy. "Told you I'd catch up," he said.

"You're in a hell of a situation," Hodges said to Tommy. He held up the draft notice.

"A hell of a situation."

"I'll talk to him," Gannon said.

"Yeah," Hodges replied sadly. "I suppose that's only right." Finally he reached into his waist and pulled out the cell keys and unlocked the door. The bars opened with a groan. "C'mon," Hodges said. "You're hereby evicted from my hotel."

Tommy continued sitting on his cot. "What if I don't want to go?"

"No choice," Hodges said.

"What if I don't want to go with him?"

"Still no choice," Hodges answered. "But life ain't never really ever been about choices. Did you choose to be here? Did you choose to look the way you look or think the way you think?" He licked his lips the way he did before when he talked about the war and about responsibility. He was ramping up to something. "And even when you make a choice, do you ever really make it? Isn't everything a person chooses to do just the end result of everything they've already done?"

"What?" Gannon asked.

Hodges waved him off. "I'm making a point," he said boldly. "This is my station and I'll say what I damn well please."

Gannon lifted his hands, giving up.

Hodges turned back to Tommy. His jaw

clenched. He took a deep breath, held it, opened his mouth to speak . . . but nothing came out.

"It's okay," Tommy said. "I know what you mean."

"Do you?" Hodges asked. "Do you really?"

Tommy nodded. "Yes, sir."

"Good," Hodges said. There was solemnness in his voice. "Good." He stepped away from the door. "Take care of yourself."

"Yes, sir, Mr. Hodges," Tommy said.

The hotel was a small mom-and-pop affair just off the highway in the shadow of the Smoky Mountains. The couple who owned it was in their seventies and they bickered now and again — just like any other long-married couple — as they booked Tommy and Gannon in, but they were nice enough. They didn't seem particularly concerned about the war or The Disease. They seemed to care only about talking to people. The old woman behind the counter asked Tommy what type of music he liked and went on and on about The Beatles as she showed them to their room. Gannon booked a single room with two beds and told Tommy, "You're not going to run away." He said it simple and plainly, and Tommy found it to be true.

Though he couldn't say why, Tommy realized that he had absolutely no plans to run away. He hadn't forgotten about me, and he was worried about my being out there on my own, but now that Gannon had actually caught up to him, now that he was finally caught — something he knew that would happen eventually — there was a certain degree of freedom in it. He could stop worrying. The feeling of being chased had gone away.

In short: he felt better.

But it wouldn't last. Even though his memory was full of holes, his heart was always able to fill in those places in his mind. His heart told him that he had to meet me the way we had talked about before leaving. His heart told him that he needed me and that I needed him. His heart told him that we were all each other had in this world.

The old woman showed them to their room. "Not many people come through here anymore," she said. Then: "Story of life, I suppose."

The motel was a long rectangle that looked as though it had come out of some movie in which people hid from the bad things they'd done. "Picked these out myself," the old woman said when she opened the door. She pointed to one of the paintings on the far wall. "I used to paint when I was younger. Got pretty good at it too. Maybe I should take it up again, considering how much those things cost to buy. Could save a whole lot of money if I just painted them myself."

"Yes, ma'am," Gannon said.

"But then I'd have to do all of the work," she said, chuckling.

"Yes, ma'am," Gannon repeated. "It's good to see some type of normalcy in this world. I didn't know it existed anymore."

"What do you mean?" the woman asked.

"Well, you know, with everything going on the way it is."

The woman clucked a laugh. "We don't worry about the world," she said. "It never makes it this far into the woods. No matter what happens out there, nothing ever changes in here."

"But aren't you afraid that it might one day?" Tommy asked.

The woman's brow knotted like an old tree. Then it relaxed. "Everything always comes out okay," she said. "It's like that climate change stuff the people kept saying would come get us. Never did. Both world wars stalled out long before coming here.

No, sir, this place is immune to the world." She smiled a wide, proud smile. "So I bet you and your son are heading down to Florida like everybody else."

"Yes, ma'am," Gannon replied. "And there's my father out in the car. I'll be bringing him in shortly."

"It's a good time of year for it," she said. "Weather's a bit more sane down there. Too cold for me here these days. I don't suppose you're going down there for that big rocket launch, are you? And don't you dare say 'yes, ma'am' again."

Looking at Gannon just now, really trying to take in who he was at this particular moment, all Tommy saw was a man who was hung up on something and never willing to let it go. Every day of his life the shadow of something hung over his head, haunted his footsteps, made him into someone he might not otherwise have been.

And all Gannon had to do, Tommy knew, was let go of it. Release the past. Release the future. Give up them both and just try to exist. Tommy did it every single day of his life. Though it was easy for him. Just like I had my Memory Gospel, Tommy had his ability to forget anything.

"Point of fact," Gannon said to the old woman, "we are going down to Florida."

The old woman clapped her hands together in excitement. "Holy Moses! That's just so exciting! I never thought I'd live to see something this important happen again in my lifetime. Seemed like for a long time there everybody forgot how to get excited about anything. After we went to the moon and found out it wasn't made of cheese we just lost all of our desire." She laughed then, a long, hard laugh.

Tommy took off his backpack and slumped down on the bed. It smelled a little bit like mothballs and cheap air freshener. But it wasn't totally unpleasing.

"I tried to talk that husband of mine into going down there. Tried to explain to him why it was important. But talking to him is like talking to a mule." The old woman stood in the doorway, lost in her own train of thought. Tommy guessed that she and her husband didn't get many visitors.

"That's a shame," Gannon said.

"That's exactly what I said to him," the woman replied, her voice full of sudden pride and energy, as though God himself had validated something she had known since birth.

"Well," Gannon said, "I suppose we'll just go ahead and get settled in now. It's been a long day."

"Oh yes," the woman said, embarrassed now, "I apologize for keeping you. I should let you sleep. I don't know why I babble on the way I do."

"It's okay," Gannon said.

The woman began to speak again, but then she stopped herself and looked even more embarrassed than she already was. "Okay," she said, and then she left.

"Not a bad place," Gannon said once the woman was gone. Then he went out to the car and brought his father in while Tommy prepared a place on the bed for the sick man. Once Bill Gannon was situated, Gannon thanked Tommy and switched on the television and took a seat on his bed. "Not a bad place at all. What do you think, Pop?"

Bill Gannon offered no reply.

Tommy stretched out on his own bed, rolled over and turned to the wall. He wanted to let Gannon know that he was still holding a grudge on account of how he had taken him away from his sister. But at the same time, he was also just plain old tired.

"Talk to me, Tommy," Gannon said.

"Talk to you about what?"

"About your sister."

"Why?" Tommy asked. He rolled over and looked at Gannon. "You're not going to be able to find her before she gets to Florida.

And even if you drive all the way down there you still won't be able to find her. Not with all of those people that are going to be down there." Tommy pointed to the television. "Just look."

On the screen the news showed throngs of campers who had come to Cape Canaveral to watch the launch. Titusville, the small town around Canaveral, was overflowing. All of the hotels were full and people had begun renting out their houses at exorbitant prices. It seemed as though everyone in the country was there. And whoever wasn't there was already on the way.

"I don't get it," Gannon said. "With all the other stuff going on in this world, I don't see what all this Europa fuss is about. It's not like there's never been a rocket launch before."

"Not one like this," Tommy replied. "This is the last beautiful thing. That's what Ginny told me."

"Bull," Gannon said. "Ain't that right, Pop?" Still Bill Gannon did not speak or nod or do anything other than what he had done for the last two decades since his stroke. But his son seemed undeterred. "There have always been moments like this, Tommy. If Pop wasn't sick he could tell you about it. Happens time and time again.

Sputnik. The moon launch. Hubble." He shrugged his shoulders. "There's always something that's the newest, biggest mission or whatever. A whole bunch of eggheads sit around and tell us that something is important and we believe them. They tell us that something is revolutionary and we believe them. But how often is any of that true? How often are there really any big moments? And I'm not just talking about in the country. I'm talking about in life. How many moments are really important? The moment you're born and the moment you die. Period." He squinted at the television, as if accusing it of something. "They give us dreams just to distract us from the dying."

Tommy swallowed. His brain was full of things he wanted to say. Things that I had told him about why the Europa mission was so important. Things our father had written in his letters to the two of us. But Tommy couldn't organize his thoughts into any cohesive manner. "It's not like that," is all that he could manage.

"It's not," Gannon said.

"No," Tommy said. "It's big. It's important. People need to know that it's important, even if they can't really say why it's important, even if they can't find the words."

"You've been listening to your sister too much," Gannon said.

"It's not about her," Tommy replied.

"Your whole life is about her, Tommy. You know it as much as she does."

"Whatever," Tommy said. He turned over again and stared at the wall.

"I'm trying to find out what you want out of your life, Tommy." Gannon sat up and looked at Tommy. "What do you want to do?"

"What I want doesn't matter," Tommy said after a moment.

"Why is that?"

"Because," Tommy replied. He sat up on the bed and looked back at Gannon. The man was tall and square and intimidating in most situations, but just now, for the first time since Tommy and I had first come to live with him, Gannon looked like a man. Not a cop. Not a foster father. Just a man who looked nervous. Maybe afraid. Definitely concerned.

"How did it feel when you got the draft notice?" Gannon asked.

"Why?"

"Because I want to know. I can imagine how it felt, but I want to hear your version of it."

"It's hard to say," Tommy began. He

243

didn't trust Gannon. It was as though he could hear my voice inside his head, pointing out all the things wrong with Gannon, all the nights when he had gotten drunk and started fights and yelled and slumped in his chair in a heap. I was in Tommy's head, trying to make him remember. But Tommy was never any good at remembering. So, all of a sudden, Gannon was just a man sitting before him, asking how he felt. Which was something people rarely did.

"I guess I was scared," Tommy said. He lay back down on the bed and turned away from Gannon.

On television the killing was still happening. The bombs were still falling. The Disease was still claiming its share of the world.

Tommy heard Gannon reach into a pocket. He fumbled with something that sounded like paper.

"I was supposed to go off to the military myself, you know," Gannon began. "Pop was in the national guard when I was a kid. He'd done six years in the marines beforehand. So he wasn't just one of those weekend warriors like everyone else."

Tommy rolled over and found Gannon staring at the draft notice.

"Back then there was fighting but there

wasn't really a war," Gannon continued. "At least, not officially. There were plenty of people being killed. There were bombings and mass shootings and things like that, but it was all just starting. It was like a lightning storm with no place to call home. A flash over here. A boom somewhere else. They came and went and didn't hold any particular pattern. Like fireflies or something. And this disease or whatever didn't even exist. The world, as bad as it was, was something a person could get their head around . . . Or maybe it all just seems that way in memory."

Gannon's face seemed to dance in the light of the television. Still he looked at Tommy's letter.

"Each year it got a little worse. But we always thought it would get better. We always figured it would just get fixed, you know? Like there had been a switch thrown that had started all of this and so it made sense that it was just a matter of time before somebody threw the switch again and fixed it all. But then, month after month, nobody ever pulled that second switch. The whole country, the whole world, just slid further and further downhill."

"My dad used to say something like that," Tommy said.

"Smart man," Gannon replied. "As for me, I was going to sign up for the military. But then my dad got sick and my mom was already dead. Somebody had to take care of him. And by then, hell, I'd met the woman that was going to be my wife. She had nothing against the military, but she didn't want to be a military wife. She didn't want to do all of the moving around, all of the waiting for the phone call that one day comes. So I let go of thinking about the military and I watched the war on television just like everybody else. Figured that the politicians and boots on the ground over there would fix everything. But then nothing ever did get fixed and I was stuck in a small town being a cop in a place where nothing ever happened and I never really made a difference, all the while Rome burning down around me. I resented her for that."

Gannon's voice trembled and it surprised them both. He cleared his throat.

"She was the one that wanted kids," Gannon continued. "For me, I was on the fence about them. Didn't have any real dislike of kids, but neither did I feel any particular need to raise any. Kids, for me, were just something that existed. And having one of my own was something I could take or leave. But not her. She said she'd dreamed about being a mom ever since she was a kid herself. Said that as far back as she could remember, she had seen her life filled up with them. A house somewhere just flooding over with children. Five, six, seven of them. As many as a house could hold. And when I asked her why they were so important to her, why it was such a hot topic for her, all she could say was 'Because that's what life is supposed to be.' "

Gannon waved his hand dismissively. "Foolish thing if you ask me: for a person to grow up thinking that the world is supposed to be any one particular way."

"Why are you telling me this?" Tommy asked.

"Oh," Gannon said. He seemed to have genuinely forgotten his point. "What I'm trying to say is that a person can make a difference in the world. A person can change things, even though it might not seem like they can. But they have to be able to go into it with both eyes open. They have to know why they're doing something. And they have to do it for their own reasons and not for anybody else's. You can't live your life for anybody else and you can't make decisions if you don't have all of the information."

"Okay," Tommy said, still not understanding where Gannon was going.

"Do you want to join up?" Gannon asked. "I mean, do you really want to be in the military? Do you really want to go off to the war?"

"I got drafted," Tommy said.

"That's not what I asked you," Gannon replied.

"It doesn't matter what you asked me," Tommy said. "I. Got. Drafted."

"Damn it, boy. Just answer the question."

Tommy thought for a moment. He imagined the way things would be when he finally joined up. He saw himself marching in a sea of other young faces during basic training. He saw himself running, jumping, all of those things that people did when they first joined up and had to become a soldier. And then he saw himself in the war. In the desert. He saw himself carrying a rifle. Firing it, being fired at. Back and forth. Bullets whizzed past his head. He returned fire. And on and on it went until, like a movie, the firing became louder and the explosions hit closer to home, and finally he saw himself being shot. In his imagination, he fell into the dusty earth, moaning and screaming and a fellow soldier tried to save him. But of course, it was to no avail. The lights all went out. Blackness. He was dead.

When Tommy finally drifted back from

the throes of his imagination, Gannon was still there. Waiting for an answer and watching him all the while. The room was still too small and the bed still smelled of mothballs and cleaning supplies. The art hanging on the walls was still tacky and beautiful all at once. The war was still playing out on the television. The sky was still the color a sky was supposed to be.

But somehow, something had changed.

"If I hadn't got drafted," Tommy began, ". . . I don't know what I would have done."

"That sounds like an honest answer. Keep going."

Tommy's face twisted in surprise. "Why?" he asked. "Why are you asking me this stuff? The fact is that I did get drafted. So what point is any of this?"

Gannon held up Tommy's draft notice. "It's a fake," he said.

"What?"

"This draft notice. It's a fake, Tommy. She forged it."

The air was suddenly too thin for Tommy's lungs. "Bullshit."

"Not at all," Gannon began. "That sister of yours needed to get you moving. So she forged a draft notice. She lied to you, Tommy. Turns out Uncle Sam doesn't want you."

Tommy trembled.

"Now," Gannon said, "tell me where we can find her."

To My Children,

Nothing was getting better and there was nothing anyone could do about it. So people took up art as a means of getting by. It was a strange and wonderful time. "Art stems the tide" someone famous said, and for the next few years you could almost believe it. Celebrities took up pottery. Construction workers took up painting. People wrote poetry on the walls of bathroom stalls. I once went into a gas station bathroom and found Robert Frost scrawled into the place usually reserved for racism and misogyny. It was beautiful and unexpected — to go in there that way and find those soft words in a rough place. Everyone was trying to take away the fear, all of us together, holding hands as we felt the earth falling away beneath us, trying to flap our arms and create wings from the beautiful things. What else was there to do?

Your mother and I took up knitting. Something about the tying together of the strings. A cliché and trite metaphor, but not the kind of thing you worry about in times like those. You exist to survive. You survive to exist.

So we knitted and we sewed and we

made colors and, eventually, we put on an exhibit. You wouldn't think people would come out to that type of thing, but they did. They came out in droves. Lining the streets and filling out the thoroughfares, all for the sake of knitting that was terrible and badly done. Everything, even the small things, could be handled if all we did was create enough art.

But there wasn't enough art. Not really. Art only ever goes as far as we are willing to take it. And in spite of the fact that we were all loving and needing art, we weren't doing anything with it. It was only another way to hide within ourselves, to tell ourselves we were safe, that we had built the levees high enough and locked all the doors tight enough as we watch through the windows of our lives and see the storm swirling.

So the world continued on the path it had chosen.

Your mother and I kept knitting, kept tying strings together, kept making small things into long, elaborate, large things, and the process kept working. We were happy.

I spent more time learning about the Europa mission that was being planned.

It began to feel like another piece of art. Some interplanetary painting that was being thrown across the face of the sky, swelling up around us all like some voice in the early throes of an aria.

Debating on the existence of life beyond earth became the nation's favorite pastime. The fundamentalists said that there would not be any sense of unity or family to come from the search for life. We would all only come to realize that we are less than singular, that we can be mass produced. The discovery of life is the end of life, some people said.

"We've got a whole planet full of people who think they're alone in the universe, and all they can do is try to kill one another. So just imagine what they'll do if they find out they're not special. Just imagine the killing." That's what your mother said to me late one night.

I was groggy and uncertain from sleep. "People have always been the way they are," I said, not really sure what I meant by that.

"Can you imagine what it might be like?" she asked.

"What do you mean?"

"If they find something there," she

said. "Something alive."

"Don't bet on it. Life's a hard thing to create. It's a rarity, not a given."

"You can't know that," she said. "No one can. It's all too big. It's like standing in the middle of the desert and saying that the ocean doesn't exist. Just because all you see is sand doesn't mean waterfalls don't exist."

I took a deep breath and swallowed.

"I'm leaving you," she said without warning.

I trembled. Somehow I had known all along that it would happen.

ELEVEN

The name of the town was Broken Boot. It sat in the palm of Georgian foothills barren of trees but full of life. I came into the town in the cab of a pickup truck driven by a woman named Cassandra. She was a long, gangly woman full of sharp angles, like an egret crafted by Picasso. She spoke in riddles and hummed to herself. There was just a couple of days left before the launch. Not long now. But there was Tommy to think of. We both knew where we were supposed to meet, but I was worried that he would forget. Because that was what Tommy did best.

But more than that, I thought about what Gannon would have already told him by now.

I rode with Cassandra for two hours, taking in stories of the Gothic South. She was a researcher, focusing on the oral tradition. "The South is full of ghosts," she said at one point, staring into the rearview mirror as the small truck trundled along the narrow, two-lane road. Cassandra watched the rearview mirror as much as she watched the road ahead. What was chasing her was difficult for me to say. "The North's full of ghosts too," Cassandra continued. "The West. The Pacific Northwest. Whole country's haunted." Cassandra made a sucking sound with her teeth. "Whole country's full up with the dead," she said. "And getting worse every day. We can't let go of them and they can't let go of us. Nothing ever ends. Not even people."

"I suppose that's true," I said.

"Of course it is," Cassandra replied.

It went this way for hours. Cassandra made points about the existence of ghosts. I confirmed it. Cassandra reconfirmed it. Eventually I closed my eyes and tilted my head back against the smelly headrest of the smelly truck. It wasn't long before I was asleep.

Dreams and The Memory Gospel mingled together in my mind like always. In my dream, I was five years old and sitting on my father's lap, watching television. On the television the planet Jupiter came into view, roiling and golden, the Great Red Spot spinning like the angry eye of some ancient god. On the television the camera pushed closer to the planet and my father sat with held breath and a slight fidget in his knee.

"How big is Jupiter's red spot?" he asked.

"It changes. But usually it's about twice the size of earth," I answered.

"The exact numbers."

"Forty-thousand kilometers tall and fourteen-thousand kilometers wide," I said. "But it fluctuates."

"And where did you read that?"

"The book you gave me: *Our Solar System.*"

"What page?"

I sighed.

"Come on, honey," her father said. "Indulge me. Please."

"Page 83," I said.

Then he kissed the top of my head and chuckled to himself. "You're going to take the world by storm," he said. "Do you know that?"

Down the hall in the kitchen Tommy was crying.

"You're going to be more than anyone else can even imagine," he said. "More than I can imagine. Maybe even more than you can imagine."

Then he wrapped his arms around me and hugged me again before turning his attention back to the television, back to Jupiter, back to the world that was far away from his own. "You're going to do what I never could," he said. "Aren't you?"

"I guess so," I said.

"You will," he replied.

Down the hall Tommy was still crying. A long, lonely wail.

When I opened my eyes Tommy's wail had become the whine of a police siren. The lights flashed in the cab around Cassandra and me. My stomach tightened and dived into depths of me that I didn't know existed. Cassandra, just as she nearly always did, had her eyes glued to the rearview mirror. "Didn't think I was speeding," she said, slowing the truck.

"Don't stop," I said, looking back over my shoulder. It wasn't Gannon's car, I knew that much. And the figure of the man behind the wheel didn't match Gannon's silhouette, but I couldn't get caught. Not now. Not when I had made it this far. Not when I knew that I had to find a way to meet up with Tommy the way we had talked about.

"We all have to do what we have to do," Cassandra said. The right two tires of the truck crunched in the soft gravel along the roadside.

"Please!" I said.

Cassandra finally took her eyes away from the mirror and stared at me. I could see, even more than before, the ethereal, avian-like quality the woman possessed. She seemed more like a creature from a dream than reality, something to be discovered rather than met. Yet here she was.

But before the truck could rumble to a stop, the flashing lights behind us shifted position like the setting sun. The lights swept around the car and Cassandra and I both turned to watch the police car turn around and race down the road.

Cassandra continued to bring the truck to a stop. The truck sat idling for a moment, with Cassandra still looking at me. "If you're running," Cassandra said, "don't tell me. I'll take you down to Broken Boot like you wanted, but you can't tell me that you're dodging the draft. That's all I ask."

"I'm dodging the draft," I said.

"Why would you do that?" Cassandra asked. Her eyebrows rose up like clouds climbing the blue sky of her eyes.

"Because I think I've lied to enough people."

Cassandra clicked her tongue and sat with her foot on the brake and the truck rumbling beneath her. I could think of a dozen different things to say to her to convince her not to turn me in, but I said none of them. The words piled up in my throat like bricks at the bottom of an abandoned well. For once, I was going to do nothing but wait. Wait and decide. I opened my mouth, mostly by reflex, like a flower in the early hours of the morning calling out to the sun.

There were no words.

The world would now decide my fate.

Then, having made its decision, the world gave out a low growl and a belch of smoke and started moving past me as Cassandra steered the truck back onto the highway, heading for Broken Boot.

We rode the rest of the way in silence.

I made it to the Broken Boot fairground in the late afternoon. Cassandra wished me well and said a prayer of good luck for me. Then her truck trundled off into the overcast horizon. I waited there for hours, making my way through the quiet husk of the past. I tried to imagine my father here, walking in the places I walked. Perhaps he had come with my mother as well. I could see the two of them walking past the place where the cotton candy would have been sold. The old Teacup ride sat dark and abandoned now, but it didn't take much effort for me to close my eyes and see the lights sparkling like candy. To hear the music grinding out of the overhead speakers, tinny and sibilant, but still beautiful in the way that only such odd things are.

I walked through the overgrown grass imagining how things would be again when the summer came in proper and the townspeople returned to the fairgrounds and reclaimed everything. The grass would be mowed. The machines all uncovered and oiled. Bird's nests removed from the Pirate Ship ride.

Once everything was cleaned and washed and prepared, the power would be restored to the fairgrounds. The Ferris wheel — which, right now, sat tall and dark, like some ancient weapon — would begin to glow in the setting sun. The lights would burn and the gears would once again swing into action and the whole world would rise and fall and rise and fall, over and over again. There was nothing else in the world quite like the sight of a Ferris wheel lit up in the twilight. Nothing else made such a promise of nostalgia and happiness.

That was what my father must have felt when he came here all those years ago. That was the reason for his article. The reason he talked as much as he did about the past and about how the world could be changed by something as simple as cotton candy and people willing to walk away from the lives they were leading for a few hours. He wanted to believe that there was always going to be hope.

But he couldn't have known about the rise of The Disease. He couldn't have foreseen the war, not really. He couldn't have understood that his children would march off into a world he could barely recognize, both kids heading to the same place now but ultimately somehow heading in different directions.

And when I thought back on it, Tommy and I have only ever been stretching apart, pushing away from each other, held together by the orbit of our shared genetics.

It was when I came out of the haunted house that I saw my brother. He was walking along through the narrow lanes of the fairground, looking at everything with a sense of wonder. He stared up at the Ferris wheel the same way I had.

I came out and walked over to him, each step a little slower than the last, like the heartbeat of a dying animal.

"This is it, huh?" Tommy asked.

"Yeah," I said.

"I wasn't sure it would still be here." He looked around at the rest of the fairground, his eyes flitting from one to the other. I've always wondered about the gap between what we see and what others see. I wondered what ghosts Tommy saw. Did the parents in his mind look like the ones I saw?

"They still use this place?" Tommy asked.

"Yeah," I replied. "The woman in town told me that it's a big deal here. World famous, in fact. All because of Dad's article. He's kind of a big deal here too."

Tommy's face was tight with thought. Then he turned to me. "How are you?" he asked.

"I'm okay," I said.

"Not long now until the launch," Tommy said. "You still think you're going to be able to make it in time?"

"I'm sure that I'll be able to find a way," I replied. "If we have to we can get on a bus. We'll just have to be careful when we buy the tickets. And maybe we'll have to use a fake name for you. That could actually be kind of fun. I've always thought you looked more like a Peter than a Tommy anyway." I laughed, but it was not genuine. I could tell that Tommy knew it.

"I guess you did it because I didn't want to come along," Tommy said. He looked down at his feet, as though they might tell him something that he did not already know. "Maybe you could have talked me into it, though. I mean, if you'd really tried. You're smart enough to talk anybody into almost anything. So why'd you have to do it this way?"

"I did talk to you, Tommy," I said. No matter how much I wanted to, I couldn't get away from the ball of guilt welling up inside of me.

"No you didn't," Tommy said. "You told me what to do. That's not the same as talking to somebody." Finally he took his eyes away from his feet.

"You just didn't understand how important this is," I replied. "That's always been your problem, Tommy. You don't understand how important anything is. That's the reason you can't remember anything. You choose not to. Because you don't want to believe anything is important."

"That's not true," Tommy said. "It's just that I'm not like you. I'm not special like you."

"Stop saying that."

"Stop saying what?"

"All of it. Stop saying that you're not like me. Stop saying that I'm special and you're not. I'm tired of hearing that. I've been hearing that all my life. I'm tired of being special. I'm tired of being alone. You're just as smart as I am but you don't want to show it. That's all it is. This is just an act that you put on so that you don't have to stand out, so that you don't feel like a freak the way I do. And I hate you for it. I've always hated you for it."

The words came out faster than I could recognize them. It was like watching rain fall. Each word linked to the other, and all of them linked, eventually, to a part of my heart that I hadn't known existed. Like suddenly opening a closet door in your home and finding a tunnel leading into darkness. You wonder if it had always been there. You wonder how it went unnoticed for so long. You wonder what that says about you.

"I'm not special," Tommy said. "That's the thing that you've never really understood about me. Sometimes I just feel like an animal. There's nothing in front of me, nothing behind me. I'm just here, in this moment. Sometimes it feels good, you know, to be able to cut away everything else around me and just exist in a certain place and time. And other times it's the scariest thing in the world because I never know where I've been and I never know where I'm going. And nothing ever really seems to matter. It's like floating in the middle of nothing." He sighed and looked at me. "But the one thing I always knew was that you were there with me, in my corner. And because you had The Memory Gospel, we could always find out the truth. I could always know the facts of what happened. I could ask you about a certain day and a certain time and you could tell me everything. You'd be able to say where I had come from. And maybe even where I was going. And I always loved you and trusted you because of that. You guided my life. The thing I used to navigate everything that I otherwise couldn't navigate. I trusted you. I trusted the fact that you were special to make up for the fact that I wasn't special. The fact that I was just something that everyone would forget about one day. And maybe that's the way it's supposed to be, you know? There are always people that matter and then there's everybody else."

"Stop saying that!" I shouted. "Stop saying you're not special. Stop saying you don't matter."

"So you're going to tell me that everybody matters? That can't be true."

"Not everybody. Just you."

Tommy flashed a smile, but it was gone so quickly it seemed like an illusion. "That can't be true either," he said.

"I didn't do it to hurt you," I said.

"You just don't know what it's like," Tommy replied. "To know that you're never going to matter in the world. To know that you're never going to be famous. That you're never going to have a great life. That you're never going to see the world. To know that all you can really expect is to get a job somewhere and, if you get really lucky, maybe you don't completely hate it. And then you spend the rest of your life doing that job and then one day you die. That's the future for me. And I'm not being pessimistic. I'm just being realistic. That's what life is like for most people. Most people live desperate lives in the darkness. And that's the kind of life I'm going to live and I know it. I'm only ever going to be one of the people in the background of the photograph when something great happens. I'll never be the person up front. I'll never be the person to do the great thing."

"Tommy . . ." I began. But he held up a hand to stop me.

"But when that draft letter came," Tommy continued, "I actually felt special. I know everybody is getting those letters and that I'm probably not really special just because I finally got one of my own, but that doesn't mean it didn't feel good. For once, I felt like I had really been chosen. I felt like somebody had said, 'Yeah, we want Tommy.' I thought I was gonna go off and be a soldier. Make all these friends in training and in the war. Be a part of something. And I'd always be able to share with them the fact that we had been chosen. And that would always bind us together. It would be special in its own way. We would make it special in its own way." He shook his head. "It really felt like something."

"I'm sorry, Tommy," I said.

"Do you know how stupid I felt when I found out it wasn't true?" Again there was the brief flash of a smile, but this time it was pained. "I argued with Gannon for almost an hour until, finally, I went and looked it up myself at the Draft Board's website. Put in my Social Security number and waited for the result to come back. And boom, turns out I wasn't there. Turns out I wasn't chosen, after all. Turns out I wasn't special, after all. And it was all your fault."

"I didn't mean to hurt you, Tommy. I just needed you to go with me."

"Why?"

"Because you're my brother. You're my family."

"You just needed a strong back to help

make sure you got there," Tommy said. "That's what I think. You needed someone to protect you and keep you safe. Watch out for you when you weren't watching out for yourself. And I guess I was a good choice." He forced a small chuckle, even as he wiped a tear from the corner of his eye. "I guess I'm special so long as I'm useful."

A moment of silence came and went between us. Tommy took a long look around the fairgrounds.

"This isn't what I expected," he said.

"I'm sure it's prettier when it's all lit up," I replied.

"Better be," Tommy said. "After everything Dad said about it . . . I wasn't even sure that you'd be here."

"Are you going to come with me?"

"I'm going back to Gannon," Tommy said. "This is your trip now."

"I need you, Tommy."

"I don't need you," he said. "Not anymore."

And then Gannon was there.

"Virginia," he said, stepping out from behind one of the nearby rides. He stood with his thumbs-in-his-belt look, the way policemen did on TV. "I believe you've got something for me." He took his right hand out of his belt and patted the empty gun holster.

"No," I said, flat and even as Euclidean geometry. I reached inside my coat pocket and, as always, Gannon's gun was there, heavy and constant, impervious to doubt and weakness. I was invulnerable as long as I had it. It steeled me in ways I didn't know were there, in ways The Memory Gospel couldn't. After all, memory was protection against the past. The gun was, in the end, protection against the future.

Gannon took a step toward me.

"Stop," I said, my hand tightening on the pistol.

"Ginny," Tommy said. I had forgotten he was there. When I looked at him now he seemed small and frightened, caught up in something he couldn't understand or control. Which was, of course, the story of Tommy's life.

"Don't worry, Tommy," Gannon said, taking another step forward. "She's not going to do anything. She's too smart for that. Aren't you, Ginny?"

"Only Tommy can call me that."

"Okay," Gannon said. He looked around for a moment, taking in the sight of the abandoned fairground. "I imagine it looked a bit better back in its prime."

"It was beautiful," I said.

"That so?" Gannon replied. "How do you know?"

"Our dad told us about it," Tommy interjected. He had a thin bead of sweat on his upper lip and his eyes were darting from me to Gannon and back to me.

"Why'd you bring him here?" I asked, finally looking at my brother, though my hand remained on the gun in my pocket, my finger rubbing back and forth against the trigger. It was soothing and terrifying all at once.

"Because this can't go on," Tommy said.

"Of course it can," I said. "Nothing ever ends. Somebody told me that recently."

"Okay," Gannon said, exhaling like a bull, "that's enough of this." He started walking forward.

"Stop," I said, almost in a whisper. My voice trembled and my hand shook, so I pulled my hand from my coat pocket, finally showing Gannon the gun.

It didn't stop him.

He took another step toward me, certainty in his eyes, the war in his eyes, swirling about him. Suddenly he was everything in my life that had gone wrong. My dead parents, the foster parents, The Memory Gospel, all of the days of my life that I would never forget, all of the moments that couldn't be put away, all of the times that things hadn't worked out, all of the times that life had been sad and broken and full of pain and someone said, "Time heals all wounds."

Time can't heal my wounds because, thanks to The Memory Gospel, time didn't exist. The wounds were still open and they always would be. And just now, Gannon was all of that. He was proof that the past couldn't be put away, that it would always come for me. The only difference was that, with a small twitch of my finger, I could send him away forever.

My finger tightened on the trigger.

Gannon came closer.

I held my breath, anticipating the sound of the gunshot . . .

And then Tommy leaped forward, his fist swinging in a hard, wrathful arc that struck Gannon square across the jaw and knocked him to the ground. In my pocket, my finger twitched in surprise and the gun fired and blew a hole in my pocket.

Gannon and Tommy both thumped to the ground and scrambled back, staring at me, wide-eyed and motionless.

My breath caught in my lungs.

"I . . . I'm leaving," I managed. "Just let

me go," I said. "The both of you . . . Please."

I backed away, slowly, carefully, the barrel of the gun poking out of my pocket like the snout of some strange, hard animal. Then I turned and raced away and was soon swallowed up by the surrounding forest, hoping that it would take me away from Gannon, from Tommy, from everything.

ELSEWHERE

The house was empty now and that kept her up some nights. As with all empty houses, it's not the space that bothers us so much as it is the sound of our inability to fill that space. If we were bigger, somehow, more than we are, then we could fill those ringing empty spaces and there would be nothing to keep us awake at night.

But she couldn't fill the spaces no matter how much she tried. And she did try.

In the beginning, back when the hard decision she'd had to make still stung the inside of her heart, she invited friends over for long, free-spirited stays. It was an easy way to fill the space because everyone was scared back then and fear is always lessened by the sounds of laughter. So she and her friends stayed together for weeks, spending their days at work and coming home and cooking dinner and laughing and living the way they did back in college. Some of them she hadn't seen since graduation even though they all lived in the same town, but now that the world was falling apart they had reconnected and, before long, they were all having a wonderful time and were able to ignore the television, the newspapers, the internet, the chatter about the war and The Disease and Embers and the time when only children would be left and the time after that when not even children would be left.

She and her friends were able to push all of it away for a glorious, intransient time.

But one by one, they all found reasons to leave. For most of them it was family. For others it was work — even though she tried to convince them that there would soon be no point in going back to the way things were. Before long, she was alone in the empty house.

After a week of it the space was getting the better of her again. She had trouble sleeping. She took to making love with men from her past who came over and then left. None of them thought much of it. They weren't the only ones in the world making love to beat back the fear. Whether they stayed for days or left before the night was through did not matter. All that mattered was that for a short time she was able to breathe again. She was able to fill her lungs with air and drift away and that was good enough for her.

But the lovemaking didn't last either and she found herself wandering the empty house, afraid and regretful and sometimes crying. Trying to convince herself that she had done the right thing.

Some days she was able to believe the voice inside her head. And other days she covered their photographs or simply turned them down so that her parents couldn't look on her. But the bigger problem was the house itself. Her parents had built it together and there was no way to forget that. The only option would be to move away and she didn't have the means. Fact of the matter was that the fear of The Disease had become unbearable and when she looked at her parents she no longer saw the man and woman who had loved her and cared for her through the entirety of her life, but instead only saw potential carriers of a plague that could one day infect her and bring her thin life to a sudden end. It took all the money she had to get them taken away and set up in the home that would keep them there without many questions asked.

But living here alone like this was getting unbearable.

The empty hallways, the wall in the kitchen where they had, every year on her birthday, marked her growth like the rings of some tree. All of it was unavoidable and it told her, again and again, day after day, "You've betrayed your parents."

But what else could she do? It was a proven fact that her parents' generation were the primary carriers of The Disease. She couldn't take the chance of being around them until people understood better how The Disease worked and how to prevent it from progressing further and coming for her one day. Thankfully, she hadn't been the only one to feel that way. There were places that would take people of a certain age in, just as a means of quarantining them, whether they volunteered for it or not. In the same way that you could check a person into a psychiatric ward, so too could you check candidates of The Disease into rest homes where they were monitored until they fell asleep and did not wake or until someone found a cure for all of this.

The former was more likely than the latter.

And when the people came to pick her parents up — without their knowledge or consent — Angela's parents opened the door and saw the policemen wearing their gas masks and they knew what their daughter had done. Their reaction wasn't one of anger or surprise or fear, but simply one of love. Her mother turned to her and said, as gently as the time she had broken her mother's favorite vase — the one that had been in the family for generations and yet, next to her daughter, meant nothing — "It's okay, Angela. It's all okay."

Some nights, now that she was alone, she still heard those words, and they twisted her up into knots and she wept and called her mother's name but there was only the empty house and the sound of her own voice echoing back to her.

TWELVE

"Why'd you do that?" Gannon asked. The sun had only just risen and the world was still gold and amber and cold and blustery. Everything seemed drowsy and forlorn to Tommy.

"I don't know," my brother replied.

"You've got to know that it's not good for her to go out there on her own like this. I'm trying to help her."

"This isn't about trying to help her," Tommy said. He rubbed his knuckles. They were sore deep down inside. He wondered if something might be broken. "Are you okay?" he asked.

Gannon rubbed his jaw. "I'm fine," he replied. "You really do have a career as a fighter if you ever wanted. You swing well above your weight."

In spite of himself, Tommy grinned. And then the grin faded away. "I don't remember my dad," Tommy said.

"Well, it happened when you were pretty young."

"That's not why," Tommy said. He continued rubbing his knuckles. He folded his arms over his chest, suddenly cold. "I have trouble remembering things."

"I know," Gannon replied. "Retrograde something-or-other is what they called it the day I first got word about you and your sister from the social worker. Something related to amnesia." He offered a stiff laugh. "I feel like you should have been treated differently in school. Like you should have been in special classes or something."

Tommy flinched.

"Not those kind of special classes," Gannon replied. "I'm not saying you're stupid or anything. You seem just fine at figuring stuff out. I mean if a person can't remember people or things after a certain point, I can't imagine how that can pass for normal. Can't understand how you'd let that person go on mingling with everyone else like it was just the way things were." Gannon pulled up more tufts of grass and tossed them. "You're something special," he said.

"I don't think I've ever been called special before," Tommy said. He looked over at the man. Gannon seemed smaller than he had only a moment ago. Tommy could see the place on Gannon's jaw where his fist had landed and he felt a sudden twinge of remorse. He took a deep breath. "I don't think that what I have is the way everyone says it is."

"What do you mean?"

"I mean it's not that I just forget everything. I'm not an animal." Tommy's jaw tightened. He took a deep breath to loosen it up again. "I mean that I can decide what I want to forget."

Gannon's head turned quizzically.

"It's like throwing rocks into a lake." He reached into the grass and found a small pebble. "Let's say that this is everything that happened tonight. Even this conversation we're having right now." He rolled the pebble around in his hand. "I can feel the weight of it, feel the hardness. The little prickly points that if I squeeze my hand real tight will turn around and stick into my skin." He held the rock between two fingers like a grape. "But if I want to," he said, "I can toss it so far away I'll never find it again. Sometimes it'll leave imprints in my hand. Sometimes I'll feel like I know it's been there, but I'll never really remember it. Not really. I won't remember the shape or color of it. I won't even remember the way it stuck into my hand when I squeezed on it too tightly." He made a fist around the rock and squeezed his hand. "I can just let it go if I want to." He took the rock and tossed it away. It sailed through the air and disappeared into the glare of the morning sun.

"Always been like that?" Gannon asked.

"Far back as I can remember," Tommy said. He smiled because he had meant it as a joke. But it didn't seem all that funny.

Gannon's body seemed to tighten. He exhaled. "I wish you could have seen Pop back before . . . well, before," he said. "He was the sheriff. I told that sister of yours all about it once. Long time ago. But I know that she remembers everything so I'm sure she's still carrying it around with her. I told her different things about him. Once I told her Pop was a hard son-of-a-bitch. Not mean, exactly, but hard. Like sleeping on the floor every day of your life and then, once you got older, you suddenly discover the softness of a bed." He cleared his throat. "And maybe he was. But he was other things too. He was nice. He laughed. But it wasn't until he couldn't do any of it that I realized. I wasn't glad about it, you understand. I was just . . . well, I just felt differently about him after he was gone. And I'm never really sure how I should feel about the fact that I felt differently."

"Ashamed or guilty?" Tommy asked.

"I'm never really sure there's a difference between the two," Gannon replied.

Finally he was done sawing at the grass. He stood and brushed off his pants and rubbed his jaw one final time. "Come on," he said. "Just because you're not going to tell me where she might go along the way doesn't mean this train ride is over. I'm still responsible for the both of you. You're still mine. So we're going to go all the way. We're going to finish all this out."

He started walking forward toward the car. Around him the fairground was awakening with the dawn. The sunlight glimmered over the abandoned Ferris wheel. Here and there rabbits made their way out from homes built into the antiquated and rusty machinery. The wind came up out of the south and warmed the air a little and rustled the banners promising, in bold font, A Show Like You've Never Seen Before!

After a few steps, Gannon stopped and looked back at Tommy. "For the record," he said, "next time you decide you want to hit me, it won't go unanswered. And don't you forget I said that." He started walking again and his head dropped a little, as if he was ashamed of the words, as if they weren't his own but someone else's. His father's, perhaps.

"Okay," Tommy said.

For the first time since he'd known the man he felt sorry for Gannon. He wondered who Gannon would be if he was able to forget his life, forget whatever he heard inside his head when he spoke in that voice that didn't seem to be his own, that voice that was full of someone else's timbre and anger. If he could forget it all, what kind of man would he be?

Tommy stood and brushed off his jeans. He took one final, long look around the fairgrounds and tried to remember some of the things his father had written about the place. He could almost see the words and letters inside his head, could almost hear my voice as I read them to him, over and over again, through the years of foster homes and foster parents and siblings and social workers and new schools and old bullies and everything else.

Almost.

But in the end, no one was there. The fact that our father had even written about this place at all was something that, just now, he wondered about. Why had he written about it? What exactly had he said? It was all a soft gray shadow in Tommy's mind, like so many other things.

What he needed was for me to come back to him, to tell him why this place was important and holy and sacred, why this specific spot on earth had meant something to our parents.

If I had been there and told him why, he would have believed me. Because, after all, I remembered everything. I filled in the craggy patchwork of his mind, his world. And now that I wasn't there, he could feel the tendrils of doubt creeping into his mind.

Maybe this place isn't so important, after all, he thought. *Maybe nothing significant ever actually happened here.*

The truth was he knew that this place, that everything in his life, could only ever have meaning if he decided it did, if he hung on to the memory. Action without meaning is simply a thing that happened. It can never become sacred. It can never drive behavior. It can never make a person decide to do something to someone else or to themselves.

The letting go of things was Tommy's greatest strength and he feared it so much that a chill ran down his spine and made his body tremble.

He could let me go too if he wanted. He knew that now.

■ ■ ■ ■

When they were back at the car, before getting in and starting out, Gannon went to the trunk and opened it. After a few moments of digging around he came up with a small metal lockbox. He fumbled with his ring of keys and, eventually, opened the box. He removed a fist-sized metal object and stuck it into his pocket.

"What's that?" Tommy asked.

"She shouldn't have kept my gun," Gannon said. "The two of you had to know I'd have a backup. Didn't you?"

A chill ran down Tommy's spine. His face went flush and his fists tightened.

"I'd never hurt her," Gannon said, anticipating the boy's rage. "But when we catch up to her again, it can't go down the same way. It just can't, Tommy."

Then he closed the trunk and got in the car and started it. For a moment the engine idled and Tommy stood looking at the car, deciding what he could do. His mind ran from idea to idea to idea, but in the end he only got in and shut the door and wished that he was the type of person who could think their way out of such things.

They stopped off for food at the end of the day. They were somewhere in southern Georgia. Not far left to go. They could have kept driving straight through, but there was still a whole day and a half before the launch and there was no sense in racing ahead. The only time they actually had to be there was when Virginia would be there: at the time of the launch.

That's what Gannon had said, at least.

Tommy caught sight of the boys as soon as they pulled off the road and into the restaurant's parking lot. They were getting out of a truck, all wearing their uniforms. Five of them. They were a mixed bag. Not a single one of them any older or larger than he was. Two blond-haired boys whose perfect features made them seem to reek of wealth. A black boy with a wide nose. A Hispanic boy with the darkest hair Tommy had ever seen, even though it was cut short. And last, one final boy Tommy couldn't figure out. Whether he was black or white or something else, Tommy couldn't say. He had a scar in the back of his head that he probably usually hid under a full head of hair, but now that he'd gotten his military buzz cut the old scarred skin shone in the daylight like a landing strip.

They piled out of an old Jeep that was on its last legs, like so much of the rest of the world. But they were five vibrant young soldiers leaping out of that dying world, hungry and shaking with life.

Tommy watched them with the fascination of stumbling across a dragon.

"Tommy!" Gannon shouted. Maybe he had been calling for a while. Tommy couldn't quite say.

"Yeah?"

He nodded at the boys. "Go talk to them if you want. Maybe it'll do you some good."

Tommy didn't even bother to argue. Fact of the matter was that he did want to go and talk to them. He knew it the second he saw them. They were like living and breathing mirrors. Seeing them was like seeing himself, split into five parts.

He stepped out of the car, heading toward the restaurant and the five parts of himself. Gannon came behind soon, carrying his father in his arms, like always.

The young soldiers were seated in a booth in the back, loud and boisterous. A pair of withered old men stood at the side of their table, laughing and shaking their hands. "It's a great war," one of the old men said.

"You're a lucky boy. I wish to God I was younger, able to do more than stand around and complain about my arthritis." He laughed.

Then the other man added, "You should have seen the soldier I used to be." He reached into his back pocket and pulled out a large crackling wallet. He flipped it open and gazed at a photo. Tommy couldn't see it, but he could imagine what it looked like: the man standing in uniform, the American flag boldly flying behind him, a stern expression on his face but tinged with the undercurrent of a proud smile.

"I tell you," the man said, "I was something back then. And talk about the women! You boys ain't had women until you got into that uniform. They come falling out of the sky, each one prettier than the last."

More laughter.

"We're going to do something amazing," one of the perfect blond boys said. "We're going to go out there and change the world."

"That's exactly what the world needs right now," the first old man said. "Change. Things have been sliding too far for too long, and it's good to know that, finally, things are going to get back on track. I just wish I could do more than sit around at home. I wish I could be there." His hand suddenly became a fist and slammed against the table. The boy jolted a little.

"Well, we'll leave you boys to it," the second old man said, folding his wallet back up but keeping the picture out in his hand. He looked at it for a moment. Then they both nodded and walked away.

The new recruits, now that they were alone, looked at each other and laughed. Whether they were proud or mocking the old men was hard to say. Tommy walked over to the table.

"Army?" Tommy said.

"The uniforms with the army logo didn't give us away, did they?" the Hispanic boy said. The table laughed.

Tommy smiled, but only because it felt like the thing to do. "Are you on leave?"

"Two for two," the Hispanic boy said. His uniform said "Rodriguez." More laugher from the table, but softer this time.

"Come on," said the boy Tommy couldn't figure out. "You know that the sergeant said we're always representing the unit. And we're the best goddamn unit on the planet!"

"Hoo-ahh!" shouted all the boys in unison, loud as trumpets.

"Can I sit down?" Tommy asked.

"Go for it, Slick," the black boy said. He was looking at the menu and salivating, as if he hadn't eaten in years. The others seemed to notice his hunger and find their own at the same time. They all turned their attention to the menus as Tommy pulled up his chair and sat down.

"So, when do you ship out?" Tommy asked. "I'm guessing you guys just graduated."

"Two days," one of the blond boys said proudly. "Two days and then it's the beginning of the end, eh?" The others erupted with noises of agreement.

"What do you mean?" Tommy asked.

"What he means," the other blond boy said, "is now that we're getting into this war, shit's about to stop. The war ain't never seen the likes of us! The *world* ain't never seen the likes of us. I promise you," he continued, "six months from now there's going to be world peace, long and everlasting."

"You're so full of shit, Hammond," the black boy said, still staring at the menu as if he could smell the letters that described the food he would soon order.

"Yeah," Rodriguez said. "I've got a bet going that you piss your pants as soon as your boots hit the sand, you pussy!"

More laughter all around. Tommy only smiled to let them know that he was in good spirits, just as they were. "So you're not scared?" Tommy asked.

"Shit no," someone at the table said, but it came so quickly that they all seemed to say it at once, as if they had all said it without any of them moving their lips.

"I think I'd be scared," Tommy said.

"That's because you're a civilian," one of the blond boys said. "We're a different breed than you. We're the people who make the world safe. We're the people who make changes. We're the life takers and heart-breakers!"

"Hoo-ahh!" shouted the table.

"I still can't believe that would make you not afraid of going over there and getting killed, though."

Rodriguez turned and looked at Tommy. For the first time, the unremittent bliss of the young recruit seemed to crack. "What the hell are you trying to say, man? Are you saying we're not well trained?"

"Training keeps you alive," the black boy shouted, but it was in a hard, rehearsed voice, as if it had been told to him a thousand times and he had no other way to think of the words than with total and complete faith. There was a religion to his devotion.

"And we're all going to make it home," one of the blond boys said. Then he looked around the table, eyeing each of his fellow soldiers. They all nodded in turn, confirming and affirming not only what he had said, but what he believed.

"But you can't know that," Tommy said.

"What the fuck!" the mixed-looking boy at the end of the table shouted. Suddenly the whole restaurant fell silent. Everyone turned and looked. "What the fuck are you trying to do, asshole! Are you one of those pacifist fuckers? You trying to talk us out of defending our country? Of doing the right thing? Of protecting people?"

"Something the matter here, boys?" came a voice from behind Tommy. It was the old man who had shown the boys his picture. He stood just behind Tommy's right shoulder, looking down at him with a slight scowl on his face.

Tommy never got to see who hit him first. There was only the hard thud of the fist landing against his jaw.

He could have sworn there were twenty of them. Just a blur of hammering pain. There was a good blow to his head and a few to his stomach that made him curl up into a ball in the middle of the restaurant. Whether it was just the boys who were beating him or the old men or the entire world, he couldn't quite say. All he knew for certain was that it was all crumbling down around him. He struck out a couple of times, like trying to punch a hurricane, and with almost as much effectiveness.

Back when he was wrestling he had learned that the only thing a person could do when there was more pain than logic was drift away from it. Curl up inside themselves and go far, far away from everything. It was almost like forgetting, like giving up everything that had happened to them, like turning away from the world and disappearing, finally and thankfully.

It was the sound of thunder that brought him back.

But the thunder turned out only to be Gannon's voice. "Hit him again and I will open fire!"

The beating stopped. Tommy looked up through bloodied eyes and found Gannon standing in the doorway of the restaurant, holding his gun on what seemed like the whole room. The five boys were still huffing and panting from the exertion of beating Tommy. The two old men, thankfully, didn't seem to have taken part in anything.

"Step away from the boy," Gannon barked.

The five soldiers took their steps back.

"He started it," shouted one of the blond boys, his fists trembling at his sides. But he still wasn't able to take his eyes away from Gannon's gun.

"You okay, Tommy?" Gannon asked.

Tommy spit, finally uncurling from the ball. His spit came out as blood. "I didn't start it," was all he said. He rose to his feet on weak legs.

"Outside!" Gannon barked.

Tommy did as he was told and started toward the door.

"All of you," Gannon added. Tommy turned back and watched the confusion spread through the soldiers. All except the two handsome blonds had their hands in the air above their heads. Rodriguez looked as though he wanted to cry.

"Outside!" Gannon barked again.

In a long, slow train, Tommy led the five boys outside, followed by the two old men. Gannon carried his invalid father, still managing to keep the boys in the field of the gun barrel, and when they had reached the back of the diner he found a decrepit old chair to set his father in, as if the man could watch and enjoy the show.

Gannon ordered the boys lined up against the stone wall of the restaurant. They did as they were told. "You got a weapon on you?" Gannon asked them each. They all said no. Rodriguez had gone from almost crying to sobbing softly. The black boy hissed for him to stop.

After they were searched, Gannon barked for them all to turn around. Finally he holstered his gun. One of the blond boys started to speak but Gannon barked for him to shut up and the boy instantly fell silent.

"You okay?" Gannon asked Tommy in a whisper.

Tommy looked away as he spoke. He didn't want to look Gannon in the eye. He was ashamed of something, but he didn't know what it was or why.

"I'm fine," Tommy said. His voice was soft.

"What happened?" Gannon asked.

"They started it."

"We didn't start shit," the mixed boy yelled.

"Shut the fuck up!" came Gannon's reply.

Silence from the soldiers.

"Let me see," Gannon said.

Tommy lifted his chin. He could feel the blood trickle from his mouth. He spat on the ground and it came out red again. A car drove past the diner just as he spat and Tommy wondered what he must have looked like to the people in it. Gannon held up three fingers. "How many?" he asked.

"Five of those fuckers," Tommy replied.

Gannon chuckled. He grinned for a moment. Then the grin faded. "Okay," he said.

The soldiers looked at one another, each seeking the answer as to whether they should be afraid or confused.

"Now!" Gannon barked.

"Five of y'all and one of him," Gannon said, pacing in front of the boys, his hand on his holstered gun as a reminder of his authority. "My granddaddy used to call that a dogfall."

Tommy watched, now and then dabbing the back of his hand to his lip to staunch the bleeding.

"Take 'em off," Gannon said. The five boys looked at one another. "The uniform coat and tie," Gannon continued. "Take 'em off. They're just going to get in the way of things."

Reluctantly, the boys began taking off their jackets. The two old men — who had followed the action from the beginning — took the jackets and held them.

Rodriguez, who had finally stopped crying, suddenly began to sob again.

"So here's what's going to happen," Gannon said. "Five of y'all chose to jump on my boy here. The only type of people that do that type of thing are those who know they can't handle themselves one-on-

one. Cowards. So we're going to try this again. One-on-one. Tommy against all five of you."

Tommy's eyes went wide. As did the rest of the boys'. Except Rodriguez, who only closed his eyes and continued to sob.

"Now, look, mister," the black boy began.

"This isn't a debate," Gannon said. "It's just a fair fight. That's all."

"I don't want to do this," Tommy said.

"Yes you do," Gannon replied in a low whisper.

Tommy knew he was right.

The taller blond boy was the first one to step forward. He had a hard voice and blood on his knuckles from when he had busted Tommy's lip in the restaurant. Tommy thought for a moment that the boy might say something. Call him a name or something to get himself ready for the fight. But the boy never did. He only raised his fists and stepped forward, and after a moment, he and Tommy began circling each other.

Tommy couldn't decide what to feel. Sure, there was fear, but only because there were five of them, each one waiting one after the other. He had wrestled long enough that he was confident he'd be okay, but still, five people was a lot to handle.

But then again, there wouldn't be any break when the war finally came for him.

The blond boy started things off with a quick punch aimed at Tommy's eye. A nice light jab. Tommy backed away. The boy threw another punch and Tommy backed away again. The other soldiers started cheering for their friend, seeing that he was taking the initiative and Tommy seemed hesitant.

"Kick his ass!" shouted the other blond boy.

"Fuck him up!" added the mixed boy.

Rodriguez had stopped crying. Maybe his friends gave him courage. Maybe that's how things would be when Tommy eventually got in the army: he would do things for his friends, not because of the war, not because of ideology, but because of the person next to him, the person getting shot at, the person walking each day through landmine-filled terrain, the person who cried with him in the late hours of the night when the fear couldn't be quieted and all anyone wanted was to go home to the life they remembered.

It was the blond boy's jab finally finding a home in Tommy's eye that brought him back to the moment.

Tommy beat the first blond boy, but it took

a long time. And when it was over, Tommy's left eye was almost swollen shut. His knuckles were bleeding and his left ear was ringing from a sweeping hook the boy had thrown that had made Tommy see stars for a few seconds. But in the end, the blond boy lay on the ground, huffing and gasping for air with his hands held over his face saying, again and again in a soft voice, ". . . you win . . . you win . . ."

Tommy won all four other fights.

But it was never the boys Tommy was fighting. Nor was it Gannon or the draft or the war or our dead parents Tommy threw himself against that day. It was the sister who had betrayed him. It was the sister who had spent a lifetime being jealous of the fact that he was easier to understand for most people and that was why the families always wanted to adopt him. It was the sister who had spent a lifetime reminding him that even if he was the one people liked, he could never be as smart as me. If the war didn't get him first then his life would flow down one tributary of mundanity until it joined with all the other lives in this world that came and went without fanfare or exception, all those lives that were a type of grinding, day after day, grinding against the promise of TV and movies and magazines and books that all said that things should be full of magic and fantasy and that declared that, deep down inside, we were all entitled to stories worth telling. "Movie moments."

The stranger that leads to love. The scenic countryside where all a person's cares drift away because, after all, beauty and pain can never coexist in the movies and books that lull us to sleep some nights.

Tommy fought against a sister who had given him this demoralizing speech for years by reminding him just how smart she was and how she remembered everything and how, in the end, life would be better for her than it was for him.

Even though he never meant to, Tommy had believed all of it. And now, with those boys right there in front of him, he could see his own fate. He would go to the war just like them. No better. No worse. And when it was over the rest of his life — if he happened to get one — would be just like there. No better. No worse. He would always bear the sin of being normal. And I spent my lifetime making him hate himself for that.

So every time his fist landed into one of those boys, it was my face he saw on the other end of his knuckles.

■ ■ ■ ■

When it was all over the five soldiers sat on the ground together in varying stages of defeat. And when Gannon came over and patted Tommy on the shoulder and told him it was time to leave, all of the boys stood — even Rodriguez, who had stopped crying and, when the time came, had turned out to be the toughest fighter of them all — and walked over to Tommy and, one by one, shook his hand.

"I'm sorry," they said, each one in his own voice.

Tommy didn't reply. He only shook hands until there were no more. He was only there in body. His mind was far, far away. Everything hurt and everything felt fine. It was like floating and falling all at the same time. For a long time he stood with his eyes closed, trying to resist the urge to slump to the ground and pass out.

"Come on," he heard someone say as he lingered in the darkness.

When Tommy opened his eye he was in a bed in a small motel room. He could see only darkness through the nearby window. He heard the passing of trucks as their tires moaned over pavement of the world. There was no pain until the moment he tried to sit up. Then it ran through him like lightning. There wasn't a single part of him that didn't hurt. It was as if someone had hollowed him out and filled him up with rust and salt. The pain made him tremble.

So he closed his eyes and went back to sleep.

The next time he opened his eyes Gannon was squatting in front of him. "Here," he said, holding a bottle of Gatorade and two pills. They looked like ibuprofen.

Finally Tommy sat up. The fiery pain was still there. But it was a little bit more manageable. He could smell the sugar in the Gatorade and so could his body. His body wanted it, no matter how bad he felt.

When he lifted his head from the pillow it stuck to his mouth from dried blood that had seeped from his lip as he slept. It hurt as it pulled away from the wound and left a dark splotch on the pillowcase.

"Cleaning lady's going to think there's been a murder," Gannon said with a chuckle.

Tommy hurt too much to smile. But not too much to take the ibuprofen and chug down the Gatorade in one long, continuous gulp.

"I can imagine how it feels," Gannon said.

"Hurts," Tommy replied.

"That's what I imagined."

Gannon took a seat next to his stretched-out father on the other bed in the room. It was dark outside and there was the sound of traffic, but it was quiet. Tommy guessed it was very late at night.

"Hell of a show, wasn't it, Pop?" Gannon asked his father. Then, to Tommy: "I brought you something." He reached across the bed and retrieved a McDonald's bag.

Tommy's stomach immediately growled.

He couldn't eat the food fast enough nor could he eat enough of it. The whole moment was a blur of moving hand and endorphins rushing throughout him. And when it was over he was drowsy and drunk all of a sudden.

"Anything broken?" Gannon asked.

"Don't think so," Tommy said. He tried to ask his body if the answer was true, and when his body told him no he mostly believed it.

"You did good today," Gannon said.

"Why?"

"Why what?"

"Why did you make me do that?"

"Because you needed to," Gannon replied. He grabbed the remote and switched on the television. Then said, "And because you wanted to."

"I didn't want to fight them," Tommy said, defensive as a rattlesnake.

"It wasn't about fighting them," Gannon said.

"Then what was it about?"

"It was about knowing that you would be okay. That's all any of us are ever doing: trying to be okay."

Gannon flipped channels and didn't bother looking over at Tommy as he spoke.

"This doesn't make anything better," Tommy said.

"I never said I was trying to," Gannon replied.

"Just because you think you're being nice to me doesn't mean I'm just going to forget about everything that's happened."

"I know what you mean." Gannon rubbed the back of his head where Tommy had hit him. "Didn't I tell you that you had one hell of a punch, though?" Gannon smiled, still never taking his focus away from the television.

Knowing that it wouldn't be seen, Tommy flashed a grin.

"He's a hell of a fighter, huh, Pop?" It was a childish and goofy thing to say, but Gannon said it anyhow.

"Why do you keep talking to him like that?" Tommy asked. "He can't hear you."

"You don't know that," Gannon said.

"You don't know that I'm wrong," Tommy replied.

Gannon sighed, then thought for a moment. Finally he said to Tommy, "I guess it's different for you on account of how your parents died when you were so young. But family . . . family's all a person has. And with this Disease, people are learning that."

"Is that why you take care of him like you do?"

"Maybe," Gannon said. "But maybe I take care of him because I know the person he was when I was a boy. Yeah, he did some things wrong, but he did some things right too. And since I've been a parent to you and your sister I've done some things wrong and some things right too, so maybe now I know how the old man felt." He swallowed. "They shouldn't just be tossed out when they're of no use anymore, Tommy. Whether this is the end of everything or not, that's one thing this world got wrong."

"What makes people like this?" Tommy asked.

"I don't know what you mean," Gannon replied.

"You know what you did to us," Tommy said.

Finally Gannon switched off the television. He dropped the remote and turned and faced the boy. But his face was not hard or cruel, only worried. Perhaps wounded. "That's just what your sister told you," Gannon replied. "Tell me something, Tommy . . ."

Tommy felt his body tightening. "Yeah?"

"What did I ever do to you?"

Tommy thought for a moment. But for the life of him, he couldn't remember. Tommy understood, then, just how much of what he felt about Gannon was because of things that I had told him over the years. Gannon wasn't just a foster parent, he was the latest in a long line of them. And I had picked each and every one of them apart because I needed Tommy to stay with me. So when we finally got to Gannon, the seeds of that failure were already sown. Tommy understood all of that once he had a chance to think without my influence. Tommy was, for maybe the first time in his life, truly free. That's what life without memory is: freedom. Pure and untarnished.

How could I ever compare to that?

To My Children,

After the two of you were born, there wasn't enough of anything anymore. Not enough good news. Not enough sunsets. Not enough stories told by strangers. Not enough wind in the late afternoon. Not enough meteor showers. Not enough conversations about theories none of us understood. Not enough insects hovering together in the evening sun like small galaxies.

Now that our house was full there wasn't enough of anything anymore.

I trained myself to keep an eye out for unequal doting. Maybe I'd give all of my attention to the son who would carry on the family name. The family legacy was never something I'd actually cared about until now. I thought about my father and my grandfather, the fact that they had literally lived and died in order for our specific genealogy to march forward, generation after generation, and that history, all those stories and sacrifices, were contained in our last name.

It mattered, all of a sudden.

And then there was the dream of Daddy's Little Girl. TV commercials were the best at stirring this sentiment: a man stands in the middle of his kitchen, four daughters racing around him, laughing, fluttering around him like humming-birds. In another scene they're painting his nails. In another scene the youngest daughter's voice comes in with the image of her father cooking dinner and says, simply, "My daddy is everything."

I wanted what the television told me I could have.

Meanwhile I was still writing my articles on the good things of the world. I wrote a two-part story on newly minted fatherhood. My readership emailed me with their support. They called it "the greatest journey." Clarence came into my office on the day it was published and said, "You realize you're done now, don't you?"

"I guess it all had to end eventually."

"Nothing will ever be the same," he said.

"That could be said of anything, really."

He wiped the top of his balding head and rested his hands on the paunch of his belly. "I'm trying to tell you something."

"Am I fired?"

"Hell no," he said.

"Then what are we talking about?"

"We're talking about the future," he replied. He was beginning to sweat. Beads rose up on the top of his head like fog on a window. "We're talking about life. We're talking about the things in life a person is supposed to talk about. If there's one thing I can't stand it's conversation about nothing."

"But so far, all we've talked about is nothing."

"That's not the point," he said.

It went this way for more than an hour. He fired volleys that hit nothing but air. I fired back, landing blows but never really being sure exactly what I was hitting or why. At the end of the day I went home and your mother was asleep on the floor of the living room, sprawled out like a murder victim. The two of you were on the couch, also asleep. I tiptoed into the kitchen and sat at the table and tried to replay the conversation with Clarence, trying to find something akin to meaning. But nothing came to mind.

I checked the news and there had been another bombing. Death had become the weather. Overcast skies and stabbing in Los Angeles. Rain and mass shooting in Denver. There was always a chance of clouds and gunfire, no matter where you lived. So when your day was done and you'd made it through, you came home and tried to see how everyone else had made out. Tornadoes and gunfire at a Kansas school. Which one had killed the kids would take weeks to sort out. If ever.

In our world that day there had been only light fog and a drizzle of rain and gray skies and a car crash.

I sat in the kitchen and listened to the breathing of three people in the other room. Your mother came in after a little while. She hadn't left the way she'd promised, but knowing that she wanted to was enough to create a trap door beneath both of our feet. We kept waiting, day after day, for the fall to come.

She looked haggard, as though she'd lost a great battle. She flashed a weak smile. "I forgot to read the horoscopes today," she said.

She forgot to read them more often as time went forward. Eventually she gave them up completely. Maybe she just felt overwhelmed by the reality of things around her. Or perhaps, she was just trying to think less and less about the prognostication of life. The past and present were tumultuous enough without adding on the pressure of trying to divine what might happen in the future.

She told me more often that she loved me.

I replied in kind.

Between confirming our love to one another we poured those words into you two. The books talked about all the different ways that people show their love. Words, actions, time, on and on. Love was a list of languages that we all spoke in our own way, and we felt it vital that the two of you, who were still too young to speak, be told in all possible languages that you were loved.

So every day the words "I love you" buzzed about our house. Every day actions of love filled up the corners and spilled out of our windows and we swam in love, trying to smother you two in it.

"I'm so tired," your mother said often.

"It'll be over soon," I replied.

"I'm just so tired," she repeated.

"I know."

We said this to each other almost every day, in secret. The two of us still tiptoeing over that trap door that threatened to end our marriage. Sometimes we switched the roles around.

It wasn't until Clarence died that we understood we couldn't give you the world of our choosing, only the best of what was left.

THIRTEEN

It was right where I had left it in my backpack. The letter from the Draft Board. I
couldn't say why I suddenly felt the urge to
stop and look at it, but I did. I was almost
to Florida now, on a back road in Georgia
lined with soybeans and old barns and
pictures of the way things used to be back
before the war. There weren't many places
like this left. Everyone lived in the cities, it
seemed. The countryside was a dying breed
in America. I thought back to that word
PEACE that I had seen painted in the
middle of a crossroads in the middle of
nowhere. I wished I had enough paint to
spread that word. To write PEACE in places
it didn't belong.

The letter was folded and creased and a
little soggy from where I had gotten caught
in the rain a few hours earlier. I had mostly
dried out but the backpack was still moist
in places, like a sweaty shirt that had been

folded and left in the hamper.

On the front of the letter was The Free Chicken, the presidential seal that verified the recipient had been selected by the president himself to go off to the war and get themselves killed. It gave a person's ending a sense of meaning and importance. At least, that's what I figured the letter was supposed to do.

I had a hard time deciding whether or not to tear the letter up or hang on to it until the end. The fact that I had carried it this far seemed to be an indication unto itself of what I was going to do. There was little point in ripping it up now and pretending that it wasn't real. All it would take was a single police officer to check my name in the database and everything would be laid bare.

I was three days overdue now. That would be the end of it if I was found out. Three days overdue is officially dodging and the courts — as well as the people a person met in the day-to-day of the world — weren't particularly kind to dodgers.

I stood and watched the letter in my hands for a moment, as if it might suddenly transform into something else — a bird perhaps — and flutter away.

But it never did.

■ ■ ■ ■

His name was John Dini and he was famous for saying, "It's easy to see God in life, but more difficult to see God in death. But He's there, just like He's always been."

John Dini had served three tours in the war and had come home without a scratch. Not even a bruised knuckle. And to make matters even more dramatic, it was soon discovered that he could write rather eloquently about what he had seen in the war. He'd written two memoirs and seventeen articles on the subject of the war and of survival, and I had read and relished all of them. So I took it as a sign of predestination that when I came into Jacksonville, Florida, I saw posters advertising that Dini himself would be holding a reading at the local bookstore.

For a while after our meeting I had been worried about encountering Tommy and Gannon again. But the world, small as it sometimes could be, was big enough for me to get lost in, if only for a little while. More than that, there was a part of me that wished that Tommy and I could go our separate ways. That we could leave one another alone and that he wouldn't be there in Titusville when I got there to see the launch. Maybe if my brother got away from me before the war, he could be happier. He could be better. Maybe the only reason he forgot everything and thought so little of himself was all the ways I had taught him to do that. Maybe Tommy was "less" because I had tried to convince him that I was "more." Even though, in the end, all I really wanted was to fit in the way he so easily could.

But these are the types of things a person realizes too late.

I knew that Gannon and Tommy would find me. But I knew it wouldn't be now.

The sky was black and rain fell in a stiff wall ahead of me when I arrived at the bookstore. A crowd was gathered out front, some of them protesting, others counter-protesting. A lone police officer stood by the door of the bookstore with his arms folded and his attention elsewhere, as if his job wasn't worth doing anymore.

The inside of the store was small and cluttered with books, as most bookstores tend to be. There were long, winding aisles just barely wide enough for two people to pass one another without bumping. The entire placed smelled of mildewed paper and parchment mites. At the far back of the rectangular building was a large chair on which the war writer sat. I made my way to the back of the store, squeezing past the other people who had come to hear his reading.

Most of the people who came to see him were around my age. There were a few older people, many of them war veterans who wore their uniforms out of respect for the war writer. But for the most part, it was the young who came to hear him speak because, more than anyone, the young were the ones being the most affected by the war. They were all within a year or two of being draft age. Why wouldn't they want to hear more about what might be waiting for them if their name came up in the lottery?

The area around John Dini was small and crowded. He was a small man with a leather, pockmarked face and a wiry gray beard that hung down from his face like moss. His clothes were too large for him, which made him look even smaller. He looked as though he was happily shrinking into oblivion and he wanted everyone to know it.

There was nowhere to sit when I finally made it past the crowd. The bookstore owner pointed at me and hissed for me to find a place to sit. It seemed that I was holding up the start of the reading — or perhaps had even interrupted its beginning. I looked around but there was no space. Dini cleared his throat and pointed at a small circle of carpet at his feet. It was the only unclaimed spot left, and I took it.

Dini began to talk about the final hours of a man named Phillip Horowitz and the end of his life: "In his final moments," Dini said, "Phillip became a poet philosopher. We could hear the gunfire and explosions coming closer, and I told Phillip that it would be better if we kept moving, but he was in no shape to move. He clutched at my hand — his blood slippery and warm in both our palms — and he looked up at me. 'Write this down,' he begged. 'Get all of this. I've figured it all out.' He choked on his blood for a moment, then continued: 'It's all a dream — every flicker of it. We dance and we dream and then the dream dance ends. I'm not immortal,' he said. He repeated it again and again: 'I'm not immortal. I'm not immortal.' It was as though Phillip had reached into his pocket and found the sun hiding there — among keys and lost change and lint and unused condoms. There was wonder in Phillip's voice. Wonder and awe and reverence. 'It all ends,' he said. And then, after a few pulses of resistance, for him, it all ended."

The reading concluded not long after that.

People struggled to find questions to ask and Dini struggled to find the desire to answer them. So, slowly, the crowd dispersed.

It was after the crowd was gone and the bookstore was locking the doors that Dini finally came walking out. He looked smaller than he had only a little while ago, as if being out in the real world had reduced him down into himself, inch by inch. He carried a leather satchel slung across his shoulder and he kept his eyes lowered as he walked to his car. Perhaps that was why he didn't notice me as I came walking up behind him.

"Excuse me?" I called.

He jolted, turning on his heel so fast he nearly lost his balance.

"I'm sorry," I said. "I didn't mean to scare you."

Dini looked me up and down. "It's okay," he said. Then, "So which is it going to be?"

"What do you mean?"

"You're either here to start an argument or ask me for advice." He shifted his shoulders beneath his overcoat and sighed. "So which is it?"

"I'm not really sure," I said truthfully. I didn't know exactly why I had waited around for him. I only knew that there was something I wanted to ask him. Exactly what that something was, I couldn't say.

"Well, suppose you buy me a cup of coffee until you figure it out," Dini replied. "I could use something to drink."

"Okay," I said.

The coffee shop was small and smelled like bread and cinnamon. A couple sat in the far corner, holding hands across the table and whispering to one another through thin smiles. They looked a little like my parents once did.

"Over here," Dini said, heading for a table in the window. "I like my coffee black."

I nodded and got his coffee. When I came back I found Dini staring out the window. It had begun raining again, coming down in long, heavy streams that flickered in the lamplight like moths as they fell. There was the din of applause as the rain hammered the street. Cars sizzled.

"Did you like the show?" Dini asked.

"The show?"

"The reading," he said, taking a sip of his coffee. "I've never really gotten the hang of it. You probably wouldn't know it to look at me, but it gives me panic attacks. Bona fide panic attacks." He patted the pocket of his overcoat hanging on the back of his chair. "They gimme pills to help with it. There's a pill for almost everything nowadays."

"How long have you been doing this?"

"Doing what?"

"This," I said. "Writing about the war."

Dini took a deep breath and sipped his coffee before speaking. "Years. I try not to keep count of it." His mouth tightened, then relaxed into an embarrassed smile. "Used to didn't think I'd actually live to see thirty, much less wake up one day having spent just that long talking about the same thing over and over again."

"I suppose it happens fast," I replied. "At least, that's what my father used to say."

" 'Fast' isn't exactly the word I'd use," Dini said. "More like it happens suddenly and all at once. You try to keep up, but then you can't. It just all kinda stacks atop itself, one piece at a time. One day you're coming out of high school and joining the army. Next thing you know you're almost sixty and you've been doing nothing but talking about a time in your life that happened so long ago that when you see pictures of yourself, somebody else has to convince you that it's actually you." Dini laughed then, a loud, deep bellow.

"It sounds like you don't really enjoy it," I said.

"I'm not really sure what that word means anymore," Dini replied. "I do it because it's what I do. It's who I am."

I looked out of the window and into the city. A woman jogged past, ignoring the rain and cold, going about her exercise as if it was high noon on a spring day.

"Does it ever get any easier?" I asked.

"Does what get easier?"

"Remembering."

Dini thought for a moment.

"I'm not really sure," he said. "Remembering things is never really a hundred percent. So I'm not really writing about the facts. I'm just writing about everything that I think happened to me. Sure, sometimes I get things right — but it's not a guarantee. And I've come to accept that."

"But what if you didn't ever forget anything?" I asked. "What if you'd actually known, going in, that you'd be able to recall every second of every day you spent in the war just the way it had happened . . . would you still have gone?"

Dini's face tightened in thought. "That implies that I ever had a choice in going in the first place."

"But you weren't drafted," I replied. "You didn't have to go."

"Yes, I did," Dini replied. "There were a lot of bad things happening back then. My only option was to join. I knew since I was a kid that I would one day enlist. I just didn't know what I'd be getting into. But I guess a person never really knows what they're signing up for, not even when they do something simple like meet a new person. You never know who you're meeting when you shake the hand of some stranger. So, for me, joining up was just like that: shaking the hand of a stranger."

"But you still didn't really answer my question," I said, quick as a flash. My hands tightened into fists. "If you knew that you would never forget what you saw there, would you still have gone?"

"Yeah," Dini said finally. "I suppose I would have."

"Why?"

"Because it was the way my life was meant to go," he said. "And maybe never forgetting is the way it is for all of us."

I sighed, frustrated. "That's stupid."

"Is it?" Dini replied. "We're made of the days and weeks and months and years that came before. We're all built from everything that's happened to us, everything we've said or done. It's all there, knocking around inside, making us act the way we act, making us do the things we do and say the things we say. You think I'd be sitting here with you right now if my life hadn't had an impact on me?"

"That's not what I'm talking about," I replied.

"I think it is," Dini said. He reached down and brought the coffee to his lips. "Let's say for a minute that you *can* truly remember everything, that every single second of your life is right there for the taking." He tapped his forehead. "Always has been and always will be. And every day — every second — the book of your life grows a little larger. So what? How does that change anything in this life? How does that exclude you from going to the war if it's where you're supposed to go?" He shrugged his shoulders. "Whether you remember none of it or remember all of it, it's your life. We're all afforded that."

I clucked a sharp, derisive laugh.

"So, when did you get drafted?" Dini asked.

"Was supposed to report in three days ago," I replied.

"It's not the end of the world." Dini folded his arms across his chest, looking chilly more than judgmental. "Are you going?"

"I don't know," I said. I wiped a tear from the corner of my eye. It's hard to say when I had started crying. The thing about a perfect memory is that it doesn't mean you see everything. There are always things you don't notice until you're wiping them away from your eyes. "I keep hoping that it'll all stop, that someone, somewhere, will throw a switch and everyone will decide that there are better things to do with their lives. I keep hoping that people will just start talking more and shooting less. If I wait long enough, maybe someone will fix us all." I looked down at the table. Where I had poured out the sugar packet I had etched the word PEACE into the sugar with my fingertip. "My dad used to say that things were different back then. Everything was better."

Dini was just about to reply when the bomb went off.

ELSEWHERE

For those who could afford it, there were other alternatives to wasting away from The Disease. There were places you could take your sick, slumbering loved one, places where they would be cared for in their unconscious existence with a degree of pampering and beauty that rivaled anything they had seen during their waking lives.

Her name was Amber Shaw and she worked at one such place.

For twelve hours a day she pampered those affected by The Disease. It was the quietest job she had ever had. She roamed the halls of the facility, checking in on the ever-sleeping-yet-still-alive patients. She turned on their favorite television shows or their favorite music so that they could hear the things they had most loved before they were afflicted. The facility where she worked did a wonderful job of producing pamphlets and brochures touting the theory that people in comas could still hear and feel and smell, that it filtered in somehow. It was all making a difference, the way rain three thousand miles away can dictate the weather for the rest of the world weeks later.

She wasn't very educated but she had heard someone who was call it The Butterfly Effect. She thought that was a beautiful name, and it made what she was doing feel beautiful, which was something she had never felt before.

Day after day she came and went through the halls. She created playlists of music — something she took great pride in — and she would run the music for a few hours and then come back in and ask her patients what they thought of it. They never answered, but she decided that they enjoyed it.

That was something that she had agreed upon a long time ago: even though the afflicted were perpetually sleeping, they were happy. Whatever dreams they were having — something else she had decided all on her own — they were good dreams, remembrances of their favorite moments: a kiss at the height of their youth, some small yet unfathomably important victory, the scent of the world in summer after the sky had broken open and everything is wet and lush and beautiful.

Her favorite patient was Mr. Smith. He was

in his midsixties and still handsome in that elusive Hollywood way.

She knew for sure that he would have liked her. They had the same taste in music and movies. When she set up his TV for the day, she sometimes would sit there for a few moments and watch along with him — even though he wasn't watching, only sleeping, constant and steady as a mountain. It felt good to be there with him. He liked absurdist comedies the most, like *Airplane!* and *The Naked Gun.*

And those same movies had always been her favorites as well.

If she'd been a few decades older or he a few decades younger, then maybe something could have happened between them. Something wonderful and glowing, something she had never been lucky enough to have on her own.

So she would sit there with him and smile at the jokes she already knew and laugh at the jokes she had forgotten. And then she would go out and take care of her other patients, but when she had the chance she would come back by and look in on him — in her heart, even though she didn't know it, a part of her was hoping to find him awake, sitting up in his bed, not necessarily waiting for her, but able to look at her with groggy, tired eyes and maybe say something nice to her like, "I dreamed about you."

She knew it was a silly and selfish thing to think, but maybe the end of the world was the best time to be silly and selfish.

As things outside the facility got worse — bombings, the economy on its last legs, the war, The Disease spreading further and further into the populace — she was falling in love with him, whether she wanted to or not. But in this world, as everything seemed to be fading, what was wrong with love?

FOURTEEN

One of the few things Tommy did remember clearly — that had not drifted out into the sprawled sea of his forgetful mind — was the time he and I spent in the group home. For just over a year we had lived there, suffering beneath the weight of loneliness and lack of family along with nearly eight others — the numbers fluctuated, children came and went, sometimes being adopted by families but, more often than not, they simply ran away. It happened most in the spring. Tommy wouldn't have thought that running away could have its season, like swimming, but it did. The long, hard winter always brought the bitter cold. So the children who wanted out were usually forced to endure until warmer weather. But their intention to leave was easy to see, even for someone like Tommy, who always struggled to know the minds of the people around him. Since he kept forgetting what people had done before, he had even more trouble predicting what they would do next.

But over the course of the winter he would see some of the others in the group home separating themselves from the rest. They suddenly became fascinated with maps, with cities and towns in faraway places. They would sometimes sit in the window and watch the traffic trundle past the old, rickety group home and they would stay there for hours, sometimes counting off the number of cars that passed. Other times, at the end of the day when dinnertime came, they would talk of license plates they'd seen. Always it was the plates from the faraway states that caught their imagination. Texas. Washington. Maine. Anywhere but here.

After the winter snows and long, dark nights, one morning springtime would come knocking at the front door and the house would wake to find an empty bed and that would be the last anyone saw of the child.

When he first heard the term "group home," Tommy thought it implied a sense of community. It made the notion of living with people you didn't know seem like something that could be tolerated, maybe even enjoyed. But if he could remember back to the beginning of his life, back to the crash and the time just after, he would find that foster homes, much like group homes, were about anything other than family.

Tommy came out of that crash with a pair of dead parents and a scar on his outer thigh that, over the years, would recede so much that people — including him — would hardly be able to notice it. Someone had to know it was there, had to know the exact coordinates upon his flesh, and even then, it could have been waved off as just some type of beauty mark. Sometimes even Tommy had a hard time remembering that it was there and where it had come from. Sometimes he could convince himself that he'd simply gotten scratched taking a tumble on a bicycle, or horseplaying with me, or fighting with some bully in some school somewhere. It could all be explained away as anything other than the remnants of his fallen parents.

Forgetting how the scar came to be made Tommy feel better about the fact that he didn't remember his parents' faces, the sound of their voices, the way it felt when they hugged him, or even if they had ever hugged him in the five short years he'd gotten to spend with them. A part of him knew that of course they had. But without the memory, without the ability to feel it in the pit of his stomach, to close his eyes and see them, it was just as easy to believe none of it had ever happened.

In fact, sometimes forgetting was a blessing. A person couldn't regret what they couldn't remember.

Tommy did not remember how, in the immediate days after the crash, the scar was just that: a scar. He did not remember how it was nearly an hour before the crash was found on account of the weather and the lack of traffic on that particular stretch of Colorado road. It was a young woman traveling alone who came upon the mangled metal barrier and the car that was beginning to disappear beneath the snowfall. After calling for help, she maneuvered down the slope and found the car on its roof and Tommy and me in the back.

Tommy also didn't remember how, not long after the crash, he and I had been put into a foster home but that I had been too much to handle and so Tommy, because he loved me and would not be without me, became too much to handle as well. Not long after that, we were both put into our first group home.

At the group home children sorted themselves out based on a general scale of size — height, weight, build — more so than age. The teenagers were kept at a different group home on account of a public safety law that came after a fifteen-year-old boy was found in a closet with a nine-year-old girl.

Tommy didn't remember any of the kids he met at that first group home. He couldn't remember the ones who sat up in the late hours of the night crying in lamentation of the lives they'd lost and would never have again. He didn't remember the way I couldn't sleep at night. He didn't remember the way I would never talk about our parents no matter how many times he asked me to. He didn't remember that he had asked me to because of the fact that he knew he was beginning to forget, that they were drifting away, shrouded over by the dark nothingness that eventually consumed everything in his mind. He didn't remember how frightened he was when he first realized that, given enough time, he would forget even me.

Tommy also didn't remember the time when he was six years old and late one long winter night that stretched out like an unending highway, he awoke to the sound of my voice.

"Tommy? Tommy, wake up!" I whispered.

His eyes rolled open. For a moment I was little more than a shadow. Then he blinked again and saw me. "What's wrong?" Tommy asked.

I replied by pressing my finger to my lips, indicating for him to be quiet.

"Come on," I said, taking him by the hand.

Tommy no longer remembered how I led him through the darkened corridors of the group home that night, tiptoeing over the creaky floorboards that always smelled of mildew and exhaustion, as if the entire house had seen its share of sorrow that it could not shirk.

Tommy no longer remembered how the two of us made our way up to the upstairs bathroom, which had a window that led onto the roof. Once there, I opened the window and crawled through and Tommy followed without question or hesitation. We settled next to one another on the shingles, both sitting with our knees tucked to our chests, our eyes watching the heavens.

"What are we doing up here?" Tommy asked.

"Just be patient," I replied, looking around. Then, after a moment, I stretched out on my back with my hands behind my head and stared up at the sky.

Tommy did the same, eventually. The shingles were warm, somehow. They felt like small, hot rocks beneath his back and he found himself drowsy all of a sudden. "I like this," he said.

"It's not bad," I replied.

I closed my eyes and I heard the small sounds coming from inside the group home. There were footfalls from children not yet ready for bed and the heavier thud of the house mother, Louise, thumping around on the bottom floor. She was a heavyset woman easily irritated but, in the end, not quite as bad as she sometimes seemed. She was always telling the children at the home about the importance of hygiene and staying clean. "Nobody wants a dirty child," she would say, as though the children in her hair were applying for jobs when the potential parents came to see them.

Tommy was almost asleep when I nudged him with my elbow. "Look," I said, pointing at the sky.

Tommy looked, but there was only the clouded sky and a handful of stars — city life affords so little of the heavens — and the moon. "Look at what?" Tommy asked.

"There!" I replied, pointing a finger at the moon.

Tommy looked, but noticed nothing different. The moon was round and the edge of it was dark the way it always was. "I don't get it," he said.

"Just keep looking," I said.

And then, after a few moments, I saw the shadow at the edge of the moon slowly making its way across the surface. As the seconds turned to minutes the moon reddened and seemed to turn to blood, and all the while, the black shadow walked across its surface.

"What's happening?" Tommy asked.

"An eclipse," I said, wonder in my voice. "Do you know how much has to align for an eclipse to happen? Do you have any idea how many exact steps there are?"

"No," Tommy said flatly. "But I know you do."

"I do," I replied slowly. I was quiet for a moment. Then, when the shadow had completely fallen over the moon and the night was at its darkest, I said, "Make a wish."

"A wish?"

"Yes," I said. "It's good luck. Even better luck than wishing on falling stars. If you make a wish during an eclipse then it's got to come true."

Tommy thought for a moment. "I wish Mom and Dad weren't dead," he said.

"Wish for something else," I replied.

"Why?"

"Because that can't happen."

"But why not? It's a wish, right?"

"Wishes don't work that way," I said. "Don't be a child."

Because Tommy didn't remember any of this, when Gannon asked him, "If you could wish for anything in the world, Tommy, what would it be?" Tommy's reply, as immediately as a lightning strike, was, "For my parents to not be dead."

The three of them — Tommy, Jim and Bill Gannon — sat in Gannon's car in the middle of an I-95 clogged with other motionless cars. As far as the eye could see on the road ahead there was only the angry red glow of taillights. Here and there people stood beside their cars, talking and looking off into the distance, all trying to discern why the traffic had been stopped in both directions on the highway. The answer would come later. For now, there was only the cruelty of waiting.

Gannon took a deep breath and spat into the grass next to the highway. "I hate this shit," he said.

He looked down the road, then back to Tommy, grimacing all the while. "What would it change?" he asked.

"What?" Tommy replied.

Gannon reached into his pocket and pulled out a cigarette. He lit it and leaned his back against the seat and looked around at the other cars stuck in Park on the interstate. "If your parents were here, if they weren't dead, what would it change?"

Tommy's brow furrowed. It was rare that he was given a question by someone that was so easy and simple, even he considered it to be foolish. "It would change everything," Tommy said derisively.

"You sure about that?" Gannon replied, the end of his cigarette burning like a captured star. "I mean, can you say to a certainty what things would be different? How exactly would your life be better?"

"This is stupid," Tommy said. He stuck his hands into his pockets and tucked his shoulders up around his ears as if a cold wind swept over him. There were words he wanted to say, but they flashed in and out of existence, dancing on the edges of comprehension like the notes of a song playing from another room.

"Just think about it for a minute," Gannon said. "Really think about it." He flicked the ash from his cigarette, then stared over at Tommy. "Reality has nothing on imagination," he said. "It's the easiest thing in the world to think about all the ways things would be better if they were different. We like to think we can fix everything that's broken. We can fill all the gaps in our lives. But we can never really know." He exhaled a cloud of smoke. "The most I know about your parents is that they were smart. That's what I heard about them when Jennifer and I first got told about the two of you. The social worker kept talking about your sister, saying how smart she was, so smart in fact that it made folks find out more about her parents. Kinda like she was a genius or something and everybody had a duty to find out where she'd come from. So once we heard about your daddy being a writer, Jennifer insisted we track down his stuff." Gannon shook his head. "I've never really had a head for that kind of stuff, but even I have to admit your old man had a way with words."

"That's what everyone says," Tommy replied. He tried to remember some of his father's words, anything from the letters he had written and that I still carried around inside of me, but nothing came to mind, as usual.

"You take after him," Gannon said.

"No I don't," Tommy replied. He wanted to say something else, ask some question, but for the life of him the question never escaped his lips.

"I guess I can see why it's easy to think

341

life would be better if he were here with you right now. If your parents hadn't died in that car crash. You think about all the birthdays you could have spent together, the hugs you never got, the Christmases you missed out on. I get that. But what if gravity didn't work the way it did?"

"What?" Tommy asked.

"Think about it. What if gravity didn't work the way it did? Then nothing would be like it is. Everything would be different. And it would be so dramatically different that we wouldn't even be able to imagine the way things are right now. Everything we know and love about the world would be gone and we'd be too ignorant to even understand what we'd lost."

"So you're saying I should be glad my parents are dead?" Tommy asked. For the first time, Tommy was genuinely angry at Gannon. Throughout everything — from the moment he knocked Gannon unconscious, to the moment Gannon came and got him out of jail, to the confrontation at the fairgrounds with me, even to the fight he set up with the enlisted boys — throughout it all Tommy had never been angry at Gannon. Not really. In every case, he'd only ever done what he felt he should. There was some internal compass guiding him, telling him to protect his sister even if it meant fighting Gannon, but there was never any hatred.

Tommy was, after all, an animal of sorts. The type to act because an action needed to be taken, not because there was poetry behind the action.

"I'm not saying you should be happy," Gannon said. "I'm just saying that you shouldn't define yourself by their deaths. Yeah, maybe some things in your life would be different if they were here, maybe even better, but that's not going to happen. This world is the only way it can ever be. Wishing it away will never get rid of the moon. My daddy used to say that."

Hours later, when the traffic finally began moving again and the long line of lights up ahead started forward and, eventually, Gannon and Tommy were able to continue on their journey, they would find out over the radio that a man had come out into the middle of the highway, doused himself in gasoline, and set himself alight, all in the hopes of stopping what couldn't be stopped, wishing the world could be some way other than it was.

"The world can only be one way," Gannon said.

To My Children,

The Terrifying Nine. That's what we called the months your mother was pregnant. We bought the books. We went to the classes. We watched the videos. We listened to the tales and divinations of old women who told us that hanging garlic above the bed would make sure you were both born right-handed and that your wisdom teeth came in uneventfully. It all seemed perfectly sane at the time.

I had a conversation with my mother that lasted for three weeks. The subject: how a baby's poop is a barometer for health. We talked about colic. Tried not to talk about SIDS. College savings plans, vaccinations, hard-soled training shoes, how to get the best deal on gently used OshKosh coveralls and their legendary resilience. Topics came and went and, all the while, your mother and I watched her belly swell and heard that drum of life beating beneath and we felt small and afraid — suddenly we were children ourselves — and all we wanted was for someone to come into our lives and tell us what to do.

Neither of us slept for those nine months. Yes, we closed our eyes in the late hours of the night, and sometimes we even slipped into unconsciousness, but to call it sleep is to call a flashlight a bonfire. I had recurring nightmares: a child somewhere in the bowels of an un-navigable house; standing before two small graves, uncertain of how I got there; kidnappings; forgetfulness; distraction; all the ways that a parent could fail and a child could be lost.

Nine months of it wrung us out. We felt small and fragile. Then she started labor and the fear went away. Nine hours of adrenaline later, we had the daughter and son fate had promised us all those months ago.

Virginia, you came into this world just after sunrise. Tommy, you came just before. I told your mother that because you'd both split the light and darkness, you'd never get along as siblings. I've never been one to subscribe to omen and superstition, but it sounded a little poetic and it made your mother smile.

She slept for hours. It was a little after ten in the morning when she awoke and the nurses brought the two of you in and she held you as the television on the far wall of the hospital room glowed and the news came in.

On your birth certificate, forever and ever, it will say that you were born on September 11, 2001. But it will never explain to you how things were before that day. It will never tell you how your parents cried as they watched the world change on the day their children were born. We wept for the dead and the living, because we knew nothing would ever be the same. The two of you would never know the world as we did. And there was nothing we could do about it. From the day you were born, we knew the extent of our powerlessness.

■ ■ ■ ■

CELESTIAL
ENCOUNTERS

■ ■ ■ ■

FIFTEEN

Everything hurt and the world was ringing. That's all I knew for certain. My legs were heavy and there was the feeling of something wet pouring down on my face. It felt like a massage in a strange way, as though I had finally done something right, something that I could be rewarded for finally in this life.

It took a long time for my eyes to wind open. And when they did I found them half covered in dirt and soot and something else. When I wiped away the dirt I was finally able to see that the wetness falling down upon my face was rain, still spilling from the now black sky. The streetlights were all blown out, dark and open as a grave. Best I could tell, the lights were out everywhere across the city. The pendulum had swung in the direction it was always destined to. The darkness of the universe had come back to claim what was eternally its own.

But at least the darkness had brought the

stars with it.

That was the one thing I'd always hated about cities: they swallowed up the stars. As I lay there in the rain, looking up through a small pocket in the clouds, I could see stars again. They shone in that soft, bright way. I counted them — something I hadn't done since I was a child — and with each one I counted I felt myself coming back. The ringing in my ears lessened and, at last, there was sound.

Someone was screaming.

I turned, trying to find where the sound was coming from, but I saw only the long, heavy pile of rubble in which I was half-buried. On my first attempt at sitting up I trembled from pain and almost screamed, but was able to catch it in my throat. Then I tried again and made it to my feet.

The coffee shop was destroyed. Everything gone, wiped away, as though a great, large hand had come along and simply scooped it up out of the earth. Such things were possible in the olden days, back when the gods were still a part of the world, when a person could burn incense or slit the neck of a bull and the gods would take notice. Would come down and provide.

But the gods didn't help out anymore, I knew that. Mankind was on its own.

An angry red glare — an emergency light bleeding out from the ruptured arteries of a nearby building — lit up not far away, casting everything in a macabre, dangerous hue. Elsewhere, alarms had come together to create a symphony.

Alarms and screaming were the soundtrack of modernity these days. And somewhere behind it, there was the sound of rain, roaring like the applause of a television audience that had seen what had happened and approved.

After a long moment, I finally took my first steps into the rubble. I looked around for Dini. He had been right there in front of me before the explosion. But it was hard to even tell where the corner of the coffee shop had been. I found parts of the table, parts of the wall behind the table, glass shards from the window we'd sat in front of, but no Dini.

I limped in a small circle — clutching a stitch of pain in my side — and found someone's head devoid of its body. I never found out who they were.

"Dini!" I called out. The reply that came back was the sound of someone screaming. It wasn't Dini, but it was someone who needed help. I turned toward the voice and found a man half-buried in debris, holding his stomach. There was blood pooling thickly beneath him. The man screamed once more and then fell silent and limp.

"Are you okay?" a voice asked. I turned to see the runner from before standing beside me, her face full of terror.

"He needs help," I said, pointing to the screaming man who was not screaming anymore.

"Are you okay?" the woman asked again.

"Help him!" I shouted, pointing at the man.

"Okay," the woman said, jolting a little.

"Please," I said. "I'm fine. Just help him."

"Okay," the runner repeated. "Stay here. You're bleeding."

I reached up and touched my own temple and when my hand came back down I found it slick with blood.

"See what I mean?" the woman asked.

I nodded. "I'll be fine. Please take care of him."

The runner finally turned to the man who was silent and motionless, still with his hand over his stomach and a puddle of inky blackness dripping into the dust beneath him.

I stood and watched as the woman went over to the man and called out to him over and over again. Then, maybe just because I couldn't bear to watch any longer, couldn't bear to find out whether or not the man was alive, I turned and resumed my search for Dini.

I limped over the dune-like rubble until, finally, I found him. He was in the middle of the street, lying on his stomach facedown with the rain drenching him and a couple of people kneeling beside him. I didn't have to walk over to know that Dini was dead.

The bodies of protestors lined the streets. Some dead, others injured, some alive and seemingly too overwhelmed to do anything other than sit and hold their knees to their chests and cry. I walked through them like a ghost.

I wanted to talk to them, tell them all that it was going to be okay. I wanted to reach out and hold hands with each of them and hug them and remind them that the whole world wasn't this way. But I knew better. It was like this everywhere. And maybe it had always been this way and always would be.

Who was I to tell any of these people that everything was going to be okay?

"It's going to be okay," I said anyway to someone as I passed. Then I said it again to someone else. "It's going to be okay." Then I said it again and again. Every time I came near someone I said it and I meant it. I gave them all permission to believe that the horror of today did not have to be the horror of tomorrow. I gave them permission to remember that things, even within their lifetimes, were not always this way. I gave them permission to remember that there had been days of their lives when the sun shone and the wind was sweet and the rain felt cool falling against their skin.

I gave them permission to believe that everything was going to be okay.

And then, though I wasn't sure exactly when it had happened, I had made my way past all of the injured and past all of the rubble and into the city itself. There were ambulances finally and firemen and police officers and simply people running from their homes and into the night trying to help. There were people running away from the ruins, chasing down the memories of some loved one who may have been in the area.

On and on it went, and I did my best to stay away from the police or, if I couldn't hide from their eyes, simply to appear as just another teenager making their way across the world. I reminded myself that just because I was dodging the draft it didn't mean that everyone who saw me knew it. I was the only one who had any reason to be suspicious of me.

"Do you need help?" someone asked me. I turned to find a tall, thin man dressed in his pajamas standing beside me. Without asking he gently placed his hands on my shoulders and eased me down to a sitting position on the sidewalk.

I didn't resist. I was tired and sleepy all of a sudden.

"I'll get help," the man said.

"No!" I snapped, and I grabbed his arm before he could run off. "I'm okay," I said. I reached up and dabbed the place on the side of my head that was bleeding and just now beginning to hurt. It was quickly evolving into a gentle, dull throb deep inside my skull.

The man took off his shirt and pressed it to the side of my head. "You need to see one of the paramedics," the man said.

"I'm okay," I said. "It's not as bad as it looks. I've been hurt worse wrestling with my brother."

"So you've got a brother?" the man asked. "What's his name?"

"Tommy," I answered after a moment.

"Good," the man said. "Tell me about Tommy."

"What? Why?"

The man pulled the shirt from my temple,

inspected the wound, then pressed the shirt to it again. "I'm just trying to keep you talking. I read somewhere once that when someone gets a knock on the head you're supposed to keep them talking. Ask them questions about themselves. Make sure they remember who they are and all that."

"I know who I am," I said. "I remember everything."

"That's good," the man said. Then he took a long look around. "But maybe, if you're lucky, you'll forget parts of this."

"I won't," I said. "I won't forget any of it."

It didn't take long for me to collapse against a wall and begin crying. I cried for a thousand reasons and I cried for no reason at all. I cried because I was still in pain. My head was bleeding and there were shards of glass in my right leg. I cried because Dini was dead. I cried for the couple that had been sitting in the corner, whispering to each other. I cried for the workers who had been stuck behind the counter that was no longer there. I cried for the people who came racing up, simply trying to help. I cried because my father had told me that everything was better back then and yet here I was, stuck in the here and now. I cried because nothing seemed as if it was ever going to be okay. I cried because I wanted to wrap my arms around Tommy and hug him and have me tell him that it was all going to be okay. I cried because I wanted to go off to the war and get myself killed because maybe that was the only way I was ever going to be able to forget everything that had happened to me, the only way I would ever be able to come to terms with the way the world was. I cried because I was afraid of dying. I cried because all I wanted to do was go away and be with Tommy and sit somewhere quiet and listen to birds sing and to the sound of running water and feel the sun on my face. I cried because of The Disease. I cried because if the war didn't get me The Disease would. One day I would fall asleep and linger and linger and linger, unable to move but still be alive, alive and yet not knowing I was alive. That was what terrified me about The Disease. It was the fact that, for a few days before your body finally shut down, a person was caught in the middle ground between living and dead. Their families couldn't let go of them but were too afraid to hold on to them. People became living memories.

I cried because the sun never shines at night. I cried because my father wasn't here to see the Europa mission. I cried because my mother had never believed it was going to happen. I cried because sometimes there's nothing else to do but cry. I cried because sometimes crying is the only way to fix something that's broken.

I cried because I couldn't fix it.

It was sometime later when I finally stopped in the middle of the street and opened my arms and let the rain wash down over me. It took away the blood and gunk and debris that had covered me. I had managed to find my backpack and carried it dangling from one arm and it didn't seem as heavy as it once had.

The sunrise was still far away — assuming the sun would ever shine again — and so was the pain that had been pulsing in my head. It still stung, like a needle stuck beneath the skin, but it was bearable. And the rain had helped wash away most of the blood so that now I only looked like a girl who had been traveling alone and caught in the rain rather than a girl who had almost been killed in an explosion.

When I closed my eyes, I remembered sitting across the table from Dini. The next instant, he was lying on his stomach dead in the street and there was no time in between.

He existed in both places at once, alive and dead at the same time. And I had a hard time deciding which it was. If time really was something that left a trail behind the way it did in movies and books, something that you could go back to, then he would always be alive and he would always be dead. That's what memory of dead people was: it was Schrödinger's cat, alive and dead at the same time, just waiting to be looked in upon by those who dared.

After I had walked a little more I came across a small store nestled in the corner of a large building. I walked inside on account of how the rain had gotten heavier and I was soggy and wanted to change my clothes and pretend that I would be able to forget what I had just seen and what had just happened.

The bell above the door rang as I entered. A lone night clerk stared at me from behind a counter. He looked past me as the door swung open. "What happened?," the man asked. "Did you hear that boom? I keep seeing cops go by here but there's nothing on the news."

"Bathroom?" I said, caring nothing about his curiosity.

"Do you know what happened?' he asked, this time standing from his seat. It was obvious that he wanted to run out the door, race off into the city to see for himself what had happened. But he didn't. Maybe simply because he couldn't afford to lose his job. Or maybe because he was afraid that whatever horror had come for the people at the epicenter of the turmoil would pull him in as well.

Whichever fear it was, the fear held him to his seat behind the counter.

"I just want the bathroom," I said, trying not to sound as frustrated as I was.

"Customers only," the man said.

I walked up to the counter and picked a pack of gum and placed it on the counter. The man rung it up and I paid for it and went to the bathroom without a word.

The bathroom was small and smelly, but warm. When I undressed I noticed the blood trickling from my stomach. There was a wound just beneath my rib cage, a cut of some sort. It only began to hurt after I noticed it.

I winced as I touched it. It was deep, whatever it was. I searched my memories, trying to remember how I had gotten it, but nothing came to mind. Obviously it had come with the explosion, but it was the first time in my life that something had happened to my body that I couldn't remember.

It was the first time The Memory Gospel had failed me.

The more I inspected the wound the worse it seemed to be. As I looked at it in the mirror it seemed to grow longer and deeper. The pain from it grew more and more present in my mind and I wondered how I hadn't noticed it to begin with. It was almost unbearable.

With trembling fingers I touched the wound. The pain from it made me yell out. I clenched my teeth and tried again.

The more I dug at the wound the more it bled. I was naked now, standing in the middle of the bathroom, staring into the mirror, watching my own blood trickle out of my body and run down my stomach and down my thigh and splat in drops upon the floor.

But I couldn't stop.

I continued sticking my fingers into the wound until I felt something smooth and thick. Something that felt like the corner of glass. I was crying now. Fear and anger and rage and more fear again. I reached into my backpack and searched for something to pull out the glass or whatever it was that was inside me, making me hurt and bleed.

I found nothing helpful. So I went back to using my fingers.

It was long, painful work. But in the end I pulled a three-inch-long shard of glass from my torso and it clattered to the sink. The blood flowed and I couldn't help but wonder how badly I had hurt myself.

"You were in there long enough," the cashier said when I finally came out of the bathroom. My stomach was still bleeding and it seemed to hurt worse now than it had before. I staunched the flow of blood with paper towels and made the decision that everything was going to be okay.

"What's the matter with you?" the man asked. "You look sick."

"I'm fine," I said. I walked over to the row of coolers and picked out two large bottles of water. Then I found the row with first aid and picked up ibuprofen and bandages.

"Seems like you might not be okay," the cashier said, looking at the haul.

"I'm fine," I said.

The man began ringing everything up. "Heard what happened?" he asked. "There was an explosion! People died!"

"Yeah," I said.

"That's all you got to say? It's terrible! Everything's terrible out there, I swear."

I nodded. Once again I saw Dini — both alive and dead — in my memory. The

362

Memory Gospel had cataloged him well.

"And then there's Florida," the man said. "Wonder if they'll still launch that thing. Ain't nothing safe these days."

"What do you mean?"

"The rocket," the man said. Then he nodded to the television.

I turned and saw on the television an image of Cape Canaveral and the rocket for Europa that was waiting to be launched. Beneath the image was the heading Explosive Device Found on Launch Pad. Mission in Doubt.

"No," I said.

"I know," the man replied. "Be a damn shame if they wind up never launching that thing after all these years, you know?"

He was wrong, as so many of us were. The launch would happen on time, if only because it had to. People needed to see that there was something wondrous that could still happen in this world. And no one needed that more than me.

ELSEWHERE

It was the longest they had been alone together in years and whether it was a blessing or a curse was left to others to be decided. Mostly they agreed that the best thing to do was simply tuck themselves away and wait for it all to end. But being tucked away in a home that spent decades holding a family between its old walls, and that was now bereft of the sound of laughter and the *thump-thump-thump* of childish footfalls, was a strange type of torture.

They were in their fifties and their children had been grown and out of the house for a decade now, but at least they used to come and visit. Nearly every weekend they came by and brought their grandchildren and the sound of laughter once again rose like a tide that filled the house and spilled out into the yard and seemed to bring the very trees to life, like a summer breeze pushing away the August humidity with a soft, cool palm.

But now everything was stagnant and quiet.

They were all that was left in the house, and soon they too would pass away — fall asleep like everyone else seemed to be doing.

She was taking it all worse than he was — which was not to say that he was immune to the sadness that crawled around the edges of their world. He missed their children as much as she did. Hadn't he been there for them just as much as she had? Hadn't he had as many sleepless nights and headaches and belly laughs as she had?

But maybe she really did feel it deeper than he did. She had always been more sensitive than he was. She cried at movies even when all a person was supposed to be doing was laughing. She seemed to find a sliver of sadness at almost anything, but he had never once called her a sad person. It was simply that she seemed to feel too much.

Of course she was grief-stricken now that they had told their children to stay away.

That moment was a particular type of hell, even after six long months.

It had all happened over the phone because he knew — and so did she — that they'd never be able to do it in person.

"It won't be forever," he lied. "It'll just be until they get this thing cured."

"But you and Mom shouldn't be there by

yourself," his oldest daughter Sheila said. All three of their children — Sheila, Matthew and Paul Jr. — were on the call together, all of them yelling and talking over one another, just like they had back when they were younger. Which, of course, made it all the worse.

"We're not invalids," he told the three of them. "We're barely sixty. We've still got a few decades left."

"What about the house?" Matthew asked, pragmatic as always. "You all got things secured? There have been break-ins."

"Not around here," he said, proud of his son for thinking of such a thing, because it had been on his mind too but he hadn't wanted to bring it up. "This neighborhood has always been too boring for anything bad to happen. You three know that." And then he chuckled because he knew that they couldn't see him smiling. Neither the smile nor the laugh was genuine, but there was no way for them to know that.

"Can we talk to Mom?" It was Matthew, the youngest and most delicate of the three. He had always been the one that took the most after his mother.

"Your mother's upstairs sleeping," he said — another lie. "I wanted to make this call by myself. But she's in agreement with everything I said. It's the best thing for everybody."

"I want to talk to Mom," Matthew said.

"Not right now," he replied. "I'll get her to give all of you a call soon. How about that?"

"Is she okay?"

"Of course she's okay," Paul Jr. butted in, just like he always did. He was the type of boy who had always kept his bedroom in order, and now he was the type of man who made his children organize their Lego blocks by color when they put them away at the end of the day. He was exacting, but he loved his children and so that made him a good father. "Dad wouldn't let anything happen to Mom. You know that."

The phone call went on this way for half an hour. It was a rubber band of everyone pushing the conversation away from their mother, and Matthew — God bless him — always bringing it back again. When Paul had been bounced around too much he said, simply and flatly, "Okay, I need to go now."

"I'm coming over," Matthew said.

"No you're not," he replied. "Paul Jr., it's your job to keep your brother away. They still don't know how this thing works and the last thing I need is for any of you to somehow get it. Do you hear me?"

"Yes, sir," Paul Jr. said.

And then Matthew protested again and promised to drive over, but he had been living with his brother for the last few years and Paul Jr. was confident that he could keep him home.

But their father wasn't so confident. After the phone call was over he went upstairs where his wife was sleeping — over twelve hours now. He tried one more time to wake her and she resisted him by continuing to sleep, continuing to lie there peacefully, as if there was nothing at all wrong with the whole of the world. It was how she had always slept, which Paul had always loved about his wife. As much as she stressed and fretted and worried, she could sleep anywhere — on planes, on boats, in cars, even standing up once or twice over the years. Paul had been tortured by an inability to sleep anywhere but in his own bed. And as a result, he hated traveling on account of how he was always tired and groggy and was always tortured by the sight of his wife sleeping just as pleasantly as she pleased, while he sat awake at 3:00 a.m. watching infomercials and regretting his decision to leave home.

And now he would leave home one more time.

He lifted his sleeping wife and put her into the car. He didn't know where he would take her, but only that it would be someplace where their children would not find them. The last thing he ever wanted was to be a burden to them. He was, after all, a pragmatic man. And he knew that it was better to have them wonder, because as long as they wondered they could have hope. They would think that he had simply left to keep them safe, which was true. And he could call and maybe make up stories about why she wasn't coming to the phone. That could work for a while. And if the day came when the truth was necessary, he would cross that bridge when he came to it.

But for now, he could postpone that. He could preserve his children's memory of their parents for just a little longer.

With his wife loaded into the car he went back inside and collected their packed bags. He was tired and beginning to feel sleepy, but that was okay because once he got in the car and on the road the air would wake him.

After everything was packed he closed up the house and locked it tight and went back to the car. She was still asleep, peaceful and happy. He rubbed his tired eyes and took a seat behind the wheel and leaned over and kissed his wife once more and, before he knew what was happening, he was fast asleep.

And that was how their children — led by Matthew — would find them, propped up against one another in the car, sleeping more deeply than he ever had before, perhaps dreaming of his wife right up until the end.

SIXTEEN

Gannon and his father and Tommy were somewhere in the Florida Panhandle when the news of the bombing came over the radio. Seven lives snuffed out in a puff of wind and rubble. Gannon reached over and turned up the radio, as if hearing the news at a higher volume could do something to make it less terrible. It filled the car with dread and fear, with a sense that everything was going wrong.

The broadcast concluded with an announcement that, because of the bombing, checkpoints were being set up throughout the state of Florida. The governor's voice came crackling over the radio, warm and confident, promising that law and order would be maintained and that people in need would be taken care off. He called for prayers and offered his own. Then he was gone and, as if he had put them there himself, blue and red headlights of police

371

cars flickered ahead on the highway.

"What's the world coming to?" Gannon asked. "I can't believe this, Pop," he called to his father.

A tall, young policeman standing in the center of the road motioned for Gannon to stop as they neared the checkpoint. "License and registration," he said when Gannon rolled up and lowered his window. The air outside the car smelled of oranges and humidity, even now in the dead of winter, as if the earth needed to hold on to the smells of spring to remind itself that things would soon get better.

The young policeman's nameplate read Branigan.

"Where you headed?" Branigan asked, looking down at Gannon's license. His eyes were puffy and his voice was wet, as though he had been crying. "You're pretty far from home," he said. Then he took a step back and looked at Gannon's car, probably wondering why it was so many states from its jurisdiction.

"Searching for my daughter," Gannon said.

"Jesus," Branigan hissed. "Amber Alert?"

"No," Gannon replied. "Just a . . . well, just a kid trying to show me that she's an adult. Know what I mean?"

Branigan leaned down and shone a flashlight into the car, into Tommy's eyes. "Who's this?" he asked.

"My son," Gannon said.

"He don't look much like you."

"Foster."

Branigan inhaled, seemed to mull this over for a moment. "That true?" he asked.

"Yeah," Tommy said. "He's my foster dad. We're going down to the launch. My sister's on her way there."

Branigan paused for a moment, still keeping his eyes on Tommy. Then he nodded and aimed the flashlight at Bill Gannon in the back seat. "And this one?"

"My father," Gannon said.

"He okay?" Branigan asked.

"He's fine."

Branigan squinted. Bill only sat there, oblivious to the world, trapped inside himself. "He don't look fine," Branigan said. "He looks like he might have that disease."

"He doesn't," Gannon said. "And even if he did, you know a cure for it? We're in the car. Ain't nobody else going to catch it."

Branigan didn't seem convinced.

"It's all on the downslope anyhow," Gannon said. "Just let us go."

After a moment, Branigan said, "I got lucky. My old man died before all this." His voice was heavy again, tired, like the wind at the end of a long day of blowing against a mountain it could not budge. "Move on along," Branigan said, waving the car through.

Gannon nodded and shifted the car into gear.

In addition to the bombing that had happened in Jacksonville, the radio told Tommy about a school in Michigan where a student had walked into a basketball game and started shooting. The early reports were that two students were dead and others were injured and the gunman was still on the loose after having raced out of the gym in the midst of the panic. It was unclear whether he had planned to kill only those two people or wanted to kill many more.

In London there was a knifing on a train. In Japan there had been a mass suicide. In Afghanistan troops on both sides of the conflict had been killed but there was less insistence on keeping count of that because people were supposed to be killed in war. In California a man walked into a bank and took five tellers hostage. He didn't ask for money, but for his wife and daughter to come and visit him. When the man's family was contacted his wife refused to come see him and so the man surrendered not long after and wept when they took him away. He was heard apologizing.

The last of Greenland's glaciers melted away. The news-people called it "The Death Knell for the Planet." On a small island in the Atlantic the seawaters rose up and finally, after millions of years of failing, swallowed it whole, never to offer it back in the lifetime of humanity. Near Hawaii a volcano was erupting. Millions of tons of ash was propelled in the air and people watched as soot rained down on homes and painted the paradise gray-black and, off the shore of the Big Island, a new island rose up out of the ocean, still steaming like a foal freshly birthed on an early winter's morning. The scientists said they didn't know how much longer the earth would continue to grow around Hawaii but, already, the real estate speculators were fighting over the rights to the fresh earth. "For once," the radio quipped, "the old expression about how they're not making any more land has been tossed out of the window."

A famous singer died. Natural causes. A famous writer died. Alcohol poisoning. Tuna were put on the endangered species list along with tigers and elephants, who had spent generations recovering their numbers only to finally stop circling the drain of extinction and flush down into it.

And The Disease . . . it was raging more than ever. At the latest report, a seventeen-year-old girl had fallen asleep and not woken up. The first Ember to fall victim to the disease. Who would carry on the war now? Who would carry on anything at all?

The end seemed very real now.

On and on and on the news went, stacking up the horrors of the day one upon the other, until finally Gannon switched the radio off.

"Damn this world," he growled, sniffling not unlike Branigan had done earlier. "Just damn it all."

It was hours later before Gannon finally spoke. The sun was cresting the earth and Tommy had fallen asleep in the long, quiet period of late night. "Do you believe any of it?" Gannon asked.

"What?" Tommy answered.

"This business about aliens."

Tommy sat up and stretched and tried to clear his head. He didn't remember any conversation about aliens, but that didn't mean one had never happened.

"This whole Europa thing," Gannon said. His eyes thinned out into small dashes as he squinted through the windshield. A mist was filling up the world beyond the car, thick as soup and gray and sad. Tommy felt the car slow a little. Gannon seemed uneasy by what might be hidden on the road ahead. "I don't understand the idea that there might be something or somebody out there other than us. If you ask me, it would be a huge mistake for God to make something more than this planet. So all these scientists think they're going to go out there and dig around on some planet and find something living." He clucked a hard laugh, but it was clipped by the braking of the car as a pair of taillights swam up out of the fog. Gannon pulled at the wheel and the car lunged around the vehicle ahead, narrowly missing it.

"Virginia thinks it's possible," Tommy said. He made a fist with his hand and rubbed his thumb against his fingers.

"That cop back there," Gannon said, "the one that talked to us. He's about to lose his job. If something don't change, there won't be anyone left to pay people like him, people like me. They'll work for a while after that, but it can't go on forever. None of this can. It'll all fall apart for him. He'll linger for a while, trying to decide if this is really how it all ends, trying to live in denial, even as everything falls apart. That's what people do: we live in denial. The water around us keeps getting hotter and hotter and we don't believe it's going to boil until it's too late."

"Can't he just get another job?" Tommy asked. "Cops are everywhere. Especially now."

"You're missing the point." Gannon shook his head and squinted even harder at the fog ahead. Even Tommy couldn't ignore the fog anymore. The thick gray soup seemed to be pressing in, as if it might shatter the glass and come flooding into the car, drowning them both. "What might be out there and what he's got in his hand are two different things," Gannon continued. "And right now he's got a wife and kid at home that he won't be able to feed at the end of the month. Right now he's losing his job. Right now he's losing the thing he loved and letting down the people he loved. Right now, at this second, there's no world out there. Who's got time to dream about other planets with all of that going on?"

"Maybe that's why we should dream about other planets," Tommy said solemnly. "Maybe just because you can't see what's ahead of you or behind you doesn't mean there's not something out there."

And then, because the universe has a long ear, a hunk of metal and fiberglass in the shape of a stopped car rose up out of the fog in front of them. Gannon stomped on the brakes. The car went into a slide and there was not enough time to stop. Forward, always forward. Like everything else in life.

Virginia,

You're going to be smart. Very smart. You get it from your mother. She was a prodigy all of her life who, somehow, settled on a man like me. A man who had never done anything worth talking about. I grew up in a small house in a small town. I went to a small school and graduated. I got a small job and had small relationships with various women. Until I met your mother.

We met at a coffee shop. She was reading some book whose title I can't remember and whose subject matter I, to this day, can't claim to understand. But she looked happy. She was happy. The sunlight poured in through a high window above me, creating a long, rectangular stalk of gold that showed the thin layer of dust particles dancing in the disturbed air as the air conditioner kicked on with a thump. And it's amazing how hard it is to find someone who looks happy in this life.

It's odd that I remember all of those details. As a general rule, memory and I have always lived different lives. I can hardly remember the first girl I kissed or the first time I went swimming. I couldn't tell you the name of any of my high school teachers and I'm no good at reciting what team won which Super Bowl with which quarterback. Memory is just a long, dark river for me.

But the day I met your mother, that memory breaks up out of the river like an island, glowing and trembling with life, always in sunlight, always in my mind. The date was October 21.

On our first date she told me the story of how her parents had made her a chess champion by the age of seven. There were magazine articles written about her, more than were written about most celebrities. But because of the nature of the sport — being that nobody much cared about it these days — she lived her life and went about her business and only talked about it on rare occasions, even though she wanted, more than anything, to talk about it.

On our first date we played each other.

We sat across from one another at her apartment. Her chess set was old and worn, the pieces chipped here and there, rubbed down by repetition. "I've had this my entire life," she said, taking the pieces out of their boxes.

To say that we actually played one another is a gross overstatement. I moved pieces around according to the few rules of the game that I knew and she talked about growing up and being able to remember everything that had ever happened to her over the course of her entire life. "It's like living in a cloud of time," she said. "Every second that ever was is there, and all I have to do is turn my attention to it."

Now and again she would remember that I was there and that we were supposed to be playing. She would move a piece, almost as an afterthought, and the move would confound me for the next ten minutes. I'd stare at the board, with my stomach doing backflips because I knew it was hopeless and the last thing a man wants to do is look hopeless in front of a beautiful woman.

While I sat there perplexed at the game, feeling the failure that was coming, she told me, "You don't have to win." A small smile lit across her face.

"Then what's the point in playing?" I asked. I placed my elbows on the edges of the board and tightened my brow and squinted harder, like staring into murky water in the hopes of finding gold.

"It's the act of sharing time that matters," she said. "That's really all any of this is about."

I was too busy just then to understand that she wasn't talking about the game. She wasn't even talking about the two of us. She was a nihilist. In her heart of hearts, she didn't believe there was any point in anything. To her, it was all just time and waiting for the end of time.

The end of time always comes.

The game went the only way it could. She won. I lost.

But that never mattered to her. For her, she was simply creating a moment that she could count. Like building a totem that you could carry around in your pocket to always be reminded of something. And when the game was over and I began putting the chess pieces back into their homes, she leaned across the table and kissed me.

It was a soft, subtle kiss that surprised me so much I said "I'm sorry" as soon as our lips parted.

"What are you sorry for?" she asked.

"I don't know," I said.

Looking back on it now, I was sorry for being who I was. Sorry for being myself. She liked me and I could tell — though I could never understand why. And I knew that I had already fallen in love with her. So from then on our lives would be tied together. And I would never be as smart as she was. I could never sit with her and wax philosophical about the economy or science. At most, when I got lucky, I could string a few words together to make them sound like something special.

But even that was fleeting.

And so, when I really think about it, I was apologizing to her in advance for all the times when I would be less than spectacular. Less than brilliant. Less than the wonder that she was.

Because I knew that she would always remember them, each and every second of my banal and mediocre existence. She would catalog it and carry it around with perfect clarity and there was nothing I could do to prevent it. She would re-member every way in which I was not perfect, even if I forgot.

"I'm sorry," I said to her again.

And now I'm saying to you, Virginia, I'm sorry. Because one day you'll be like her. Smart, full of remembrance, able to look back at these letters and see the smallness of the man who wrote them. You'll look at his words and see little more than the language of a child wearing an adult's clothes.

And maybe you'll laugh at me. Maybe you'll pity me.

Or maybe, like your mother, you'll love me.

If I had my choice, though, I'd hope you could simply forget me. Forget the imperfections, let me be something greater than I am. That's one thing that memory does. It softens the edges and polishes the dullness of those we love so that we can remember them how we want rather than how they are.

But you, Ginny, you'll be stuck with everything just the way it is. And that's a heavy weight. I see it on your mother's shoulders sometimes. It pushes her down into the earth, makes her footfalls heavier.

Forgetting is a way to freedom. A way that I'm afraid you will never have.

So the only thing that I can say is to look to your brother. He doesn't have what you have. I can see it. He's like me. He's normal. He's simply a person who will come and go in this world. He will live a small life, marry, die a small death, and that will be perfectly fine. That's the best any parent can really hope for.

Stick close to your brother. Don't

think he's dumb because he isn't like you. You're twins, after all. Let the one half carry the other when the time comes.

SEVENTEEN

I had been skirting the thin tree line that ran parallel to the highway for the last few miles when I saw the lights of police cars flashing. I took a moment to think about what I should do next. There were three vehicles and one ambulance flashing silently, clogging the highway into a long disappearing line of cars as still as dead ants.

There wasn't far to go now. Only a handful of miles to Titusville and the end of this all, but endings were always a difficult thing, I knew.

The headache I'd had since the bombing was still there, as reliable as the sunrise, throbbing between my ears. It was a concussion and I knew it. And the wound on my abdomen — that was tender and seemed to be widening, bit by bit — was some type of internal bleeding. I knew that too. And the blood wouldn't stop itself. It would only continue seeping out from the insides of my body to the other parts of the inside of my body, drop by drop, like an ocean filling up the inside of a planet. I would die if I didn't get to a hospital soon.

But after coming this far, what else could I do but march forward?

When I was close enough to the lights, I was able to see it, finally: framed by broken glass, a small blue car lay on its back like an insect. Wheels in the air, a broken thorax of transmission and exhaust parts offered up to the sky. A puddle of glossy black fluid painted the highway.

Tall, long policemen in winter coats stood with their hands in their pockets, staring off down the embankment along the roadside. One of them pulled out a cigarette, lit it — despite protest from another officer — and sucked on it so hard he drained away half the cigarette's life in a single breath. When he exhaled there were tears in his eyes. He wiped them, then flicked the cigarette onto the ground and crushed it beneath his boot.

Shortly, a tow truck came along and pulled the blue car from the center of the road. The policemen watched the work with the patience of cows, each of them chewing something over in their minds as the tow truck gears whirred and groaned and some-times seemed to sing — nothing happy, only their familiar, erratic dirge to broken things.

With the car moved away the police began waving a single lane of traffic through. One by one the lone line of travelers began to move. Horns blew in celebration. People yelled from the car windows poems of impatience: " 'Bout fucking time!" and "Some assholes shouldn't drive!" Still only one police officer beckoned the traffic past. The others stood solemn as headstones.

From the safety of the trees that shrouded me, I removed my backpack and shifted on a small, hilly spot that let me get a clear view of everything but, at the same time, kept me out of anyone's main line of sight. My attention drifted from watching the police officer wave the cars through the one open lane to a large white cloth that lay in the ditch down at the bottom of the embankment. How I hadn't noticed it up until now was difficult to say.

As if he knew I was there and had finally seen the important object that I was meant to see, one of the cops standing on the embankment stepped forward. He pulled his hands from his pockets and half walked, half slid down to where the white cloth lay in the muddy, brown ditch. He stood beside it with his fingers trembling at his sides, and when a small breeze came down out of the north, it fluttered the cloth and lifted one edge of it, and I caught a glimpse of the dead body — a girl, not much older than me — beneath it.

Then the wind stopped and the dancing cloth, like a magician who's accidentally killed the dove, concealed its horror with fluttering white hands.

I scrambled onto my feet and threw my backpack on. I raced away from the road and back through the tree line. I thought I heard someone calling after me, but I could not be sure and I did not stop to look back as I broke into a terrified sprint.

I ran until my stomach hurt and my lungs refused to play along anymore. Then I stumbled and fell and cut my hand on a rock and, huffing the heavy, morning air, I coughed and the cough drove phlegm into my mouth and when I spat it out it was pink with blood. I barked a laugh and lifted my shirt. The purple-red bruise on my stomach was larger.

I swallowed and tasted blood and lowered my shirt and continued on.

My running had taken me into an open field. Hay bales were scattered here and there across the field like errant punctuation. On the far side of the field an army of pine trees stood and, behind them, cars drove southbound. It was the interstate again.

"Hell of a run," a voice behind me said casually.

I turned so fast that I lost my balance and nearly fell. But there was a man's arm there to catch me. He was lying on the ground in a green sleeping bag with his head resting upon what looked like a dress suit rolled up like a large pastry.

"Easy," the man said, sitting up now that I had regained my balance and backed away. "It's not like I came running into the middle of your camp. I was just lying here finishing off the morning sleep when you came stomping through here."

"I'm sorry," I said. "I was just . . ." My voice trailed off.

"Doesn't matter to me what you were 'just,' " the man said. He closed his eyes and yawned. "You ain't my kid so I don't particularly care what you do. How old are you? Sixteen? Seventeen?"

"Seventeen," I answered. No one ever got my age right. He was the first. It was a flash of surprise in a long moment of pain. My stomach still throbbed and I felt tired and weak. And then, in the back of my mind, there was the dead girl on the highway.

"Yeah," the man said, still speaking with

his eyes closed. "When I was seventeen I had left Georgia and was living in an apartment in Cincinnati with three women of varying ages and disposition." He paused here to chuckle. "Good times," he said. "Simply outstanding moments."

I looked down at the man, trying to decide what my opinion of him was and what his ultimate intentions might be. Men alone were dangerous things. They made girls like me disappear.

"What are you doing out here?" I asked.

The man did not answer right away, so I asked again.

"No man, or woman, is an island," the man replied with his eyes still closed, "but sometimes in life there are moments when you want nothing more than to float alone for a little while." He cleared his throat and sat up in his sleeping bag. Then he stretched and moved the sleeping bag down to his waist. He wore a T-shirt that was surprisingly clean and unwrinkled for having been slept in. "I don't suppose I'm going to be able to get any more proper sleep this morning, am I?" He did not wait for me to answer. "Well enough, though. It was very nearly time for me to get up and make efforts into taming this day." He coughed again, clearing out the morning chill from his lungs.

"I didn't mean to wake you," I said.

"Waking was inevitable," the man said. "So you did nothing that life was not, very shortly, going to do of its own accord. So in many ways, you are the thing that brought me into this world today, dear child." He paused and considered what he said. Then, as he had done before, he chuckled to himself.

"My name's Virginia," I said.

"Beautiful state," the man said. "Simply beautiful. Lived there for almost a full year. Lived with an older woman who liked cats entirely too much. Had dozens of them. Yes, ma'am, I've had my fill of cats in this lifetime. I don't wish them any harm, mind you. But I've had my fill of cats." With a few awkward movements of his legs, he managed to work the sleeping bag down so that he could properly stand. He wore a pair of black dress pants and handsome black socks and, just as with the undershirt he wore, none of them were wrinkled or crumpled. It was totally impossible to tell that he had slept in a sleeping bag the night before. He went through another round of yawning and coughing.

"Someone died," I said.

"What? Where?" the man asked.

"On the highway. A car accident."

He made a *tsk, tsk, tsk* sound. "Terrible," he said finally, looking off in the direction of the highway. "Always rough to start a day with the knowledge that someone has died. It makes things develop awkwardly from there on out. I really wish you hadn't told me that."

I thought for a moment. "Who are you?"

"My name doesn't really matter," the man said cheerfully. "You and I are strangers. And that's really all we'll ever be. So what does it matter if I tell you my name or if you tell me your name? We'll both have forgotten before the sun is extinguished and the night comes climbing over everything." He squatted and began poking about in the bottom of his sleeping bag, eventually retrieving a pair of black dress shoes that shone so brightly they looked as though they had just been polished. "I suppose I'll see about breakfast now," the man said, putting on his shoes. After he had his shoes on he picked up the roll of clothing he had been using as a pillow and unfurled it, revealing a suit coat, dress shirt and tie. And, like everything else he was wearing, the clothes were completely unwrinkled when he put them on.

Suddenly he was standing there in a full

suit and tie in the middle of a field alongside a highway where a person had just died in a car accident, and he was so immaculately dressed that he might as well have fallen out of a men's fashion magazine.

I had no choice but be intrigued by the man. He was just strange enough to appear as an illusion, a figment of my imagination. And the idea that, perhaps, he wasn't real was enough to distract me from the blood seeping inside me. It was almost enough to distract from the death I had just seen.

Almost.

But I worked hard to let him distract me, regardless of whether or not he was real.

"What are you doing out here?" I asked.

"You've already asked me that," the man said.

"But you didn't tell me," I replied.

"I did," the man said, rolling up his sleeping bag neatly. "I told you that I was sleeping, but now I'm not sleeping. So asking me what I'm doing now will most certainly provide a very different response from when you asked me before." He considered this. "Okay," he said, "I supposed it's fair that you've asked me again. As my answer this time, I'll say that I'm preparing to find breakfast somewhere around here. Yesterday, as I chose this place to bivouac, I noticed some naturally growing berries and a farmhouse less than a half a mile in the distance. Both of these should provide some type of sustenance to get me through the first third of the day. Which is really all anyone can ask for at any particular moment."

"Do you know them?" I asked.

"Know who?"

"The people in the farmhouse."

"No," the man said. "But what does that have to do with anything?"

I was beginning to feel as though I was talking to a fortune cookie. Everything that he said was both direct and roundabout at the same time. I had read stories about genies and mythological creatures who spoke this way, only answering the wording of things rather than the spirit of them. It made my head hurt, but it fascinated me as well.

"How do you make your living?" I asked finally, feeling that I had finally created a question that would offer an answer I could feel satisfied with.

"I meet people," the man said. He had finished rolling up his sleeping bag. He retrieved a small satchel from the brush from a place I had not noticed and tucked the sleeping bag into it. "I meet people and

I talk with them and, invariably, they help me."

"You're a con man," I said.

"A confidence man?" the man repeated back to me, considering the sentence as he said it. His face twisted into one of sustained thoughtfulness, as if the idea needed proper scrutinizing. "I suppose it does take a certain degree of confidence to do what I do," he said. "But I've never considered myself a confidence man. I don't take anyone else's confidence. I simply meet people, talk with them, and they tend to help me. That's all. I'm a stranger in their lives, and I've learned to take pride in being a stranger, and some people find comfort in that." He seemed to like this answer. "There is nothing more comforting in this world than a person whom you do not know and whom you know will be gone soon," he said. "They can become anyone for you in the brief time they are with you. You can tell them anything. Share anything. Give them burdens you have not given to anyone else, knowing full well that, when they leave, they will take the weight of that burden with them, leaving you lighter, more carefree, than you were before." He paused and let the words buzz about in the air like fireflies. "It's a beautiful thing, sometimes, being a stranger."

I could not think of what to say, even though it had been said before by Connie back at the hospital as she prepared to deliver her and Nolan's baby. It was as if she were there, bleeding through my memories the way my parents sometimes did.

I tried to properly understand everything that I had just heard, but I wasn't sure that I was smart enough — or maybe wasn't old enough, though I liked that idea worse than the idea that I was not smart enough. One thing that had always bugged me was people telling me that I would find some greater understanding when I got older. There seemed a fallacy in that, as if getting older was something that was promised so maybe a person shouldn't work quite as hard at understanding a thing right now, at the age they currently were. And I had two dead parents, which proved to me that there was never a guarantee of getting any older.

"So," the man said, "you've asked about the how and why of my life, so might I ask about yours? It's obvious that you're on the move. So why are you out here along this long, tumultuous road of being a vagabond?"

The man sat cross-legged on the grass where his sleeping bag had been, apparently with no concern for the cleanliness of his handsome suit. But I had a feeling that, as soon as he stood up, I would find that his clothes were perfectly cleaned and unsoiled.

"I'm going to the launch," I said.

"Excellent!" the man exclaimed, tossing his hands in the air with excitement. He whistled. "Capital idea," he said. "I absolutely love it. The whole human race is at a hell of a crossroads right now and you've chosen your path. That's just terrific! The world needs more youth like you. You're someone who's chosen life in this world." He raised a finger and pointed it at me to punctuate his point. "And make no mistake about it, that's what the launch is: a choice of life. The only other choice is death."

I started to ask a question, but the man continued:

"You know, I used to live in Titusville. Lived there for almost six years. Loved a woman there for almost twenty. I was an undertaker — though the current phrase for it is *funeral director*. But I liked it when I was called an undertaker." He smiled and stood and brushed the back of his pants. Then he picked up his satchel and slung it over his shoulder. "Well," he said, "I suppose I'll be going now. There's a living to be made out there and it can't be done without the help of others. Know what I mean?"

I waved goodbye but the man did not see me. He walked without hesitation and without looking back over his shoulder. There was nothing but the forward arc of the world stretched out before him.

ELSEWHERE

The Morgan family was an old family. Which was to say that they were a family who had come into wealth many generations ago and, in the time since, had done a lot of things with that money to ensure that the Morgan name would continue to mean something in this world. For generations they had all worked hard, one after the other, owning land, donating to causes, enabling industry. On and on the narrative of success went, and now it had come down to simply two of them.

Harold Morgan had been the first to break tradition, the first one to not buy into anything. Ever since he was a boy he had cared less about the family name and more about books. His father, perhaps also getting tired of carrying the weight of the Morgan name, had doted on his son by building him his own personal library from the time the boy was able to read.

But that was a long time ago, decades, and now the boy was an old man, well into his seventies, and his father was still alive at ninety-five years old and the two of them were all that was left of the Morgan line on account of Harold being unable to have children and, perhaps even more than that, there was Harold's general disinterest in people.

The only thing he liked about people was the books they wrote.

Books were the greatest thing humanity had ever stumbled across and, by some miracle, kept up for ages across the world. He was still indebted to his father for the library the old man had built him. And now that he was seventy the library was still his favorite place.

And now that the world was ending and his father had contracted The Disease, he could stay within his library and not feel bad about it.

There were servants to send out for food and to take care of all of those odds and ends that needed to be done. Six months ago he moved his sleeping father into the library and, each and every day, he sat and read to him for hours on end. He wasn't sure whether or not those affected by The Disease could still hear what was going on around them. All that mattered was that they were together, the last two of the Morgan line, when everything came crumbling down. There was something noble and beautiful in it.

Every day Harold read. He began with his favorites, the classics that he had fallen in love with in his youth that had stuck with him over the years like familiar friends. His father, though he loved his son, had been an aloof man, especially after it became clear that his son would likely be the last of the line. The man had seemed disappointed or, perhaps, simply sad, like realizing that one has reached the final chapter of a novel they have been enjoying and would like nothing more than for the story to keep going and going.

But all stories must come to an end. So Harold read to his father, because that was as good an ending as he could dream up.

EIGHTEEN

The boy effervesced out of the fog. Smoke and water. Nothing more, perhaps, than a vision caused by the crash. Some type of brain damage. He looked to be about eight years old and he wore a three-piece suit manicured well enough to carry him to a christening or a funeral.

Tommy waved hello, because that was what he had been taught to do.

The suited boy standing in the fog smiled and waved back.

"Hi," Tommy said.

The boy bolted.

Tommy didn't know why he felt the need to give chase, but he did. He stumbled forward away from the highway without looking back to see that Gannon or anyone else was okay. In fact, he had no thought of Gannon, of me, of the war. Tommy pursued the boy with the focus of a parent.

The ground beneath his feet was wet and

soggy, with a loamy smell so thick and wet he was not breathing it — it was simply pushing itself in and out of his lungs of its own volition. "Wait a second," Tommy called out to the boy. "Hey! Wait up!"

But still the boy charged forward through the foggy gray dawn. The suit the child wore was only slightly darker than the fog, making him disappear and reappear over and over again as the distance between him and Tommy ebbed and flowed. He was like some memory stuck on the edge, always there and yet somehow never there. Tommy had a hard time believing that the child could move as quickly as he did. Then he realized it wasn't that the boy was moving so quickly. It was simply that Tommy was moving slowly.

His legs were weak and the back of his neck hurt. His body was doing what it was told, but only barely. He listed to one side as he ran, favoring his right leg. But still he chased the boy that was made of fog.

And then the boy was gone. Finally consumed by the milky swell of air.

Tommy turned in a circle, calling out once or twice, and still he did not see him. Now far away, back on the highway, Tommy could hear the low thrum of cars stopping to see the accident, and of others slowing only to take in the sight of whatever carnage there was to see and then to leave it behind.

Tommy stood and thought for a moment, deciding between walking forward into the gray or heading back to the highway.

Going forward felt like a bad decision, but forward he went.

It was the image of the boy that drove him forward. He could still see him in his mind as he stepped slowly and carefully through the soft earth.

Again Tommy called out for the boy. He stopped walking and stood and called out and held his breath to listen upon the chance that he might respond. There was none.

It took a moment for Tommy's brain to understand that it was seeing a door. There was simply a mound of kudzu and loamy earth that rose up out of the soggy flatness of the marshland. When he first saw it, he thought it might have been an abandoned car of some sort. But as he got closer to the mound Tommy was able to make out the brush and bracken that covered it. He thought he saw movement — a shaking of some of the leaves on one of the scrubs — but left the thought as a figment of his imagination. It wasn't until he was able to physically touch the bushes that he believed what he saw was real.

Carefully, he pushed aside the bushes and found the mouth of the cave. It was a door, he understood then. The bushes were not placed there by nature, not simply the random growth of the wet earth, but placed there intentionally by someone. Designed to create a barrier of privacy. With only a slight hesitation, Tommy pushed through the bramble and entered the cave.

Long, wonderful coolness. Tommy could feel his heart beating in the sides of his head now that the cool, wet air washed across his face.

Tommy sat and closed his eyes and breathed slowly. He nearly fell asleep, then heard a sound. It was a soft thud, like a rock falling. He opened his eyes and squinted into the darkness ahead, seeing nothing. He rose to his feet — shaky, his body still in need of rest — and leaned against the wall. Behind him the dim fog pushed its way into the mouth of the cave, doing nothing to illuminate this underworld.

Like a leap of faith, he started forward.

The darkness reached for him with each step, growing around him like dark vines. He traced his hand along the wall as he walked, his body gripped with the fear of a sudden drop-off reaching up out of the blackness to pull him down to his death. The path turned gently to the left as he went along. The wall on which he traced his hand was hard and old and smooth, concrete most likely. This was no longer nature that contained him, but a structure of mankind.

Soon the fear that is latent in all of us — that fear that only darkness can bring — swelled up inside Tommy and made his stomach tighten and made each step forward into the belly of the cave more and more difficult. He could feel the cave swelling around him, as though he were descending into the belly of some immense creature. The sounds of his own breathing and footsteps took longer to come back to him. There was a sense of more air above his head.

But his eyes were finally beginning to adjust. He could make out his hand in front of him when he tried — when he stood and focused and concentrated — and he thought he could see what looked like stalagmites rising up out of the ground in the wide open room ahead of him. The sand that had been beneath his feet was replaced by solid rock and the sound of his steps echoed even louder.

Then he could see that, indeed, there were stalagmites around him. He could hear the sound of dripping far off in the distance — dripping and the sound of something else that he could not quite make out. The stalagmites looked like teeth — improperly placed — but they possessed a strange type of beauty.

Tommy's eyes adjusted more and more to the dimness. He could make out his hand in front of him more clearly. He could see the hue of his skin shining brightly in the darkness. He continued to stare at it. It looked slightly alien, as if it did not belong to him, but to some creature that existed in the darkness at the bottom of the ocean. He spread his fingers and saw his hand as a starfish, creeping along at an impossibly slow pace. The longer he studied his hand the more it became clear and visible to him, as though there were a light shining down upon it.

Tommy looked up.

Above him, somehow, Tommy saw stars. Countless stars. Glimmering and sparkling. Clustered together and spread out. He saw the Big Dipper and Taurus, and the framework of other constellations he did not know as well. Somehow, here in the belly of this cave, there was starlight, shining down upon him, some type of miracle.

"Excuse me?" a woman's voice said.

Tommy startled. Not ten feet away from him was the small boy he had seen earlier. Next to the boy was a tall, thin-framed woman with blond hair. She wore blue jeans and a denim work shirt. "Hi," the woman said, smiling.

Tommy did not know what to say.

"My name's Vivian. This is Jake. Jake says you followed him home." Vivian looked down at the boy, who was obviously her son. She patted the top of his head and tousled his hair. For his part, the boy only watched Tommy with a mixture of curiosity and leeriness.

"I'm sorry," Tommy said.

"Why are you sorry?" Vivian asked.

"I . . . I don't know," Tommy replied. "I didn't mean to . . . I just saw him and I was worried about him. That's all."

Vivian smiled wider. "I completely understand," Vivian said brightly. "Jake usually stays away from strangers. And he's not supposed to go out there on his own like that." The boy looked up at Tommy, then turned his eyes to the floor. "Are you hungry? Thirsty?"

"I suppose," Tommy said.

"Okay," Vivian replied. "Well, you're

welcome to whatever we have. After all, you were trying to look out for Jake here, so the least I can do is invite you into our home for a meal. Or at least get you out of that world out there for a while."

"You live here?" Tommy asked.

"We do," Vivian replied. "But don't get nervous. We don't eat bats and night crawlers. We've got a perfectly normal house." She paused. "Well, maybe *normal* isn't quite the word I should be using, but I think you'll get the idea once you get there."

"Okay," Tommy said. He took one final look up. "Those can't be stars," he said to Vivian.

"Why not?" Vivian replied.

Tommy followed Vivian and her son into the depths of the cave. The boy walked in silence, now and again looking up at Tommy as if trying to understand how he had come to exist in this place. "My name's Tommy," he said to the boy, offering a handshake. The boy reached out and shook his hand with a stoic visage.

"Jake can't talk," Vivian said.

"Oh."

"But don't worry," the woman continued. "There's nothing wrong with him. He's a smart little troublemaker. Just a silent one is all."

"Okay," Tommy replied.

"It's been a long time since we've had a visitor, hasn't it, Jake?" Vivian asked her son. She took his hand and squeezed it. The boy looked up at him and then nodded in affirmation. "As you can imagine," Vivian continued, speaking to Tommy as they walked, "this isn't exactly a standard setup, and so it's not often we get people that stop by unexpectedly."

Along the walls of the tunnel through which they walked there were small lights placed along the floor at distant intervals. They did the bare and Spartan job of shining out the path ahead, leading Tommy and Vivian and Jake to where they needed to go. There were no pitfalls or holes in the floor of the path as Tommy had expected. In fact, he could almost go as far as to say that he felt comfortable walking through the hallways. Perhaps he had simply spent too much time on the road, too much time along the blacktop of the highway, always worrying about the exhaustion.

This was something different. The feeling in this cave was one of cool softness, like a pillow turned over in the middle of the night.

"They'll be very excited to see that we have a guest, even if you only stay for a little while."

"They?"

"My husband and daughter."

"So there are four of you down here?"

"Yep," Vivian replied. "In fact, I imagine that you and my daughter aren't too far apart in age. At least, from what I can see of you. I'll be able to see you a little better once we get to the house. I keep telling my husband that we need more lights out here, that someday one of the kids is going to get hurt or that, maybe, just like today, some stranger will show up and find the place and get lost in here."

"Is it easy to get lost?"

"Always," Vivian replied. "Everything leads somewhere. And it's not until you've been here long enough and stumbled through enough of the wrong ways that you can really find out where anything is. Sure, the lights help, but a person is always curious about the unlit path."

As she said the sentence, Tommy became aware of a path opening up to the right. The wall simply seemed to disappear and there was a great mouth of darkness down which the dim lighting that stood along the path did not penetrate. The path seemed to go on forever. "That's exactly what I mean," Vivian said. He nodded to the mouth of darkness. "Down that way, it's okay for the most part. But there are definitely some places where you can make a misstep and have a pretty bad fall. Or even if you don't take a bad fall, there's always the possibility of simply getting turned around. That cave goes for a long way, and even though it eventually reconnects back with everything along here and will get you to safety, you wouldn't know it. You go down that way and, inside of five minutes, it feels like you're in the center of the earth, in the center of the universe even. Nothing but darkness and stone walls and no way to find your way back out. People panic in places like that."

"Then why don't you close this off?" Tommy asked. "What if Jake went down there?"

"Jake knows his way out," Vivian said. "He's been down there before and came back home, and he can do it again if he needs to." She looked down at Jake, who looked up at her and smiled.

"That sounds dangerous," Tommy replied.

"Life's dangerous," Vivian said. "And not letting children learn to face danger, at least a little bit, doesn't do anything at all to help them."

■ ■ ■ ■

It was not long before the light that Vivian promised began to appear. It began as simply a dull white glow that illuminated a bend in the tunnel ahead. But then the light began to grow as they neared it. Jake bolted ahead with the familiar excitement of children who have finally returned to the world they have left behind.

"Let your father and sister know we have a guest," Vivian called out to the boy. He disappeared around the bend.

The tunnel eventually opened up into a large, sweeping cave strung with lights from one side to the other. The lights gave off a soft, warm hue. The cave was broken up into sections. There was a living room — complete with chairs, tables and a bookcase. There was a kitchen and dining room that did not look much different than those Tommy had seen in every other home he had ever been into.

He had expected more differences than what he saw. But it was obvious that this family was, indeed, living here.

"How do you have electricity?" Tommy asked, slightly awestruck by the underground home.

"Solar panels," Vivian said. "Up above, of course. If you could go straight up, you'd see about a half an acre of solar panels standing in the middle of the Florida swampland."

"Oh," Tommy said.

"Not quite what you expected?"

"I can't imagine it is," a man's voice replied.

Tommy turned to see the boy racing back through a tunnel on the far side of the room, followed by a man and a girl. The man, who was obviously the father, smiled and waved as he came into view. He was tall and thin, like a reed that someone had given clothes and taught how to walk. He did not look like the insane save-my-family-from-the-end-of-the-world type that he obviously was.

No one is who they seem to be in this world.

"My name's Michael," the man said. He reached out and shook Tommy's hand. "I can see that you've already met Vivian and Jake." He turned and took the hand of his daughter — who seemed too shy to step forward on her own and say hello. "And this one here is Helen. Don't let her calm demeanor fool you. She's just as much of a troublemaker as Jake is." He grinned at his daughter. "In fact, I'd probably be willing to make an argument that she's even more of a headache." Tommy smiled. Helen only waved hello and seemed to be more interested in the book she was carrying with her. As soon as the work of greeting Tommy was over, Helen went back to reading her book.

"I can imagine that this is all a bit strange to you," Michael said, and the entire family looked at Tommy, waiting for him to make a comment about how they were being perceived.

"It's definitely different," Tommy said, trying to be cautious with his words.

"Don't worry," Michael said. "You're welcome to take a break from all of that and stay here for dinner."

Dinner was more normal than Tommy had expected. The family was like any other family he had met. They laughed, they made fun of each other. The food was delicious and not nearly as strange as Tommy had anticipated. Vivian was a wonderful cook and an entertaining hostess. She was a geologist and spent a lot of time talking about the history of the rocks and the land surrounding where the family lived.

For his part, Michael seemed excited by the future. He was an engineer. Anytime

Tommy saw something in the family's home that looked as though it might be on the higher end of the technology spectrum, he could be sure that Michael had created or purchased it. He was still employed by a college up in Jacksonville, where he went a few times a week to teach classes.

Tommy wondered how many people knew what kind of a house he lived in.

"Why do you live like this?" Tommy asked after dinner. The question had been burning inside of him from the very beginning and now the flame was too great to be held at bay any longer.

The immediate reaction from the family was simply laughter.

"You made it longer than we thought you would before asking," Michael said, grinning. "We actually have a little game where, whenever someone new comes to visit, we try to see just how long they can make it before asking why."

"I'm sorry," Tommy said.

"Don't be," Vivian replied. "We're not so obtuse that we can't understand just how strange all of this is."

"We're doing something different here," Michael said. "And we go to great lengths to make sure that our children understand just how different it is as well. We don't want them to grow up being so far removed from normal life that they don't fit in. After all, they're not going to be living with us forever."

Tommy was surprised by just how sensible everything sounded. "Then why are you living down here?" he asked.

"Because it's what feels like home," Michael said. He leaned back in his chair and folded his arms in front of his chest. He looked perplexed. "Actually," he said, "that doesn't sound like quite as good an answer as it always seems to sound in my head."

Vivian laughed. "We've tried to come up with better ways to explain it to people," she said to Tommy. "People always thought we were some kind of doomsday preppers — those people who think the whole world is about to end and so they move underground or into those insane bunkers and start stockpiling food and weapons to wait for some inevitable catastrophe."

Michael smiled. "Nut jobs," he said.

"There's a little pot calling the kettle black action right there," Vivian said.

"But we're not nut jobs," Michael said playfully. "We're eccentric. There's a difference."

"Shenanigans," Vivian said.

In spite of his curiosity, in spite of the

strangeness of it all, Tommy could not help but smile at the family's dynamics. They loved each other. More than that, they were happy. Even living down here beneath everything, as if they were trying to run away from it all, they were happy. More than that, they truly believed that everything was going to be okay. The Disease . . . the war . . . all of it would end eventually and the family would reemerge into a normal world, a world where their children would be loved and live long, healthy lives.

"We just wanted a different life," Michael began. "We used to live in Boston. I never could get used to the winters up there and Vivian always wanted to move out here for her field of study. More of the geological history of the world is on display out here. Back there, everything interesting has a building stacked on top of it."

"Settle down," Vivian said to her husband.

He smiled. "Sorry," Michael said. "Can you tell I never much cared for city living?"

Tommy nodded politely.

"Anyhow," Vivian picked up, "we moved out here for me to do some doctoral research. And we didn't move straight out here," he said. "We used to live in Phoenix. We had a pretty nice house on the outskirts of the city and, well, we were living a perfectly normal and functional life. This was back before the war and everybody falling asleep and not waking up." He leaned back in his chair and took a long look around at the cavern in which they now lived, as if moving back through the many veils of memory that he carried within him. "And then I was doing some research and I found out about this old military installation that was built out here in the sixties. It was a deep-drilling installation, a place where they were doing geological research. They hollowed out this section of rock and built this small network of caverns that ties back into the natural caverns. So I came out here to see it, just out of curiosity. Most people didn't even know it existed. It's one of those things that the government built and forgot about, and everyone who used to work here and who really knew about it, well, they were too old to care about it or they'd forgotten about it too. It was just a piece of the forgotten world."

Michael sat forward in his chair. "Can you believe that they could build something this terrific and forget about it?" he asked. "I mean, how is that even possible? This place is amazing!" Michael's eyes sparkled in the glow of the lamplight around the room.

"Down, boy," Vivian said.

"Yes, ma'am," Michael said playfully.

"Anyhow," Vivian continued, "we came here and found this place. I won't say we fell in love with it immediately — well, maybe Michael did. But it definitely had its charm. There was a quiet nature to it. And I don't just mean that in the literal sense. Yeah, we were away from all of the sounds of cars and cities and everything else. But there was something else. There was this overarching sense of patience, this impression of timelessness that came from standing beneath all of these rocks, these pieces of the earth that are older than our brain can really process. The whole world, in essence, began in places very much like this." She sat back in her chair and looked around admiringly. "It's a notion that sneaks up on you after you've been down here a little while. And once it does, well, everything else just feels cheap and tawdry compared to this. Even the biggest and most expensive mansion can't hold a candle to this place — in our opinion, at least."

Tommy followed the lead of his hosts and took a moment to admire the room. He still couldn't quite say that he fully understood their fascination with living beneath so much rock. After all, wasn't it just the same as living beneath the shadow of all those billions of tons of steel in the cities that Michael had mentioned? But Tommy had to admit that he was calmer than he had been in a very long time.

Perhaps it was the stones and their immemorial nature. The sempiternal way that they seemed to exist: seeing everything change around them and yet still being able to endure.

"They're just rocks," Tommy said to himself.

"What was that?" Vivian asked.

"Nothing," he said.

The rest of the evening was enjoyable enough. The small family who lived beneath the earth turned out to be much more normal than Tommy had expected. The husband and wife loved their children, the children loved their parents. The children seemed to know just as much about the world as children their age should and their views were not particularly skewed one way or the other. Tommy had heard and read about the children of people who live "eccentric" lives. The children are oftentimes brought up to believe that the world exists in a very specific way, they are taught to be a certain flavor of conservative or liberal. They are taught that one version of God is more correct than all others. They are indoctrinated in a dozen different ways.

But Michael and Vivian's children were just like all the other children Tommy had ever met except that they didn't seem worried about today and they weren't scared of tomorrow. It was as if everything in the world was only a dream down here, something to be shaken off at the coming of the dawn in favor of something more real.

As far back as he could remember — and even farther — Tommy always had trouble making friends, finding connections with people. Largely it was due to the fact that he was consistently moved around throughout his life. When he was very young and didn't understand how life in foster homes worked, he tried to make friends when he moved to a new town to live with a new foster family. He would go to school and smile and be friendly and, in general, he was very capable of finding people who liked him and who he liked back.

But then he would have to move. After the third time he moved, he began to recognize the signs of a foster family that was ready to let him go to someone else. It would begin with a subtle distancing of affections.

One couple would always come and sit on

the edge of Tommy's bed and read to him until he fell asleep. Then they would place a bookmark in the pages of the book and switch off the lamps and, perhaps, lean in to kiss him gently on the brow. In his dreams, there was a perfumed wind that fell across his face and he knew, without being aware of it, that his foster parents had given him those small, affectionate kisses. Another family would always sit with him and ask him what he had learned that day. Whatever his answer, they would try to transform the answer into some life lesson. He would fall asleep thinking of what they had told him about the nature of people or about the nature of the world. They were always optimistic lessons, things that said that kindness and polite behavior were how to make your way in the world. They created a picture of life that made sense, an image of the world in which everything was capable of working out if a person simply tried hard enough and was patient enough. *Karma* was the word that they used to describe the notion of the world being just and fair.

But eventually it always happened that, in the weeks before he would be told that the family did not want him anymore and were sending him to another foster home, the nightly attention would stop. All of the small moments, whatever they were, would begin to lessen.

It always came to pass that one foster parent was less willing to get rid of Tommy than the other. It was just the nature of how things worked. This would be the person who worked too hard in the last days of Tommy's time with them to be kind to him, to make sure he understood that the reason he was leaving was not his fault. "You didn't do anything wrong" is what they would always say to him. Each and every family said it on the day when they told him that he was being sent away. They would recite it like a mantra, something that absolved both them and him of any guilt. Something that liberated everyone at the cost of no one.

Of course, the only thing that Tommy could think was that it was his fault.

Of course he had done something wrong. Why else would they get rid of him?

That was his thinking then, as a child. Now he was almost an adult and he had a better understanding of how the world worked. He understood that there were no promises in this life, not even the promises of people who claim to love you, people who swear that they will always be with you, always a part of your life and your identity. Even if they wanted those things, there was death to make them out to be a liar.

"Let me show you something," Vivian said after the family was settled in for the evening.

"What is it?" Tommy asked.

"Something you can't see anywhere else," she replied.

"Can I come?" Helen asked.

"You've got studying to do," Vivian said politely. And then she leaned down and kissed the top of her head. The boy frowned in a dejected way, but then went off to his room to begin working.

Vivian and Tommy walked through the hallways until they reached a large, sweeping cavern.

"Here we are," Vivian said.

Around the room were small lamps along the floor that illuminated the walls dimly. "What is it?" Tommy asked.

"Just wait here a second," Vivian said. "You'll see."

Tommy watched as Vivian walked over toward the hallway through which they had come. There was a small metal panel on the wall. Vivian opened it, threw a switch, and suddenly there was nothing but complete and utter darkness. A wall of it fell across Tommy. It buried him. It was a darkness so complete and total that it made his eyes hurt.

"Vivian?" Tommy called out, fear in his voice.

"Don't worry," Vivian said. Her voice sounded impossibly far away. "Just wait there."

"Okay," Tommy said. He tried not to be nervous, but he was. He suddenly realized just how little he actually knew about this eccentric family who lived in caves beneath the loamy Floridian soil. He remembered horror movies and what happened to people who were in those movies.

He closed his eyes.

"Do you see it?" Vivian asked.

"See what?" Tommy answered. He opened his eyes, but there was still only blackness.

"Look up," she said.

Tommy did as he was told. He looked up and, somehow, saw starlight. It took his breath away.

"It was Michael's idea," Vivian said, looking up at what was, by all visual accounts, the heavens. Stars upon stars upon stars shone above Tommy's head and, for a moment, he forgot that he was buried beneath the earth in a hole in Florida. Instead, he was standing in the open darkness of space itself, floating there, timeless and ethereal.

"Michael spent months working on it," Vivian said. "Hanging little lights in the most exact locations to make it look like the real sky."

"It's amazing," Tommy said.

"It is. Sometimes I look up and I get lost in it." She paused. Then: "I don't know why you're on the road. Maybe you're running away from something or someone, or maybe you're running to something or someone. Whatever the reason, just don't forget that there are things like this out there. When you run away, you run past a lot of things that you can never get back. Don't forget that."

Tommy opened his eyes. Gannon was there, blotting out the sky, as though he had never been anywhere else. Tommy had forgotten about him. Forgotten about the car crash. Forgotten about the launch. Forgotten about the war and The Disease. He had even almost succeeded in forgetting about me and our dead parents.

Almost.

But seeing Gannon, he realized he hadn't forgotten any of it. Not really. He'd only managed to hide within himself like the family hiding within the hollow of the Floridian earth.

"He's dead," Gannon said.

"Who?" Tommy asked, still confused, as if the family he had met was nothing more than a dream.

"Pop."

They walked out of the fog together without another word. Gannon led, Tommy followed. When they reached the long, black slither of highway, it was still cluttered with police cars and ambulances and rubber-neckers all gawking at Gannon's overturned car.

They walked over to the ambulance where Gannon's dead father lay beneath a white sheet speckled with blood. Gannon trembled, standing there in the light of the brightening day. He spat. "He deserved better than this," he said. "He was my pop . . . and he deserved better."

"I'm sorry," Tommy said. He wanted to put his arm around Gannon, but it was a habit foreign to him, so he only stood and watched until Gannon spoke again.

"I wish you'd known him," Gannon said. "All you ever saw was the aftermath, like everything else in this world. But in his prime . . . Well, you would have liked him, Tommy. He would have liked you too."

Tommy nodded. He tried to imagine Bill Gannon as anything other than what he had

known — in the same way that he sometimes tried to imagine the world without
war and without The Disease, back when
"everything was simpler," as people were
always saying — but it didn't work. All he
saw was what he had been given.

"Are we going back? You should bury
him."

"After," Gannon said. "Your sister started
all of this. I'm going to see you two together
again. I'm going to see this through."

"This wasn't Virginia's fault," Tommy said.

"We'll see," Gannon replied.

Tommy,

It'll be your job to take care of your sister. That's just the way it will work out. She'll be odd, always. She'll never fit in and it'll be up to you to help her fit in and, when she doesn't, when she gets frustrated by everything and everyone — including you — it'll be your job to bear the storm of her frustration.

I hope you can do it. I know you can, but I have to hope that you'll know you can as well.

I've seen it in your mother. The way she drifts off into herself, always remembering everything as if it were actually happening right here and now. It's like someone watching television, only you can't see what they're watching. Sometimes, after she's spent too much time in memory, she will come out of it, looking groggy and far away, and she'll look at me and I can see all of the sadness that I can't imagine and I wish, more than anything, that I could take away her memories. Make her able to forget. Able to be something normal.

So when it happens with Virginia, it'll be your job.

There are rules: be patient. That's the biggest rule. Even though she's your sister and even though she will love you, she won't be able to understand why you can't see the world the way she does. Not really. She'll empathize to the best of her ability, but she can no more understand your world than you can understand hers. I suppose that's the way it is with everyone. We all exist in closed rooms behind locked doors inside our minds.

But with most of us, there's enough normalcy to understand one another. We're able to convince ourselves that the person next to us thinks in a way that's very similar to the way we think. And we're able to feel for them and they're able to feel for us and that's how we make it work.

But now that's all going away. Which brings me to the second rule:

Protect your sister.

The world you're coming into is different from the world I came into. By the time you're of age, there'll be a war on. It's the logical conclusion to the way the world is going. And the world will take you both there, take you there and leave you with only each other to seek out salvation and survival.

NINETEEN

There was nothing left to do but bleed out and die. Sometimes life just happens that way. The miles to Canaveral were long and winding and, all the while, I was bleeding and the world was getting worse. I caught a ride with a caravan of people heading down to watch what would happen. It took some work but I managed to staunch the bleeding enough that it could go unnoticed. The people were the partying type, lost in themselves and in the news that poured in over the internet about how dangerous the launch was becoming. There were threats made by terrorists and promises made by the government. The two sides both trying to convince the whole world of their sincerity.

Southern Florida is a landscape made of dreams that lead to stiff waking. The Spanish moss sags down from the branches like cloudy tears and the trees rise up like the fingers of the dead. The water holds both memory and promise, either depending on what you've come looking for.

The caravan snaked its way through the Panhandle in a long, brightly lit line of revelry and excitement. There were close to fifty cars, their headlights slicing through the waning day like candles pushing back the darkness of eternity.

I was being driven by a thin-framed blue-haired woman who talked more than she breathed. For seventy miles she talked and I half listened. My stomach wound ached but the blood had mostly stopped and there was too much else going on for the woman I rode with to notice. She sawed the steering wheel back and forth over the highway, swaying the car like a ship on unsettled seas.

A few times I felt the beginnings of nausea.

The other half of the time I was thinking about my wound and wondering if it was infected and wondering if the numbness that I was feeling was a severed nerve or just a damaged one and, more than that, I was wondering if Tommy would forgive me for not telling him that it was me who was drafted. I knew Gannon would have told him about it by now.

Tommy was known for his ability to forgive on account of his ability to forget, but maybe this would be the exception. Or, maybe worse, Tommy actually would forget but he wouldn't be able to forgive and for the rest of our lives he would hold on to something that he couldn't remember. I would always have a shadow over my head in his mind.

"Are you listening to me?" Carrol said. Her voice was like a mountain breaching from the ocean.

"What did you say?" I asked.

"You see," she said, "I knew you weren't listening. I knew I was wasting my time."

Then she reached down and turned up the radio and the news came in:

The Disease wasn't getting any better and neither was the war. The newest victim was just under thirty and all signs pointed to The Disease spreading even farther and faster than anything projected by the CDC. Within ten years there wouldn't be anyone over the age of twenty-five. Not long after that no one over the age of twenty. And so on and so forth until finally there would be no one left old enough to reproduce and then, in the end, in the final days of humanity, all you would have were children bearing witness to an ending that they were too young to understand or appreciate.

"Jesus," Carrol said. "It's just . . . it's just

too much to bear. This is how the world ends." She shook her head. "How old are you, child?"

"Seventeen," I said.

"Oh Lord," she said, shaking her head again like a willow tree. "I wonder how much longer you'll be able to make it. I wonder how long before it comes for you just like it comes for everybody else. I used to think they'd find a way to fix it, but now I know better. This is it." She wiped a tear from her eye. "And you'll have to be there for it."

"You're still alive," I said. "That's something. Maybe things will get better. Maybe you'll make it too."

"We're already gone," she said. "We knew that from the very beginning. We ain't like them rich people and politicians. We can't afford to hole up in our bunker and breathe fresh air and stave off the end of the world. All we've got are these here masks and I don't believe they'll be around much longer. No. Don't you get fooled by the fact that we've made it this long. We won't be there at the end. Lights will go out for us long before the party ends."

"Then why are you here?" I asked. "Why make this drive to Canaveral?"

"For the same reason the launch itself is

still going on," she replied. "Because it's been in the works for years and if this is going to be the way the world ends then why not end it doing something beautiful?"

"Do you even know what the Europa mission is about?" I asked.

"Why wouldn't I know?" Carrol interrupted. I realized I was being condescending.

"I didn't mean anything," I said.

"Sure you did," she replied. "But that's okay. What's a Twilight like me know about rockets and moons and everything else? And the truth of it is that I don't know a whole lot about this stuff. I know just what the news tells me and even that I wouldn't put too much stock in. I heard all that stuff people have been talking about the rocket launch and everything else. All that talk about it being some sort of secret government escape plan. But don't you get behind that. Not in the least bit."

Carrol was still shaking her head solemnly, as if the action was saying everything she couldn't find the words to say.

"But the thing about it is," she continued, "even if that's the truth, so what? What's there for someone like me to do about it? I ain't the kind of person that gets picked up and put onboard a spaceship and taken away from all of this."

"Do you really believe that's what they're doing?"

"No," she said. "But it proves my point. I'm a nobody and I've always been a nobody and that's fine with me. I've been a happy nobody."

"Don't you want more?" I asked. I felt bad about the question no sooner than I asked it.

"Why should I want more? Is any of it gonna make me live forever? And even if I could, what would it be worth? How many sunsets can you see before you get bored with them? And if you got bored with them, what would be the point of living forever? That's the old catch of life: you get all you get and you don't get any more and that's the way it's supposed to be."

"I can't believe that," I said. My stomach was in knots and throbbing all of a sudden. "People are meant to be more than just nobodies. People are meant to improve themselves. I keep telling my brother that. I've been telling him that his whole life and he doesn't change. He just keeps on being who he is. He just keeps on forgetting everything."

"You got a brother?" Carrol asked.

"Yep," I replied.

"What's his name?"

"Tommy."

"That's a good name. If I'd ever had a boy I was going to name him Tom. It's a strong name." Carrol's mouth tightened and her eyes saw something beyond me, something from her past. Perhaps it was the dream of the boy named Tom she never had. "Tell me about him," she said. "Tell me about your brother. He ain't going off to the war, is he?"

"No," I said. "Not if I have anything to say about it. But . . ."

"But he wants to go, don't he?"

"Yeah."

"I knew it," Carrol said. Her hands clutched the steering wheel. "I don't know what it is about boys always wanting to play war. They act like there's something in it that they'll find that they can't find no place else. Something that they can't find in love, in their mother, in their sister, in having a child of their own someday. They act like going out there and getting their head shot off . . . Lord bless them all. It'll all be over in another generation or two. They'll reach a point soon when the war won't have anybody old enough to run it and all them young enough to go off and get killed won't have anybody telling them to go do that.

And maybe that'll be the way the world ends. All soft-like. Just a breeze running out over a flat lake until it can't reach the other side."

Carrol's words hung in the air for the next few miles. We were silent, save for the radio and the drone of the motor until, finally, we were there.

It wasn't unlike the photographs I'd seen of Woodstock and other great parties over the stretch of modern history. The long line of cars was stopped, permanently and irrevocably. They all knew and understood that they would not make it any closer to the launch than they were and they had resigned themselves to enjoying the night, to celebrating the Europa mission in the best way they could, to making a party out of things until the moment came when the sky was lit up by the engines of the rockets and the vehicle broke the bonds of the earth, beginning its long, historic mission.

So people turned off their cars and got out and produced camping chairs and some of them even had small barbecue grills and there was food cooking and people cheering and people dressed in costumes of aliens — all manner of creatures ranging from the typical Roswell aliens to things with many legs and tentacles to things that didn't quite make sense and seemed to appear from someone's fever dreams of childhood. People cheered and drank and smoked and danced. Music blared from empty cars and the drivers got out and found other people along the road to dance and party with and everyone cheered and there were sparklers burning and fireworks being fired and, now and again, there would be some police officer who came along the road on their motorcycle. The intention of the cops were to keep things from getting out of hand, but whoever it was didn't seem to be overly worried about things. In fact, they seemed just as excited as everyone else about what was happening. One of them had taped a sticker to his helmet that read "Europa or Bust" and, from time to time, he would stop and get off his motorcycle and find someone who was cooking something particularly interesting and he would eat with them and laugh.

As I passed by, I heard someone ask him about the launch and he smiled and gave a long, detailed description of what people could expect when the rockets finally fired and the night sky became a pathway to the stars. People stood around cheering and laughing as they listened, drinking and eat-

ing and forgetting that he was a police officer. They saw him simply as someone as
excited by the Europa mission as the rest of
them. I heard them refer to him as
"Tommy."

I'd been walking slowly, taking in the
crowd. But at hearing that name I couldn't
help but walk faster. My legs burned and
felt full up, ready to burst from my skin. I
wanted to break into a run. But still, everywhere around me, the party continued,
oblivious to me and, seemingly, everything
else in the world. The cars were all empty
and the headlights still burned and everyone was out and talking and cluttering up
the street and the policeman stood among a
crowd drinking a beer and, now and again,
looking down at his watch and then looking
up at the sky in the direction of the launch
pad.

People called out to me as I made my way
along. "Come and have a beer," some of
them said. "Party's over here," some young
man yelled as I passed. I only kept my head
up and looked down the long stretch of road
and I thought I saw my parents ahead of
me, walking in the distance, heading to the
launch pad.

So I walked faster. The crowd was growing more and more excited as the count-

down came crackling in over radios and through cell phones. People swirled about, cheering and full of revelry as I swerved through and around them. I was still bleeding. And maybe I had lost too much blood, because I began to know that, if I could be fast enough, I could catch up to my parents. And if I could catch up to them, I could grab their hands and hold them and never let them go and, once again, we would all be a family again. All I had to do was catch up to them. Follow the path undistracted just as I had done since leaving Oklahoma, since leaving Tommy.

There was only the path ahead.

My arms and legs rose faster, taking me from a fast walk into a slow run. And then, up ahead, I saw my parents again. This time they were farther away, rising up a tall drawbridge that sat in the middle of the water. They smiled and my father carried five-year-old me on his shoulders and, for an instant, I was both versions of me. I was the seventeen-year-old chasing the ghosts of my parents and, simultaneously, I was the child riding atop my father's shoulders, looking out over the water from atop the bridge, seeing the glimmering lights of the city on the far shore and the flat surface of the water.

"Dad!" I called out suddenly.

And still I ran and still my parents were always ahead of me, beyond the length of my reach. When I reached the far side of the bridge my parents were far down the road, farther than they had ever been. My body was beginning to tire. The blood still poured, but I continued to ignore it.

My heart was a drum pounding against the thin walls of my chest. My lungs pushed and pulled and gave a little less with each breath. My legs were filling with sand. But still I ran. People began to clear a path for me, not really knowing why, only knowing that I was desperate. And then, for reasons I would never know, some people began to cheer as I raced past them. Perhaps it was the party atmosphere that did it. Too much alcohol and beer and food, too much cele-bration of the launch of the Europa mis-sion, too many good vibes and too much humanity. Whatever the reason, the cheers began small and grew like a storm rising up out of the west until, all of a sudden, the crowd was parted and there was a line of people on both sides, applauding me as I passed and calling ahead for people to clear the way. I was like a runner at the end of a marathon, carried not by my body but by the crowd around me, being willed to the finish line when I wanted nothing more than to give up, to stop and stand and let the pain of fatigue recede, to get my breath back, to breathe and laugh and do anything else.

But there was no time.

I lost sight of my parents and, eventually, even the crowd of people around me receded. There was only me and the earth and the rocket sitting on the launch pad at some distance ahead of me. On and on and on I went, losing more of myself with each stride. But then the pain went away. Suddenly and without warning, there was Tommy, waiting for me.

TWENTY

Tommy knew the time was always going to come when they would catch up to me. He had hoped it would be after the launch, though he didn't know why. Maybe that would be easier. Maybe then everything would make sense. Maybe after the launch I could simply keep going, Tommy thought, disappear and avoid the war.

But suddenly, he and Gannon had reached the road to Canaveral. It hadn't taken Gannon long to get another car. Not a police car, just a cheap rental, but he wouldn't be stopped. The line of cars stretching over the long waterway to Cape Canaveral had come to a full stop miles before the Cape itself. There would be only walking from there on out.

"Let's go," Gannon said. He'd pulled the car over to the side of the road and switched it off.

"We won't find her," Tommy said.

"You wouldn't have come if you believed that."

He stepped out of the car and shut the door. After a moment, Tommy followed. He jogged up alongside Gannon, scanning the crowd as they walked, not sure if he hoped to see her or not. "What are you going to do when you find her?"

"Take her back," Gannon said. "She's got a responsibility."

"She won't go," Tommy said.

"I'll make her," Gannon replied. His pace was even and heavy, like the heartbeat of an elephant, like time itself.

The audience of humanity was everywhere. Partiers, revelers, cars filled with children and old souls, picnics spaced here and there along the edge of road, small boats floating in the water along the road, decorated with all manner of colors and lights and symbols. There were dancers and the smell of food cooking on grills. There was the smell of beer and marijuana and a thousand other scents. Children raced around dressed like astronauts carrying toy rockets powered by sparklers and imagination. Music spilled out from inside cars and rolled into the thick, warm air of Florida in January.

"Fools," Gannon said, almost at a growl.

He spat on the ground as they walked. His eyes swung back and forth like those of a wolf on the hunt.

"I think it's nice," Tommy replied.

"Nobody wants to be a part of the world they were born into. Everybody wants to be in some other place at some other time, as if that'll fix the way their lives turned out. Pop told me that once. Did I ever tell you that?" His voice wavered.

"No," Tommy said.

He shook his head as a group of children passed carrying a toy rocket ship. "And then they teach it to their children. They teach them to live in a world that doesn't exist, to think of things that aren't the way they are." He spat again. "No wonder everything's falling apart."

"Virginia won't come with you," Tommy said.

"I'm not going to ask her," Gannon replied. "I'll take her back with me and she'll go and enlist like everyone else. Or she'll wind up in jail. Those are the only two options for her."

"I'll take her place," Tommy said.

"It doesn't work like that," Gannon replied. He stopped for a moment, catching sight of a girl who looked more than a little like me. She was the right height and her hair looked the same, but then the girl turned to face Tommy and Gannon and they both saw that it wasn't me. "We've all got to walk into our own destinies," Gannon said. "You should know that by now."

He continued walking forward.

It was then that Tommy slipped away into the crowd.

His heart drummed in his ears as he made his way through the crowd. "Virginia?" he called out. "Virginia!" Sometimes people turned and looked at him, trying to decide why he had come this far and what he could be searching for, but they inevitably turned back. Over and over and over again he found everyone except me.

When I found him, Tommy was standing on the edge of the waterway looking off in the direction of the shuttle, waiting patiently as the last minutes until the countdown slid away. He looked different than I remembered him. As if he was no longer the brother I had known for all of my seventeen years, as if, in the small time away, he had decided to be something other than the other half of me. And I think that was when I realized, truly understood, that Tommy and I would never be able to make things work between us. After a lifetime of sharing the world, we had grown apart. Little by little. Day by day. Him carving out his own slice of the world and me folding in on my own, buried in my memories. The both of us had always been walking away from one another, even as we walked together for all those years. All that chasing, all that trying to stay together, it had only ever been a type of stalling, just a way to try to cling to sand that was destined to slip between our fingers.

But that's the way it is with siblings, with family. We live together even as we grow apart. Babies become children, children become teenagers, teenagers become adults, and all the while we build worlds of memory and thought and imagination inside ourselves. We build oceans of life under the surface of ourselves. And those around us only get to see what they choose to see, never what we are.

But just then, I saw my brother for who he was. And I knew that we would not stay together. We couldn't stay together. In fact, we had left one another ages ago. No matter how much I remembered the way things were, things can simply be the way they are.

Tommy and I had spent our time together. Now it was all going to end.

Tommy continued watching in the direc-

tion of the rocket. I knew what he was trying to do, just like I knew everything else
about my brother. He tried to remember
our father's letters: all the dreaming the
man had done about Europa and the space
program and the importance of imagining
beyond the bonds of the earth, but all
Tommy could come up with were his own
small thoughts on things.

"You made it," I said, walking up beside
him.

"You knew I would," Tommy replied, still
staring forward, watching the crowds, the
bustling night, the uncertain future. "You're
hurt," Tommy said, looking at my bloody
clothes.

"We all are," I said. Then, "It's going to
be beautiful. Those rockets . . . they light
up like nothing else. First there's that flash
of light. Then the smoke just kind of billows
out like a cloud. It's like —"

"Stop," Tommy replied. He was cold all of
a sudden. He folded his arms across his
chest and made his hands into fists and,
finally, he turned and looked at me.

For a moment he seemed surprised, as if
he had expected me to look like someone
else, as if he had expected to look on me
and see something other than a reflection of
himself. Or perhaps that was simply my own

feelings reflected back at me in Tommy's eyes.

"I'm sorry," I said.

"Sorry for what?" Tommy replied. "I need to hear you say it."

"Tommy . . ."

"Say it, Virginia."

Nearby a family of five stood together and cheered at something coming in over the radio. Whether it was news of the launch or news of the war or news about The Disease, it was hard to say. They were simply a family, and here, at what was sure to be the end of everything, they were somehow happy.

"I'm sorry for sending you the fake letter," I finally said. "But you have to understand that it was the only way I could get you to come down here. Mom and Dad would have been here."

"But they're not here! They're dead! They've always been dead. Don't you understand that?" His voice was louder than he had ever heard it. So loud that it almost rose up over the sound of the crowd around us as the countdown to the rocket launch began in earnest. There were only moments left before it all came to pass. "They're not here anymore. We're not their children anymore. We're no one's children. All we have is each other. That's all we've ever had.

But you've never been able to believe that. You've never been able to understand that. You've spent your whole life looking for them, remembering those letters over and over and over again, as if reading them would somehow change the fact that everything is the way it is." He spread his arms wide, as if taking in the whole world. "But nothing can change the way it is. This is the world, Virginia! This is what the world is always going to be!"

"Tommy . . ."

"They're dead, Virginia! They're always going to be dead!" His lip trembled as he spoke. Whether it was exhaustion, sadness or just the weight of a lifetime pouring through him, I couldn't tell. The weight of life varies so much from person to person. For Tommy, not remembering so much, I imagine that life weighs more for him than it did for me. After all, remembering everything lets you create the world as it was, without ever losing sleep over the ways you think it could have been. The burden of forgetting the unforgettable moments of your life had to be unbearable for my brother. I understood that, there at the end of our journey together. His imagination over everything that his mind had let him lose would forever haunt him, especially as he watched me carry it all, day by day, keeping our parents inside me, with him never able to hear our father's voice or remember the feel of our mother's touch.

And through all that, the one thing Tommy ever had was the war, the belief that he could go off and be special the way the television commercials and Mitch the Bitch and everyone else in this world said he should be. He could never run off like the other Embers because that's what I would have done, and even more than he wanted life, my brother wanted to be different than me. He wanted his moment in this world, and I had made him believe that he'd finally gotten it. And then I'd taken it all away.

"I didn't do it to hurt you, Tommy." I took a seat in the low grass overlooking the waterway. Around us the crowd grew in excitement. Someone set off fireworks. A small group of policemen went over and warned them against it, but there were too many people for anyone to make a difference. So things continued on. Fireworks lit up the sky. Music filled the air. A brother and sister couldn't find enough space in the world to hold them both.

"What's the longest we've ever been apart?" I asked.

"I don't remember," Tommy replied.

"Exactly. You don't remember. But I do. Three days, thirteen hours and forty-three minutes. That's how long we've been apart."

"Doesn't seem like any time at all," Tommy said, scratching the back of his head. His body was still tight, unwilling to let go of the anger.

"Not unless you can remember every minute of it. Every second," I said. "You've never understood that, even though I've told it to you a dozen times."

"No you haven't," Tommy said.

"Yes I have," I replied. "Don't make me tell you the exact dates and times."

Tommy sighed a heavy, frustrated sigh that sounded like the whole world was sitting on his shoulders. "I get it," Tommy said. "You're special. I've always gotten that. You don't need to remind me of it."

"It's not —"

"Let me finish," Tommy said. He looked down at his hands, and then up at the sky. "Dad always talked about how special the Europa mission and everything was. At least, that's what his letters said, right? But I don't really remember. I have to trust that what you tell me about those letters is true. I have to have faith in you, or else I don't have anything that I can believe. But I do. I believe in you.

"I've always looked out for you, always kept you safe. And I did it because I've always known that you were special, that there was something big waiting for you, that one day you'd go off and do something. So it was my job to protect you. My job to keep the bullies away and to make sure you didn't go off on your own to some foster parents that we didn't know, where I couldn't protect you." Tommy finally turned and looked at me. "That's why I used to always try to get you to run away with me, because it would have been simpler. And trying to keep you safe until . . . well, until you could do whatever it is you're supposed to do was all I had. But you would never come."

"We never could have made it on our own, Tommy," I said. I reached out and touched my brother's hand. It felt like years had passed since the last time I did that.

He flinched and pulled his back.

"Maybe," he said slowly. "It was the best thing I could think of." He shrugged his shoulders. "But I guess it doesn't really matter all that much now. You've made it this far and you're still special. You're still here. You've still got something great waiting for you." Tommy cleared his throat. "But what about me?"

"Time's up," a voice said before I could answer Tommy.

It was Jim Gannon.

He came out of the crowd like something old and immortal, like a force of nature that could never have been stopped even if it had wanted to stop itself. And of course, that was truth. Gannon couldn't be anything other than what he was. "Okay," he said, walking over to us.

"It's fine," Tommy said, standing up and stepping between Gannon and myself. It was more instinct than anything else. There was no plan, no intention, only action. He could have been some animal that wanted nothing more than to protect its own. "It's fine," Tommy said. "You don't have to do this. You don't have to turn her in."

"You know me better than that by now, don't you, Tommy?" Gannon said. "We all got to see things through to the end. Pop taught me that a long time ago, and I'm not about to let that fade away now. Not after all this."

"I'm sorry about your dad," Tommy said.

"What happened to Bill?" I asked.

"He's gone on," Gannon said after a hard swallow. "Wouldn't have happened if I hadn't been out here running across this country after you."

"The Disease?"

"It don't matter," Gannon replied. "I did my duty. I was a . . ." Something caught in his throat. "I was a good son to my old man. I never put him in a home. I loved him and took care of him right up until the end. That's what children do. That's what this whole world has gotten wrong, but not me. I did my duty. And now you're going to do yours."

"I'm sorry about your father," I said, feeling my stomach twist itself with fear. "But I'm not going to the war. And I'm not waiting around for The Disease. I'm leaving, and Tommy is coming with me." I placed my hand inside my coat pocket again. There was blood and pain, but there was also the gun.

I pulled the gun and leveled it at Gannon.

"Ginny . . ." Tommy said.

"I'm sorry, Tommy," I said.

Gannon only looked at me, with something like pity in his eyes, and said, "I'm sorry." Then he walked forward toward the waiting gun.

■ ■ ■ ■

EUROPA

■ ■ ■ ■

In certain types of stories, this is where the tragic end would play out. This is the moment when Gannon would have made some dramatic lunge at me. Tommy would have dived in front, come to defend his sister. The flash of light. The clamor of the gunshot. That's the way things were supposed to have ended.

But that's not the way things actually happened.

While I had the courage to pull the gun and aim it at Gannon, I never did find the courage to pull the trigger. I'm not ashamed of that anymore.

When I didn't pull the trigger, all that happened was that life moved forward, syllable by syllable.

Gannon walked forward and took it from my hand, and I wilted as the weight of it disappeared. A few miles away — beyond the crowds of revelers and gawkers and dancers and misanthropes and believers and dreamers and desperate hopefuls who had trekked all this way in commitment to the idea that everything would work out in the end and the desperate nihilists who had come this far just to watch the final flicker of light before the fire of humanity faded and the embers burned out and there was nothing left but a lonely place in the sky where once there had been laughter — the booster engines of the rocket ignited and liquid helium expended energy and the shuttle rose — slow at first, like an idea taking root in the imagination — and soon the inches of ascendance became feet and the feet became miles and the cheers and shouts that rose up from the people were deafening and it made the air quake and it felt as though there would be no more oxygen left to breathe once everyone had let out such shouts and sighs and sobs and screams and laughter. As the rocket rose into the night sky, headed for Europa, even Gannon and Tommy and I all turned and stood in silence as though nothing that had happened before in our lives mattered.

There was only now, only this moment that stretched the rubber band of understanding, an understanding — sudden and terrible — that simply the act of standing and watching the launch was an act of belief, an act of hope. We had, all three of us, given up on hope a long time ago. Tommy and I had given up on it with the death of our parents. Gannon with his father's stroke. And now here we were, all three of us, all children of the dead, trying to hold on to this one last flicker of light burning over our heads, stretching farther and farther away by the second.

"It sure is something," Gannon said.

And then the moment passed.

Gannon eventually took us back home the way he had always promised he would. After I spent a couple of days in a Florida hospital we went back to Oklahoma, back to the small house where there was no wife or father anymore, only Tommy and me. And, further keeping to his word, he turned me in to the Draft Board a couple of days later. The thought was there in my mind of running, but I had no reason anymore.

Tommy did as I always knew he would. He went off and signed up for the war. But for a while, it turned out to be the best thing for him. They shipped him out and, for a long time, my brother became someone other than who I had always known. He wrote me letters every few days, telling me all the details of what had happened when he and I had gotten separated on the way to Florida, because he knew that he wouldn't be able to hold on to the memories for much longer. We were both surprised that he had held them for this long.

That's how I learned about his time with Gannon, the boys he fought, everything. In Tommy's letters, he took on the qualities of our father, something neither of us had known he had. He found eloquence without me. Each letter was more beautiful than the last.

And in reply, I sent him our father's letters, one by one, pulled directly from my memory, and Tommy read them and replied and told me more about his life without me. He enjoyed basic training, just like the army recruiters had always told him he would. He got to use all of his muscles and, with me not being there, he felt that he had "finally rolled out from beneath a shadow that had shaded me from sunlight." His words.

I never knew my brother had that in him.

After basic training, after writing to me and showing me all these facets of himself that I had never known, my brother shipped out and was killed in his very first battle along with a dozen other boys and girls.

And that, as people say, was that.

My brother had finally truly left.

As for me, the Draft Board didn't put me in jail the way they did with every other Ember who had tried to run away from the war. Tommy had been right all along: with my perfect memory, the government would find something else for me to do. It took them a long time. They had their hands full, after all. Over the next five years The Disease began to spread faster, catching up to the war in its disregard for human life until, finally, even the warmakers realized that there would soon be no one left to continue their bloody tradition. So the war ground to a slow, frightened halt.

I lost track of Gannon after I was finally properly drafted. For all I know he stayed in his empty home in Oklahoma and, right now at this moment, is still there, living, waiting, talking of duty.

For me, there wasn't even time enough to become embittered the way people do after they've spent time trying to kill one another. There was only time for science and research, but by then it was already too late. Science can take a lifetime to master, and with The Disease becoming more aggressive, those who were the best chance for finding a cure began to succumb to The Disease. One by one the greatest minds of generations nodded off, never to be roused again.

Meanwhile the Embers, with no war left for them to run from and no future to chase them, stopped wandering. They set up camps in secluded parts of the world. Humanity's youth returned to the forests and deserts and hidden spaces from which humanity itself had once come, all in the hopes that The Disease would burn itself out and leave them behind.

The government, with nothing else to do, reacted similarly. Youths like myself were sent into bunkers well below the surface of the earth, into places where we would not see the stars shine or feel the air push across our faces. The earth became like Europa — barren on the surface, but with something beneath that surface. And it was here, beneath the ground and at the end of humanity's timeline, that I was put to work.

Someone nicknamed me The Recorder. My job was simple: catalog everything that was. Keep track of it all. A living, breathing memory bank that would always carry as much of humanity as anything else. Mostly, in the beginning, I carried facts: water and food rations, air handler calculations, chemical equations used in the making of medicines. I was the girl who answered every question.

But then, as people grew to believe that I would never forget anything, I became the keeper of stories. People came to me and told me of their personal histories. They told me of their children, their parents, their childhoods, the adventures of their youth, their talents, their dreams, their failures. And when I asked them why they told me rather than writing it down, they said simply, "It's never the same as talking to another person."

And so I became the vessel for their lives and, all the while, I only ever wanted to tell Tommy everything. Some nights, mingled among the cluttered memories of my life and the lives of everyone else I had ever met and talked to, Tommy was still alive, still smiling, still holding my hand in all those foster homes and on that long, long road to Florida. And our parents were there too, smiling, walking beside Tommy, filling up the spaces inside me.

As for the probe that was launched for Europa, I still haven't heard about whether or not it found life there. I only know that I believe it did, just as I believe that The Disease will burn out and we Embers will emerge and humanity will survive. If memory and family can survive inside me, if

Maggie and Connie and Nolan and Gannon and my parents and, most important of all, Tommy, can live inside me, then why can't the rest of it?

I am the world's keeper. But I am, above all else, my brother's keeper. Tommy is always alive.

That's what memory is.

That's what love is.

ABOUT THE AUTHOR

Jason Mott holds a BA in fiction and an MFA in poetry, both from the University of North Carolina at Wilmington, and is the author of two poetry collections. His writing has appeared in numerous literary journals, and he was nominated for the 2009 Pushcart Prize. His debut novel is *The Returned* and aired for two seasons on the ABC network under the title "Resurrection." His second novel is *The Wonder of All Things*. Jason lives in North Carolina.